NO FUTURE

Des Hawkins

NEWTON

First published in Great Britain by
Newton Publishers (1992)
P.O. Box 1999, Swindon, Wilts. SN1 1ZA

Copyright © Des Hawkins

All rights reserved. No part of this publication may be produced, stored in a retrieval system, or transmitted, in any form, or by any means, electronic, mechanical, photocopying, recording or otherwise, without the prior permission of the publishers.

This book is sold subject to the condition that it shall not, by way of trade or otherwise, be lent, re-sold, hired out or otherwise circulated without the publisher's prior consent in any form of binding or cover other than that in which it is published and without a similar condition including this condition being imposed on the subsequent purchaser.

Every effort has been made by the author and the publishers to trace owners of copyright material.

Printed and bound by Unwin Brothers Ltd.,
The Gresham Press, Old Woking, Surrey GU22 9LH
A Member of the Martins Printing Group

ISBN 1-872308-02-3

Price: £15.50

CONTENTS

		Pages
Chapters		
	Foreword	v
1	Ops and all that	1
2	Standdown	19
3	Over the Alps	29
4	And again	43
5	Texel again	79
6	Back from leave	91
7	Recognition and promotion	101
8	Commissioning and all that	121
9	It happens to the best	141
10	Get him out of here	159
11	Finals	171
12	The aftermath	187

Every character in this book is fictitious and no reference whatever is intended to any living person. In the nature of the subject matter there may be persons who could fit their own experience into the characters simply because the way of life was circumscribed, in a close and limited circle, a way of life with minimal life expectancy.

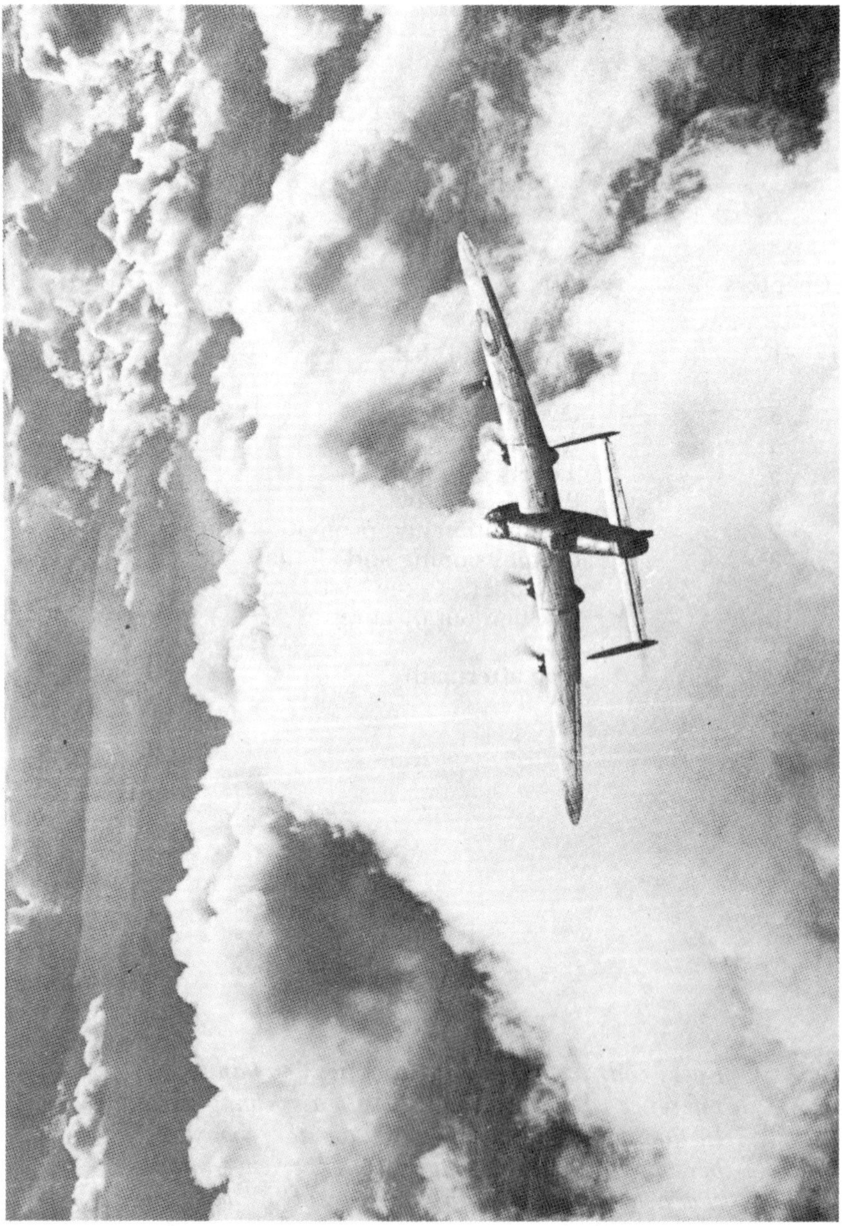

FOREWORD

During the period of the Second World War covered by "No Future" I was a schoolboy living in Lincolnshire, and from the branches of a large tree in the garden used to watch Lancasters setting out on their raids on Germany — and wishing I was on board one of them. I was already a keen student of all things aeronautical and also a member of the Air Training Corps, which had the big advantage of providing occasional access to bomber airfields in the area. Postwar I spent over 30 years in the Royal Air Force, much of the time as pilot captain of large piston-engined aircraft — though never in Bomber Command. I hope I can legitimately claim some knowledge of the atmosphere on a wartime bomber station and of how crews functioned, therefore, while still being sufficiently distanced from the subject of this book to be reasonably objective.

By 1943 Bomber Command had the necessary navigational aids and techniques to make effective attacks on German towns and cities, though small individual targets were still beyond the capabilities of all except certain elite units. "Main Force" crews like the one around which "No Future" is written were therefore almost invariably used on "area" targets of the type which have received much critical comment in many recent books and articles written by authors benefiting from hindsight, and with scant attention to the circumstances prevailing at the time. It is rare indeed that they suggest any alternative method of hitting the Germans where it hurt most — in the "Fatherland."

Led by New Zealander "Acc" Burnett, the author's fictional crew may seem to have led a charmed life, but then so did all who survived a Bomber Command tour, for the statistical chances of safely completing the required 30 "Ops" was very low indeed. Luck and acquired skill were needed in about equal proportions, but also vital was the camaraderie so well portrayed in "No Future," for it was this that enabled them to cope with the fears and anxieties which dominated the lives of aircrew, many still teenagers. As the magic figure of 30 operations got closer the tension inevitably mounted though the apparent effect on individuals could be very different. Some like "Ace" were outwardly unchanged but others, just as brave, were noticeably "shell shocked." I will never forget the sight of a Squadron Leader navigator at East Kirkby shaking uncontrollably as he gave a talk to a party of cadets of which I was one. The married men had the added strain of knowing that their wives were waiting somewhere, often far away, fearing the dreaded telegram "Missing believed Killed," while nearly all the rest had girlfriends to worry about. How many of the latter remained as unsullied as Marion in "No Future" is conjecture — but some undoubtedly did. To the modern young reader the dialogue between the lovers may seem somewhat stilted — but it should be remembered that it was a different age with different values.

An ATC camp spent at Strubby came vividly to mind as I read "No Future." We also endured cold, damp Nissen huts in the corner of a field seemingly miles from the cookhouse and the NAAFI — or anywhere else for that matter. But it was only for a week — not months on end!

"No Future" is a novel, but is obviously based on the author's experiences during the latter part of Bomber Command's "War" of nearly fifty years ago — and is certainly none the worse for that. Thankfully there are no heroics in the book — it does not need them. It is a good story convincingly told — with a very poignant twist in the tail.

Squadron Leader R. C. B. Ashworth, RAF (Retd)

No.1 Air Observer School Malton, Toronto, 1941.
Des Hawkins is fourth from the left in the front row.

NO FUTURE
Des Hawkins DFC, MID

The author lives in Newquay, Cornwall.

He was born in Warminster, later lived in Melksham and was educated at Fitzmaurice Grammar School, Bradford-on-Avon, all in the County of Wilts.

Schooldays were challenging for the school's policy was one of "Work hard — Play hard." He remembers with affection the wholly dedicated staff, remembers their names and personalities, can picture them still some 50 years on and has an appreciation of their combined efforts to knock some knowledge into resistant youth. It was undeniably a good school.

He was however unable to decide upon a career and the onset of War solved his problem even though it turned out merely to be a delaying action. He volunteered to serve with the Royal Air Force Volunteer Reserve, but it was early 1941 before he was attested. During the waiting period he played piano in local Dance Bands.

Eventually the call to arms arrived which meant reporting to Aircrew Recruiting Centre at Regents Park, London. There he suffered a course of square bashing and was fed in the Zoo. This was followed by Initial Training Wing at Scarborough, before being despatched across the Atlantic to No 1 Air Observer School, at Toronto, Ontario where there were no Blackout conditions or Food rationing.

At Observer School he was one of only four LIMEYS on an all-Canadian course where he was taught the principles of Air

Navigation, Bomb Aiming and some Meteorology together with practical morse key work. Once qualified as an Air Observer he was returned to the United Kingdom for operational training.

Operational training on Wellington Bombers lasted some three months followed by two months on a Heavy Bomber Conversion Unit. He was then posted, in turn, from early 1943 to Lancaster Bomber Squadrons 44 (Rhodesia), 630 and 625 in the single role of navigator. He was awarded the DFC, and Mentioned in Despatches. He remains proud to have been one of Sir Arthur Harris' OLD LAGS.

After demob in 1946 he joined the staff of the Corporation of Lloyd's, (Lloyd's of London) and while so employed rejoined the RAFVR for five years of flying at weekends. Upon retirement from Lloyd's after thirty four years of service he went to work for Lloyd's broker, Edgar Hamilton, Ltd, for four years commuting from Winchester, Hants to London daily.

Now in final retirement, with difficulty he has found the time to create "No Future," following up an intention that has always been in mind, arising from poignant memories of those War years that can never be erased.

He is a member of a number of RAF related associations — 44 (Rhodesia) Squadron, Bomber Command, Aircrew and RAFA. He is also a member of the British Legion and the Cornish Aviation Society.

Leisure pursuits are music, reading and walking the Cornish coastline.

Chapter 1

OPS AND ALL THAT

"Contact starboard inner." Sergeant Pilot "Ace" Burnett leaned over to peer through the Perspex into the dark shadows between the fuselage and the port side inner engine nacelle, at the same time automatically raising a thumb in confirmation of his readiness to start up. Somewhere down there was a fitter with the starter ack who, in answer to Ace's call, echoed faintly "contact starboard inner". The engine jerked through a windmilling action and then, as the compression bit and fired, the roar of the ejector exhausts crashed upon the air. The pilot breathed hard and throttled back. In a matter of seconds the three remaining engines coughed into motion and were soon running at a steady warm-up rate.

Now for the cockpit drill. Every dial, gauge and lever received his cursory but positive inspection, for every one indicated some vital function the failure of which could jeopardise Ace's part in the night bombing operation. Initially satisfied, he proceeded to rev up each engine in turn testing for magneto efficiency. Whizzo! he said to himself. All seemed to be in order. The first hurdle on this his very first operation was surmounted. The Lancaster appeared to be entirely serviceable.

It was time to turn his attention to the crew, for as skipper of the aeroplane it was his responsibility to ensure that each member had carried out their own drills, for their safety, for his and for the safety of the expensive bomber. He spoke into the microphone incorporated into his oxygen mask which in turn was hinged loosely on one side of the leather helmet with a facility for clipping on the opposite side.

"Check your equipment and respond," he commanded. From the bomb compartment Sid Marks was the first to acknowledge:-

"All systems go, Ace."

"Good show, Sid. You'd better come up now for take-off."

"On my way." Sid pushed past the flight engineer, eased past the navigator, playfully cuffed the wireless operator and went through the armour-plated door to take up position on the bunk.

"You OK, Ken?" — this to the flight engineer who was standing just aft of the pilot's position checking the panel of oil temperature gauges.

"OK skipper."

John Howard, the navigator piped up that all was in order. Taffy Williams, the wireless op who sat to the rear of the navigator's position confirmed "Oxygen OK," but added with clear concern:–

"The bloody pigeon's laid an egg and I don't like it, look you."

These then were the five crew members who had to struggle forward up the fuselage to gain their places and struggle was the word for it because they'd each had to climb over the enormous main spar which supported the 102 feet of wing span, carrying their respective equipment of which the most awkward was the parachute pack.

"What about you, Jock? We don't have all night to waste."

"Sorry mon," replied Jock Campbell, the tail end gunner who hailed from across the northern border. "Oxygen OK, but I think my electric heating's up the creek."

"God. What a fine time to find out. Sure you're plugged in?" Ace was distinctly irritable. "Check again and if its unserviceable you're sure going to freeze."

"All OK." Frank Cartwright the mid upper gunner confirmed quietly. The oxygen supply was vital and came in for general use at 10,000 feet and above. Most of the operation would take place at double that height when continuity of supply would be necessary to maintain life and efficiency of purpose. An oxygen failure might well be the cause of a disastrous error of judgement likely to consign the whole crew to graves in some foreign field. The trouble with interruption of supply at operational height was that in the first place it was hard to detect and in the second place produced a grand euphoria of overwhelming confidence, a state which inevitably produced the most shocking reactions, errors on the grand scale terminated by ultimate incoherence and death.

"Did I hear you say we've got an egg, Taffy?" Ace asked. "Bit unusual what!"

"Yes and I don't like it, look you." Taffy invariably preceded or succeeded a statement with "look you". He was a bit rattled and sounded even more Welsh than usual.

A fine start, thought Ace. He recollected that earlier in the day Taffy had displayed all the interest of a professional pigeon fancier, appearing too, to relish responsibility for the care of the carrier pigeons, which was logical enough for both wireless operators and pigeons were skilled at transmitting messages in their different ways. Indeed the pigeons were carried solely for the purpose of sending distress signals if the aircraft was obliged to ditch in the drink — a sort of delayed Mayday call. So now to hear the little Welshman referring to those aristocratic looking birds in so ungrateful a fashion was altogether surprising, simply because one of them had obeyed the dictates of nature. Of course it was plain that Taffy was superstitious.

"Didn't know you were superstitious," taunted Ace.

"Superstitious? Goodness no. Don't be daft," rejoined Taff in an aggrieved tone. "It's just that I don't — well, makes a mess, look you."

The pilot buttoned his lip. He knew full well that whatever the wireless operator felt within him, nothing more would be said. He, Ace wasn't remotely superstitious, neither did he give credence to the supposed manifestation of gremlins who, many would have, played tricks on aircraft in flight to the disadvantage of the crews, rather like poltergeists in Irish circles. Fleetingly, it occurred to him that Jock, his rear gunner, believed that fate could be circumvented by the simple expedient of toting round a lucky charm. Once at OTU he'd dropped his talisman whilst in the process of stifling an imminent sneeze. He'd scooped it up pretty smartly, unable to hide the embarrassing flush of pink on his fresh Gaelic complexion. Like most superstitious bodies he was sensitive to what even he considered was a human frailty. At this moment, at the remote tail-end of the fuselage the rear gunner could not have missed Ace's taunt and a pronounced humming of a Scottish air made it clear that he was not disposed to be drawn.

"Got the first course ready, John?" Ace was back to the needs of the moment.

"Sure thing. 102 True. Set course at 23.30 hours."

"OK. 102 T. Final time check. Coming up to 23.04 in about 7 seconds   5, 4, 3, 2, 1, now."

He signalled the duty marshaller "chocks away" and said to the flight engineer:

"Let's go, Ken. Keep a good look out to starboard. I don't want to run off the perimeter and get bogged down."

With Ken standing by peering out into the shadows, Ace opened up the port outer engine turning the Lancaster slowly on the concrete hard standing, while the marshaller signalled the way with a flashlight. The pilot gunned the starboard outer to straighten, and then again to turn on to the perimeter only vaguely defined. He swore softly. "It's bloody dark. Can't see a thing. Navigator, dowse your light for a while. It's reflecting on the windscreen." John lowered the anglepoise lamp and adjusted the blackout curtain between his position and the pilot while the latter gunned his engines to give broadly even thrust and slow progress within the barely perceptible boundaries of the perimeter, towards the distant runway in use.

"Didn't forget the rations Taffy, did you?" John asked.

"No mon, there's efficiency here."

"Probably scoffed the lot by now," suggested Sid and added "and the pigeon's egg."

"Wrap up cockney. Go back to sleep." Taffy fumbled with the signals gen on the edible ricepaper. He was beginning to feel hungry.

"Alright cut the cackle, chaps," admonished the pilot. "Seat belts. We're approaching the runway."

A red Aldis flashed out from the caravan. Ace applied the brakes and the Lancaster hissed to a jerky halt. From the far side of the runway another Lancaster had turned on ready for take-off illuminated by the navigation lights.

"Kite from 'A' flight coming from that direction," suggested Ken, to no one in particular.

The 'A' Flight Lancaster began to move away with throbbing power that completely overrode the idling murmur of Ace's aircraft and then receded.

"There's the green," reminded Ken.

"OK jokers. Prepare for take-off," warned Ace crisply. He turned on to the runway. He was as cool as ice now that the big moment had arrived. Gone were earlier doubts: he was the master. Slowly he juggled the four throttles forward holding the brakes full on. The Lancaster began to rock violently under increased power. Ace released the brakes. R Robert moved forward slowly, all too slowly it seemed, but gaining speed nevertheless. At a speed of 50 knots the pilot eased the control column forward off his chest to bring the aircraft into flying position with the tail up, at the same time moving the rudder bar to maintain a straight run between the flares. Full power and boost. Ken's left hand had been behind Ace's right on the throttles and now, on his pilot's instructions, laid on full take-off revs and boost. More right rudder, Ace breathed as he detected an early swing to port as a result of torque effect. The Lancaster bumped slightly as the wheels just left the runway, bumped again before finally staggering into a slow climb. The navigator logged the airborne time automatically.

"Wheels up," the pilot curtly commanded. The engineer swiftly complied.

"Flaps up." Again Ken complied. The whole crew breathed again as Ace began a climbing turn to port striving to turn on to the reciprocal heading, parallel to the runway flares in order to keep the airfield in view. It was not yet time to set course and the aim was to gain as much height as possible in the meantime. A mile or two away the sharp wink of the airfield identification pundit monotonously threw out its two letter morse characteristic. With ever increasing height the airfield lights were now no more than fairy rings. Up above the stars twinkled — Ace was seemingly climbing up to them, trying hard to put into effect *per ardua ad astra*, and yet the aim was only 20,000 feet. It was ludicrous that the Lancaster conceived by puny man was making such hard work of climbing to this modest height while the heavenly bodies above were virtually at infinity.

"Time to set course in 2 minutes," warned the navigator. "Course 102 True."

"OK navigator, turning slowly now on to 102 T. We'll just about be over the airfield in two minutes." It was important to get a good start from an identifiable datum point. "On course now navigator," he said at last. "Right over base. Height 5,500 feet."

John logged time of setting course and glanced at his repeater compass just to make sure that Ace had got it right. There was no room for errors. The Lancaster headed broadly eastwards still climbing towards the dim outline of the Wash visible only because of the distinction between land and water, and then only just so. Skegness was out there somewhere on the port side but unseen. Soon they were running roughly parallel to the northern face of the East Anglian bulge and to blacked out Sheringham, the first turning point.

Settled on to the new course, Ace adjusted climbing revolutions slightly together with the trimming tabs and made an attempt to make himself more comfortable. Of itself the air cushion on which he sat should have been comfortable enough, but with a parachute pack between cushion and posterior it was hardly a luxurious situation. With arms resting firmly on the elbow rests he allowed himself a period of relaxation. The passage of the Lancaster was smooth enough in the cold night air, wholly free of turbulence, conducive to sleep, but he dare not relax some sort of vigil for there must reasonably be a number of other bombers in the vicinity. Some 600 bombers were setting out for DUISBERG although they were not all beginning their journey from Lincolnshire and would approach the Dutch coast on different tracks. There would also be variations in the courses set by the navigators at different times due to the experience of differing wind velocities and directions at different heights.

Suddenly Lancaster R Robert began to rock violently under the impetus of unexpected turbulence.

"What the hell's going on?," queried Jock from the rear gun turret. "I'm going up and down like a yo yo."

Ace wrested with the controls and when R Robert had regained stable air he answered the rear gunner:–

"Don't panic, Jock. We were in another kite's slipstream. Keep a good look out, Ken, and you, Sid." It was a new experience that could only arise from flying in a concentration of aeroplanes, and a worrying one too. In the pitch black night a collision had to be a strong possibility despite the bigness of the sky.

"OK Skipper." Sid confirmed that he was not asleep. "At least it proves we're going in the right direction and not on a reciprocal course."

John did not go much on this implied lack of professionalism but he forced good humour to the fore:–

"Don't worry, Sid. I've already checked the position of the Pole star." While there was nothing ahead but a black void, to the rear airfield identification beacons still winked out in friendly fashion.

At 10,000 feet the pilot switched on his microphone:

"Oxygen on, button your masks and keep it that way. Cut out any cackle and dowse that fag, Sid."

From the nose Sid groaned to himself but carefully stubbed out a dogend. How the hell did Ace know he was having a draw?

"It's getting bloody cold." Jock could no longer hold back his complaint. "My heated suit is not working."

"Yah. You ought to be used to the cold, mon, where you come from." Taffy could not resist a dig at the Scotsman.

"Cut the cackle I said." Ace was getting a shade annoyed. A few vague mutterings surged backwards and forwards for a few seconds before tailing off into what would have been silence if it were not for the steady roar of the four Merlin engines which helmet and earphones were no protection against. The pilot had got used to vocal outbreaks from his crew. What else could one expect from four Englishmen from different parts of the Country together with one fiery Welshman, one equally fiery Scotsman and he himself, a phlegmatic New Zealander. The latter realised that these verbal flurries did little harm. Indeed they acted as safety valves.

Keeping a comprehensive roving watch over the cockpit instrument panel Ace's eyes moved into the forward darkness and then to each side. He was able, however, to allow his thoughts to wander back to Jock Campbell in the rear turret who had the dubious pleasure of being styled officially as "rear gunner" or in the vernacular variously as "tail end Charlie" or "ass end Charlie". Whatever one called him did not make a scrap of difference to the lonely discomfort he bore. Some 69 feet back from the nose of the Lancaster the power operated turret into which he was wedged was just about the coldest and draughtiest position in the aeroplane, and, with his electrically heated suit unserviceable, or only partly efficient, Jock must be feeling very cold indeed. When they reached the operational height of 20,000 feet the outside temperature would be in the order of 20 degrees of frost. He was surely going to have a job to avoid frostbite. Even so, sitting behind four 303 machine guns he must never relax constant vigil for if trouble came from an enemy fighter it would generally come from the rear and from the very dark segment underneath the turret.

Ace decided to check up on Jock.

"Are you still cold?" he asked.

"I'm cold, but I think my suit has got some heat."

Further forward in the mid upper turret, just forward of the rear entrance Frank Cartwright manned twin 303s. He was undisputably the baby of the outfit and looked it. He was fair haired, palefaced, had adolescent acne, was barely out of school and scarcely detached from his mother's apron strings. Of all the crew, Frank had taken the shortest cut from civvy street to operations, being the product of a rapid intake occasioned by the need for extra gunners when Wellington and Manchester bombers were replaced by the bigger four engined Stirling, Halifax and Lancasters with the additional gun turret. In the RAF for little more than a few months he had risen from the lowest rank of AC2 to Sergeant in one fell swoop, with pay of course. So far on this trip Frank had not said a word. No doubt, thought Ace, Frank was overawed and who could blame him.

The skipper's cogitations emigrated a span further forward, over the main spar, through the armour plated doors to the wireless op's position. Taffy was Welsh, of course. The English equivalent of his name was William Williams and according to the rest of the crew that was too ridiculous for words. It had been proposed and seconded that he be renamed Taffy. Like Ace, whose proper Christian name was Gordon, also heartily disliked by the crew, he was reborn. He was, like Jock, on the slim side, with a mop of dark curly hair; unlike Jock who was fresh-complexioned; he was on the pale side. His somewhat tight lips were surmounted by a hawk nose both of which features gave a clue to his largely taciturn character. He had one basic weakness. He could not resist rubbing Jock up the wrong way. For all that, he and Jock seemed to get on quite well with each other in a sort of love-hate relationship. What was absolutely certain was Taffy's dedication to his chosen skill. He was a shit-hot wireless operator.

At Ace's side sat Ken Ward, the flight engineer. Ken was short, relatively broad on the beam, brown haired and brown eyed. If his stature was disproportionate his features were square and strong. He wore a ready smile which seemed to attract the fairer sex all too easily. He joined the RAF as an apprenticed fitter, went through Halton and then for reasons he could not adequately explain had volunteered for aircrew. From Ace's point of view there was a particular advantage in having an aero engine fitter on tap, so to speak, for if the engines ran rough, Ken would have a pretty good idea of the extent of the problem.

Then there was John Howard, the navigator. Ace understood how the latter ticked because their working relationship had to be closer by reason of each other's dependence on the other's skill. John had gone to the right school and the right college and had, in his own words, received an education of decent mediocrity. He was stocky in stature, red haired and blue eyed, handsome enough in the eyes of the opposite sex although not easily disposed to take advantage of it. He could flare up to match the colour of his hair, although such occasions were rare. He had, Ace knew, got his navigation pretty well wrapped up considering the difficulties that wartime flying imposed. If he had a particular fault, it was a lack of confidence in his patently obvious ability. Once Ace had tackled John on the subject practically accusing him of displaying an inferiority complex. The navigator had replied without heat. "How can one have a complex if one is inferior?"

Finally there was Sid Marks, the bomb aimer, or horizontal Sid as the rest of the crew referred to him. He was a mousey haired Cockney and a right handsome fellow. It was thought he had a wife, but no one knew for sure. At all events he showed little interest in women and any courtesies to be extended tended to be on the heavy side. He could be extremely voluble in his cups. On the other hand he could lapse into prolonged silence. He could achieve absolute relaxation without significant effort. If he could lie down rather than sit, he would and if he could not be found it was a fair bet that he was in his billet, horizontal on the biscuit mattresses, with eyes discovering something totally absorbing in the rafters, or closed, smoking the inevitable cigarette. It is probable, Ace thought, that even at this moment Sid would be having a quiet kip. He decided to find out:

"You awake Sid?" he asked.

"Wide awake, Ace," was the immediate response from which the pilot deduced that Sid the nonchalant was having a spell of operational tension.

Ace's reflections had raced through his mind in bare minutes. I'm pretty lucky, he mused. Could easily have had the misfortune to be crewed with a less competent lot. His cogitations were interrupted by the navigator:

"ETA Dutch coast 10 minutes."

"Right navigator," Ace replied. "Peepers wide open. They know we're coming and are out looking for us."

"Pinpoint the coastline, will you Sid," requested John.

"No dice, Johnny boy. Cloud below. No vision."

"OK. Navigator to pilot, alter course to 123 True." John directed confidently. He knew they were pretty well on track for he was still just able to identify the co-ordinates on the Gee box, but navigation was a belt and braces affair. If Sid could have come up with a pinpoint on the coastline, tracking would have been doubly confirmed.

Out to starboard there was a steady glow like searchlights trying to pierce unbroken cloud. It meant land and it could only be Holland.

Those searchlights aren't there for nothing, mused Ace and then aloud:

"Someone must be stooging several miles to starboard. John are we on track?"

"Dead on track, Ace — no problem."

"Probably some Yankee kite got lost on a training stooge," suggested Jock.

"Come off it, Jock." Sid could be very sarcastic when he liked. "Yanks are like birds, bloody sensible — don't fly at night."

Ace grinned into his mask. Sid was wide awake still and that was comforting. What's more, Jock had just piped up. That was equally comforting. Maybe they were too cold to drop off, for whilst the rear turret was always cold, so could be the bomb compartment. It was 20 degrees below outside and this was causing a thin film of ice to form on the inside of the windscreen tending to obscure the pilot's vision.

"Dab a drop of glycol on the windscreen, Ken." The engineer was at the ready. R Robert droned on seemingly alone until eventually, ahead and slightly to starboard the red tracking marker laid by Pathfinders force burst and continued to burn with amazing longevity. It was also clear that the cloud was no longer in evidence.

"Whacko," breathed John as Ace communicated this information. It confirmed that his own tracking was pretty accurate, unless of course Pathfinders were up the creek, so to speak. He needed this confirmation for the G. Box was now out of range or at least very weak signals were obliterated by "grass." He barely had time to pass to the pilot a new course before an excited but urgent voice came onto intercom in a pronounced Scots accent.

"Skipper, unidentified aircraft 150 yards to port — same heading, same height. I can see the exhaust manifolds. Stand by, but prepare to dive port."

"Standing by," replied Ace coolly. He took a firmer grip on the control column.

"Whatever it is, I don't believe he's seen us," suggested Jock. "Can you see him, Frank?"

"I've got him, Jock. Maybe a JU88." Frank for all his youth seemed controlled. There was very little warning. Jock spotted movement as the two engined aircraft lifted the port wing:

"Dive, dive port go, go," he yelled at the top of his voice.

Ace threw the Lancaster into a steep dive to port, just in time to avoid a vicious stream of tracer which curled away over the top of his aircraft. The crash of Jock's 303s resounded down the fuselage and a strong smell of cordite was evident.

"OK. We've lost him for the time being." Jock was calmer now having taken comfort from blasting off his guns.

The pilot hauled a resisting aircraft out of the diving turn into a slow climb for height, correcting his course to starboard to make allowance for the wild deviation to port. His stomach had momentarily reached up to his mouth and he experienced a redigestation of earlier eggs and bacon that was not a bit pleasant. During training he had often practised the standard evasion pattern but it was altogether a different kettle of fish with a bomb load underneath. For a short while as he had pulled out of the dive he could feel the weight of the bomb load striving to rip out the belly of his aircraft and strip off the wings. But if his stomach failed him, he was in total command of mind and limbs. He even enjoyed a mild sense of elation at having staved off the first enemy attack, but pure logic insisted that they might not get so much warning another time and there was a long way to go yet.

"Eyes skinned, Cobbers," he gritted it out between the teeth. "It's the bugger we can't see I'm worried about. I'm banking to port and then starboard. Take a gander underneath gunners. We need a bloody periscope on this kite, upside down." He dropped the port wing heeling over so that the whole wing section was practically vertical and then over to starboard.

"All clear," called Frank from the mid upper turret.

"All clear." Jock couldn't agree more.

The navigator came on intercom:

"ETA target 0150 that's zero hour plus 5. Spot on."

"Good show, John." To say that Ace was pleased was a masterly piece of understatement. He was of course aware of the navigator's tenet "that man is not lost". He was equally aware of the imperfections of navigating in war time conditions.

Ahead a few searchlights had begun to flicker into the sky waving around seemingly aimlessly and then starlike flashes began winking away. Pathfinders must be there trying to identify the aiming point.

"Five minutes to Zero hour," warned the navigator.

"Right John. Give me a course for when bombs are away."

"Short leg for ten minutes — 191 True."

Dead ahead a group of red target indicators flowed out, blood red waterfalls of sheer brilliance turning night into fire.

"There go the reds," shouted Sid. "Boy! what a sight." And what a sight it was. With the outflow of markers the German defence knew exactly where the attack would be made. Up shot the searchlights in massive numbers and the flak bursts were more than catching up. There were also the insidious bluer searchlights, radar controlled and probing. In one such beam was a flash of white as it homed in on a Pathfinder aircraft and immediately other searchlights swung round to latch on, but just as quickly the trap was eluded.

"Hey Johnny," Ace called. "Come up here for a minute will you."

Very smartly the navigator dowsed his lamp, parted the curtains and bobbed up beside the pilot. He plugged into Ken's intercom make and break joint.

"Are you sure we're not ahead of time?" the pilot went on. "We're almost on top of the reds and the greens haven't gone down yet."

John pushed Ken out of the way and peered down into the bomb compartment where Sid was at full stretch watching the reds move towards his bombsight. "S'OK Ace. Distance is deceiving at this height at night." He wasn't all that confident, but he was pretty certain his timing was right. In absolute confirmation the greens cascaded out in a brilliant shower almost right on top of the reds.

"We're OK," Sid added. "Bomb doors open. A couple of minutes yet."

"Bomb doors open," echoed Ace and the belly of R Robert opened up.

"There go the first bombs," Sid advised while John felt it prudent to retreat behind his curtain. He'd better recheck his calculations if only to take his mind off what was going on outside. The target area was a massive pyrotechnic display. As the bombs crashed down there was a continuous flashing of exploding bombs and photoflashes, the latter each of 2,000,000 candle power, whilst all the way up from ground to operational height it was almost like daylight.

"Left, Left," intoned Sid. "Steady, keep it there, Ace." Sid was resolved to put his load in the right place and Ace was really concentrating.

Still more searchlights swept the sky, intersecting to form cones of light, silhouetting the bombers, while flak was being pumped up like water from hoses. R Robert rocked violently as a shell exploded near at hand and slightly ahead, while ominous puffs of black smoke drifted by.

"Keep her steady, Ace," called Sid. "Right a bit — hold it," and then "Bombs gone. Keep her steady for the photo."

The Lancaster shot up like a cork as the bombs tumbled away.

"Course 191," reminded the navigator.

"Course 191," said Ace. "3000 revs, Ken." The engines roared a protest at being asked for full power while Ace turned slowly on to the new course. Once again R Robert was rocked by a heavy explosion, but there seemed to be no obvious damage. At least the fans were turning alright.

"What's it look like Jock?" The rear gunner now held the grandstand view.

"Looks bang on — really concentrated." Jock was really jubilant. "Cripes! Kite exploded to the rear. Just an almighty flash and then nothing. Must have hit the petrol tanks and disintegrated. Flak's died down though."

"Right. All eyes out. Fighters." Ace's warning was brisk.

The ten minutes up the navigator came up with a new course that would be positively directed towards home and as far as he was concerned the coast or at least the theoretical coast (they had not seen the coast on the way out and probably it would be the same on the way back) could not come too quickly, although even then it could not be assumed that they were safe, for without a doubt the bomber stream would be pursued to the extreme range of the enemy fighters. But the coast would be a comforting milestone to achieve. John was determined to take his worries in stages, equating them, so to speak, with each leg of the route. His one rapid look outside on the bombing run had been, if not exactly frightening, sufficient to inspire a hasty retreat to his office. Logic told him that the office afforded little protection from heavy shrapnel. For that matter it occurred to him that en route to the target he had for the first time in his career sat on top of a 4000 lb bomb together with a goodly number of incendiaries, which was a thought far from comforting even though that danger was now past. To avoid morbid cogitations he took new refuge in the science of navigation. Odd he thought, that his Mercator Chart, the prime means of directing the bombs to the enemy had been the brainchild of a Flemish born German cartographer. It was a strange sort of "chickens coming home to roost."

Ace turned carefully on to John's new course for home, reduced the engine revolutions to 2300, the airspeed to 165 knots, which meant the aeroplane would, with a headwind, be tracking across the ground at round about 145 knots. There was little to be gained by streaking flat out for home base, losing the protection, however nebulous, of other bombers in the vicinity. Moreover, there was still a long way to go and to flog the engines unmercifully might store up trouble for a subsequent trip.

Out to port there was a sudden gush of flame which then began to fall towards the ground, seemingly very slowly. Just for a moment there was the outline of a stricken bomber in the engulfing flame. Then it was swallowed up.

"Fighters," murmured Ken, the flight engineer. It was obvious but the remark served to remind the pilot of a necessary exercise, while John logged time and place.

"Banking port, then starboard," advised the pilot. It was a directive to the gunners to keep their eyes open. The mighty Lancaster rolled over to port, stabilised and then over to starboard. With bomb load gone, it was easier to handle as well as being a less tiring manoeuvre.

"All clear," called Jock from the rear turret.

"No sign of trouble," confirmed Frank, the mid upper, who having said very little all along was almost eloquent.

Luck there had to be, all of the good variety. The Lancaster roared on gracefully through stygian darkness. Once, Ace diverged slightly from the course to avoid a group of waving searchlights on what had to be the Dutch coast.

They finally crossed the English coast by Skegness. Ahead was the exhilarating sight of airfield beacons winking sharply from the proximity of the many Lincolnshire bomber bases. In due course Sid identified the home beacon cleverly despite the fact that his morse left a lot to be desired.

"There it is. Dead ahead," he advised.

Ace ran over the beacon, turned onto the QDM. He switched on to Radio Telephone just in time to hear C Charlie calling the tower for permission to pancake. Whereas for take-off RT silence was maintained, now for landing full verbal control would be available and exercised. Ace was a shade disappointed. We are not first back he realised, but not far off for the flare path had not long been lit. Going wide of the flarepath he stabbed the transmission button.

"Manger Robert to Bakewell. Permission to pancake." He released the button. Up from the ground came the soft mellow voice of the WAAF R/T operator.

"Bakewell to Robert. Receiving you loud and clear. Your turn to land no. 3. Circle at 1000 feet."

"OK Bakewell. Robert at 1000 feet upwind."

"Hello," said Sid to no one in particular. "Somebody else in the circuit." Out of the darkness they heard the unspecified aircraft call:

"Sugar clear of runway." Then flying control was on the air again.

"C Charlie clear to land. R Robert prepare to land."

"Robert preparing to land," echoed Ace. So the Flight Commander, Sqn Ldr Denning was first down for Sugar was his kite. Ace hoped he could keep Robert, which had served him well on this his first operation. He had the obscure feeling that Robert would be a lucky kite. He quickly turned his attention to the landing procedure in respect of which the greatest care together with first class judgement would be called for. Landing a big aeroplane at any time was a pretty skilled business, but at night on a poorly lit narrow flarepath when the diagonal approach between the vertical and horizontal planes could be very deceiving, was altogether more hazardous.

"Robert clear to land," came the call from flying control. Acknowledging swiftly, Ace turned sharply from downwind tracking to line up upwind, losing height slowly all the time.

"20 flap," he rapped out.

"20 flap," echoed the flight engineer.

"Wheels down," Ace directed and as Ken obliged Robert nosed up a shade while the speed dropped off.

"Revs up. Radiators closed." The pilot's instructions were clipped and again:

"Full flap." He had cut it a bit fine. Again the nose moved up perceptibly, the speed falling off. Again he got the revs up. "Call the airspeed navigator."

"110 .. 105 .. 110 . 110 .. 105 .. 100"- the navigator intoned the ASI readings from his own panel.

"Cut throttles when I call, Ken," reminded Ace. He expected the engineer to be ready and waiting, but they were all tired with the result that reactions could be slow, so a reminder did not come amiss. Slowly the Lancaster lost height over the leading glims. Then they were over the flarepath.

"Cut". Ken snapped the four throttles back. The engines popped and spluttered. Robert floated just above the deck and then touched down on all three points with scarcely a bump followed by a mild squeal of protest from the big wheel tyres.

Jock's praise was earnest. Sitting more or less over the tail wheel he was in a good position to judge the landing.

"Wizard show, Ace. Couldn't have done better myself."

A buzz of conversation broke out once the pilot had cleared the runway, but it dried up quickly as Ace concentrated on carefully negotiating the perimeter. It was a hell of a long way to 'B' flight dispersal but eventually the torchlight signals of the marshaller showed the way to Robert's hard standing. Ace turned into wind and shut down engines.

You could have heard a pin drop. The silence was absolutely uncanny after 4 hours and 18 minutes of flight. After suffering the drumming engines for that length of time the silence was, well loud. Certainly no one wanted to say anything. The relief of having completed their first operation was absolute. They were content to strip off helmets and wipe down faces that were still sticky from contact with oxygen mask rubber. But a move had to be made. It was time to collect the paraphernalia of flying and await the truck that would be already on its way to collect them for debriefing. On the morrow flying log books would be written up faithfully with date, time of take-off, Target, bomb load and total flying time.

In the Intelligence block, in the hours of pre-dawn darkness the reception committee awaited the returning crews. There present were the senior officers and section leaders who had been present at briefing together with some ladies of the WAAF complete with cocoa and biscuits. Humanly the latter were there to get the job over with so that beauty sleep could be regained, the flyers to welcome comrades in arms, the weather man hopefully to have his earlier forecast confirmed, the medical officer to see whether he had any clients and, of course the intelligence officers to glean the success of the operation or otherwise and any other gen relevant to the present and future conduct of operations. This was the time when the big boys were largely uninformed. Earlier at briefing the latter had been in secret possession of the pre-op plans while, at least at first, the crews had been in the dark. Now the reverse was the case, the crews had the gen which the big boys eagerly awaited, and the first three crews down were ready to spill the beans.

Ace Burnett and his crew took seats around one of a group of tables presided over by an intelligence officer, smartly avoiding the imminent attentions of the MO who was mooching around to justify a reason for being in attendance. After what the IO considered adequate time for the crew to settle and gather their thoughts, he addressed them with a series of questions, the answers to which would form the basis for analysis of the success, or otherwise. As was his privilege as captain, Ace did most of the talking in a dry crisply presented style, occasionally calling for confirmation from crew members or elucidation of particular matters. For example John, whose job it was to log events, times and places, was asked for their position when attacked by the night fighter and Jock, who had the best view of the target situation from the rear turret was asked his view as to the concentration of the attack. Were there any particularly heavy explosions? It all took about 10 minutes, the interview terminating with Ace signing the captain's report.

Squadron Leader Denning, "B" Flight Commander, who had been debriefed first was standing talking to the Wing Commander, but when he spotted Ace and his crew about to slink off to breakfast he detached himself from the CO's company and strolled over.

"How did it go, Burnett?" he asked.

"OK Sir." Ace could be like an oyster at times, needing to be prised open.

"No trouble?" The Sqn Ldr was persistent.

"One fighter attack." The way the young pilot said it implied it was a consequence scarcely to be considered, but in fact he was desperately tired. For several hours he had manhandled his Lancaster without let up, because, while George the automatic pilot was installed, no self respecting bomber pilot would be sufficiently audacious or foolish to relinquish control to an automaton over enemy territory.

"Good show boy." The Sqn Ldr sounded as if he did not expect anything else from his "B" flight crews, but Jock was unable to resist putting his Scottish oar in.

"First saw this JU88 out on the beam. Parallel course. Thought we hadn't been spotted, but he attacked on the port beam."

"Why didn't you fire when you saw the enemy?"

"Well Sir," Jock wished he had kept his trap shut. Now he had to go through with an explanation. "I was almost sure it was a JU 88 but it could have been a Mosquito or Beaufighter."

The Sqn Ldr smiled understandingly.

"You'll have to accept that if you see a twin engined kite near you, or single for that matter, it shouldn't be there as far as you are concerned and is an enemy. Take no chances lad."

"Right Sir." Jock was pleased not to be balled out.

The Flight Commander turned to Ace:

"You've had your baptism and at least you won't run away with the idea that just because everything seems quiet there's no danger. Right? OK, shove off for breakfast and get some sleep."

GET SOME SLEEP. It sounded fine, but it was not as simple as that for six of the seven man crew were absolutely bursting for a PEE, a situation arising from the problem of attending to nature's calls in flight. Jock's position in the rear turret ought not to have been too difficult because the Elsan was nearby, but of course it was because the bulkiness of his electrically heated suit together with the fact that the turret was cramped anyway, made the first entry a struggle let alone having to get out and in again in flight. Frank, in the middle turret would have found the situation easier to manage, but he had foreborne. In the case of Taffy, John, Ken and Sid, each would have had to detach themselves from the main oxygen supply, connect up to portable bottles, struggle over the main spar, only to find it was so bloody cold 60 feet back in the fuselage that one could not perform anyway.

Then there was the long journey back to gasp breathlessly over the main spar again. On a relatively short trip of some 4 hours it was far better to keep the cork in the bottle, so to speak, the more so since a man out of normal crew position weakened the defensive cohesion of the seven man single unit. Only Ace had the convenience of a flexible tube and funnel since under no circumstance could he leave his seat. He had actually used the tube with instant regret for, by reason of slipstream vortices, he had well and truly got his own back. Now with the experience of continuing dampness he reflected on the old adage that one should never piss against the wind.

Chapter 2

STANDDOWN

John Howard woke at the comparatively early hour of 11 AM to find that he seemed to be the only one conscious in the hut which slept two crews of Sergeants, but as he languorously surveyed the scene he became aware of a throat tickling sensation. Someone else was awake, smoking a gasper and a pretty foul blend at that. His eyes traversed the two rows of bodies over which bedclothes were in total disarray. From Sid's bed a swirl of smoke curled slowly towards the ceiling. If Sid did not appear to be awake for his eyes were firmly closed, he was conscious enough to contrive spasmodic efforts to draw on his fag.

"Wonder what's on today, Sid," John ventured. Sid's facial muscles twitched slightly and an arm arced out to flick ash on to the floor.

"We are I expect, old boy," he murmured matter-of-factly.

"The worst of being on a new unit is we don't know the form." John was speaking quietly enough, or so he thought until a strange voice grumbled from out of swaddling clothes:

"The form is to bloody well belt up — the Tannoy'll blast us out if we're wanted." The grumbling tailed away into an inarticulate murmur, finally stalling in regained unconsciousness.

"Now you know," admonished Sid, still with eyes closed.

"Nice cheerful Sod," replied John. He glanced around taking in the detail of their sleeping quarters. It was only the second night and altogether a pretty poor show. He and the rest of the crew had arrived on one day, fell into bed that night too tired to look around, on ops the next night and again too tired to care where they were accommodated.

The big prefabricated hut housed 14 beds. At the ends were two separate rooms. In the centre of the hut was a coke stove. It was the kind that blazed away producing a hot fug and just as easily burnt out prematurely leaving the air as cold as a witch's kiss. There was a door at each end of the hut and above one was the Tannoy speaker designed to muster personnel from the various dispersed sites.

About the ceiling were suspended bare light bulbs only roughly central and altogether it was no palace, merely functional, the

19

abode of aircrew Sergeants where they needed to recoup energy for the next bombing operation. It was a depressing thought that over on the Base station, a peacetime establishment built with bricks and mortar, the aircrews slept in centrally heated Messes with hot and cold water immediately available without having to go to a different building for ablutions.

Ace and crew made it to the Mess on Sid and John's instigation. It had not been easy to get them all out of bed without causing upset to the other crew, although Ace had been easier to handle simply because he had been crafty enough to bag one of the two end rooms. It was pretty muddy up the lane leading to the Mess and it seemed a shame to have to walk over the well polished floor of the Sergeants Mess in muddy shoes.

The newspapers announced that "A large force of our heavy bombers attacked Duisberg — 32 of our aircraft are missing," and a puckered frown on Sid's forehead indicated that the thrills of JANE in the Daily Mirror had been eclipsed by the more potent news.

Ace had read the headlines too. What was obvious to him was that the business of being bomber aircrew was stuffed with "No Future" unless he and his crew could keep their fingers well out and experience a goodly share of luck.

An hour passed before anyone else put in an appearance. Those that did were stuffed with lassitude. Whilst it was scarcely likely that the increasing odour from the kitchens had spread the quarter mile to the sleeping quarters, some anticipation of the approaching meal was evident from a steady influx of bodies. Even so aircrews were normally conspicuously lax in so far as arriving on time for meals was concerned, a circumstance that caused the catering staff no end of irritation. So there had to be a motive. With the passage of time it was becoming possible that the prospect of night ops was fading for the Tannoy maintained an impressive silence. If preparations for the evening were not actively in hand they were certainly in mind.

The sudden entrance of Texel Hanson, Sqn Ldr Denning's flight engineer, displaying a wide mouthed grin complete with tombstones, confirmed the expectation.

"STANDDOWN chaps. Weather's duff."

"Whizzo!" whooped one Sergeant.

"Butch Harris must have overslept," said another.

Such remarks swiftly merged into relaxed conversation, both general and particular until finally the dining room door swung open and there was something of a concerted rush.

Texel latched on to Ace and his crew. It was pretty noisy at first and very much a cross to bear for the waitress.

"Get up them stairs, Dora," Texel advised the waitress as she asked if he wanted soup.

"I don't like stairs, Tex." She was pretty quick off the mark with her rejoinder. Knowing the worthy Sergeant she probably came armed with stock answers.

"Well I'll do you in the basement then," he suggested.

Dora was substantially built, the top half of her obtruding amply. She was congenial enough, usually advertising a ready smile, but on this occasion Texel distinctly nettled her. Her voice moved up an octave preceded by massive indrawn breath.

"You're incorrigible Texel," she neighed and throwing back her flowing mane with a sweep of the hand she stalked into the kitchen.

"Must have had a bad night too," said Texel blandly. "Which reminds me. You chaps ought to get acquainted with our local pub, so what about a beat up at the "Old Cow". There was general assent.

The heavy rain that had built up during the daytime had ceased by evening giving way to a miserable drizzle that was just as forbidding, but in the little village pub a blazing log fire threw out a come hither welcome.

Texel briskly wished the publican the time of day, while the latter merely nodded, content for the moment to polish the glassware until the clientele had taken up their positions. He knew exactly what Texel wanted and the manner in which the order would be presented.

"Eight dirty great pints of wallop, Bert." Texel peered around in a proprietorial way before adding, "meet your new clients. Baskets all. This here pipsqueak of a navigator plays piano so we're going to shake the dust out of it."

Bert cast a quizzical look at the little group of Sergeants. They were no different from the others who had passed by, mere boys in uniform with faces of innocence.

"S'alright with me," Bert replied. "But keep it clean or you'll drive away my regulars".

"No cause for alarm. We're going to have some sloppy sentimental stuff. Take you back to your courting days. Zat so, Johnny boy?" Bert pulled a wry face; he could still appreciate a trim female figure and imagine his youth, but dreams were all he had left.

"Don't rush me, Tex," replied the navigator, "I'll need a pint or two to work up enthusiasm." But he really could not resist the opportunity for practice and once conversation had got under way he sidled up to the piano. With some dubiety he ran tentative fingers over the keys and much to his surprise the piano was

21

in a fair state of tuning. Increasingly relish superseded earlier inhibitions. He started in with "We'll meet again" followed by Glenn Miller's "Moonlight Serenade" and other evergreen favourites, oblivious of the interest of a now expanded audience. He was relieved to be away from the natter of Service life that was in turn relevant and irrelevant, sustained or fragmentary and when fatalism and cynicalness were not only partners but habits of mind.

As the noise in the bar escalated in tune with the number of pint mugs lifted, John turned to view the scene. A battle royal was in progress. A writhing sea of blue sought attention at the counter where the publican, now reinforced by a pair of comely wenches, was fighting a losing battle to keep abreast of demand. But Bert had to be happy for the clientele were free with their flying pay although the prospect of running out of beer was a frequent worry that aggravated his stomach ulcer. John with no such ulcer decided he did not want one either. It was time to stop playing louder than the background noise, so he rejoined his group by dint of some considerable pushing and shoving.

The plaintive, barely audible "Time Gentlemen Please" call came all too soon, but the mood of the gathering was such that the publican's plea was substantially lost in the pungent atmosphere. Besides, where were the gentlemen? Subsequent pleadings had much the same negative effect, until, simply because the liquid supply dried up, there was no further reason for the assembled company to outstay its welcome.

Out into the night Ace and Co spilled although the means of exit was no simple matter, for somewhat implausibly, as if a complicated pattern of thought transference had intruded, a bulky group of bodies chose to make an exodus at precisely the same moment. It was all a question of whether bone structures would be impacted or the door would take leave of its massive hinges. Fortunately for the war effort there seemed to be no casualties requiring hospitalisation.

"Well what now?" asked Texel breathlessly but clearly of the view that he at least had not the vaguest intention of terminating the jollification just because the Licensing Laws left a lot to be desired.

"Lets go see we can keep the mess bar open," suggested Ace with the air of having produced an absolutely brilliant original idea. Since the idea was latent if otherwise unspoken by the rest, there were no objections and Sid deciding that the proposal should be positively seconded, said so.

It was dark. No lights were visible in the village. The incumbents of the little cottages had achieved a near perfect efficiency in blanketing in every possible chink of light, or they lived in fear of a particularly diligent ARP officer, or just simply got up with the light and retired at sundown, like birds. An uncertain moon peered very faintly through fast moving cloud, so uncertain indeed that the light from it was non-existent. So out came the torches. At least it was not raining.

Just about spitting distance from the pub door, Sid said quickly, "Last at the bar buys the drinks all round," and set off like a greyhound, torch held out like a knight's lance before him. John gave himself a shock by passing Sid just outside the main entrance. He had always been a good long distance runner, but unrecognised as a sprinter, so as he forged still further ahead he reflected that his current superiority had to be due to alcoholic stimulus or to his crew mates' singularly low standard of athleticism. With the arrival of his second wind the exhaustive reaction on respiratory system lessened and he tore round the narrow pathway towards the Sergeants' Mess entrance in a headlong process that gained momentum with every loping stride, lunging finally through an unaccountably open door with only half anchors on. At first he thought implausibly that someone had had the forethought to open the door for him. At it happened he was brought up very sharply by the reverse situation. Someone was coming out, which circumstance caused him to lose total control. He tripped on the step and measured his length on the hall floor. Just for one fleeting moment he spotted a body trying desperately to avoid him and as he heavily got back on to his pins he took in the vision of a WAAF Sergeant standing with arms folded, gazing at him impassively.

"Gosh! I'm awfully sorry. My brakes failed." Ruefully he rubbed a knee, while casting the lady an apprehensive glance, certain that she might be on the point of beating him over the head. In a thousandth of a second he realised that that danger was not imminent. Now with hands on hips she was surveying him like a schoolmistress about to upbraid a recalcitrant pupil. In a further thousandth of a second he took in the whole view that was wholly satisfying — a rare specimen of WAAF, a Sergeant, and young at that. A head of jet black hair above the biggest pair of soft brown eyes he had ever seen, topped a trim, slim, but well-proportioned figure. His gaze became prolonged though there was nothing remotely indecent to it and he was inclined to wish he could go through the same motions again if only to allow further appreciation. This notion he disregarded as it occurred to him that his continued interest was already on the verge of rudeness.

The WAAF, by way of a suitable response gave John a straight look in mute reproof of the latter's admiring stare, but soon there was a trace of a smile that reached those wondrous eyes. She eyed him with genuine curiosity. When she spoke her voice was mellow contralto.

"I should jolly well think you would have the grace to apologise. Apology accepted, with reservations."

John groaned within for it seemed he was about to get chapter and verse in terms of the reservations, but the danger was averted by the tardy arrival of Sid, Texel, Ace, Frank, Ken and Taffy with Jock bringing up the rear striving to the last to avoid having to pay for the drinks, in keeping with his National trait.

"Hello Marion, my love," said Texel breathlessly. "I see you've met one of us already."

"Ah. Now I see." Marion looked straight at the navigator. "If you're mixed up with Texel there's no telling what you've been up to."

"Meet Ace Burnett and his crew." Tex nominated them one by one and then went on: "Jolly good chaps. We have been on the razzle, sweetheart."

"So it seems. How very unusual!" You could almost feel the chill in her voice.

"Well, they're new to the squadron. Had to show them around a bit." Texel was all innocence.

"You drink too much. You probably all do." Marion continued to act the schoolmarm.

"That's because my love is unrequited. I open my heart to you. You turn my heart to quivering jelly and my legs to water and what happens, I'm spurned and have to turn to drink." To listen to Texel made one want to cry but the only effect it had on Marion was to make her angry. She cuffed Texel about the ears.

"Enough of that," she warned severely.

"Oh. Alright love." Tex was in no way abashed. "I was just beginning to get warmed up. Chaps, this is Marion Hall, one of our two operations watchkeepers. Dates can be arranged by whistling or emitting wolfish howls beneath the window on the port side of the control tower, but candidates are requested to confirm application on Form 000, in triplicate." Texel remained in fine fettle, but in contrast she maintained an unnerving calm which was a shade surprising when, whether in fun or not she was so paraded before strangers. It was to be assumed she was accustomed to hearing him rabbit on.

"What is Form Treble 000?" she asked, puzzled, and even Texel showed some embarrassment for he quickly realised he had gone a bit too far.

"Don't ye know love?" he almost whispered. He looked around at the little company who were by now shifting their feet. "Shall I tell her boys?"

"No" they replied as one.

"In that case I'll tell her. One can always learn. It's that stuff — yards of it with "Air Ministry Property" stamped on each piece and usually found in the t—"

"That's enough. I am fully informed. Knowing you, I should not have been fool enough to ask." She gave him a really poisonous look. "You *have* had much too much to drink."

"Have a heart, sweetheart. We've only just begun. We only die once. Have a drink with us. I apologize, I grovel."

"No thank you. I'm off."

"Just a teeny one. I promise to be good," cajoled Texel.

"Please do." John bit his lip. He felt the blood rush to his face.

Marion gave him a look that reflected some interest. The navigator had given her the courtesy of a suitable apology, he spoke in a cultured manner and his manners were probably impeccable.

"Well, just a shandy then, please," she said after momentary hesitation.

"Good girl." Texel was genuinely pleased. He moved quickly towards the hatch to pre-empt possible closure, quite forgetting that Jock, who was last in the race, should have bought the round. Needless to say, Jock was not doing any reminding.

"Texel said you were an ops watchkeeper," Ace questioned conversationally. "We're a bit green. What do you do?"

Marion favoured him with a gracious smile.

"I sit up in a little room in the control tower and write down the ops gen as it comes through on the scrambler — target, route, bomb load, petrol load, in fact the lot, but not as Texel suggested, open to dates."

Ace nodded, ignoring the sting in the tail.

"In every sense you are wise before the event. Sounds like you have a heavy responsibility on your shoulders."

"I like to think so," she replied modestly enough. "The work does not admit of error as you will readily understand. That's why I am, like you, favoured with 3 stripes."

Texel returned from the hatch and handed over the drinks, being very careful to follow the courtesy of "lady first."

"Just caught Charlie about to close up," he said.

"I like this station," Marion said, still speaking to Ace. "It is well away from Lincoln and that suits me. It will begin to be lovely here by the end of this month and more so when summer arrives, but then I'm a farmer's daughter and it is natural for me to appreciate the countryside." She got into a discussion with Ace on the respective merits of the English countryside and the New Zealand counterpart, while John studied her covertly with mounting interest. He noted that she was well-spoken with no noticeable accent. Since she was hardly the rustic girl of John's limited acquaintance, she just had to be of good family with a perch fairly well up the social ladder. Here in the mess she was the odd one out amongst so many men from varying walks of life and yet so confident and self-possessed.

It was clear that the rest of Ace's crew were fascinated by her presence and her easy discourse with Ace, as if she had known him for years. They were content merely to listen.

"I didn't much like the look of it here," John put in when Ace and Marion paused for breath. "There's so much mud about and so far to go from one part of the airfield to another."

"You can have a bike issued." Marion felt she should be helpful. "Most of the personnel prefer biking to walking. Just draw one from stores."

"Well thank you, Miss." Frank was rather nervously correct and won an attractive smile.

"There's certainly an atmosphere of friendliness." John was determined to keep her eyes on him. "Not like the OTU."

"I've been told before that life on an operational station is superior to other units," she said. "Better, easier atmosphere, better food and very little discipline. I think you will all get to like it here, especially when the weather improves."

"I haven't pedalled a bike since I was a kid," Ace mused aloud, but clearly he had latched on to Marion's suggestion.

"Don't fall for that one, Marion." Texel had had enough of the background. "He just wants you to show him how — you can see it in his eyes. 'Sides, you've got your work cut out darning my socks."

Marion did lose her cool and wagged a finger at the flight engineer so furiously that he shied away in alarm. Her eyes were arctic.

"Yes and now you HAVE put your foot in it. In future you can wash them, or at least soak them first. I swear that the last pair you produced had been worn for at least a year. I burnt them on the stove."

"What? My favourite pair? My lucky pair? How could you wilfully destroy them?" Texel looked so pained that the little group burst into laughter. Even Charlie poked his head out of the hatch and thereby introduced himself.

"I've got my own mending to do and so I must really go." She unhitched hat and coat from a peg and turned to wag a final critical finger at Texel. "Think well on your sins — you will be the only loser. Thank you for the drink."

"Shall I see you to the WAAFery." Texel tended towards the contrite. "It's pretty dark out there."

"You're not such a bad scout, Texel." There was a smile this time. "But no thank you. I've got my bike and a good lamp to guide me." With a final wave and a goodnight to all she was gone.

"Nice girl that," murmured Tex and lunged at his pint as if he had sorrows to drown.

"Quite a peach." Ace just had to agree. He had enjoyed his chat with her. John gazed thoughtfully at the closed door. That girl was a beauty and it was more than just skin deep. How old would she be, he wondered. Perhaps she touched 25 but one could never be sure of girls in uniform. Some looked older, some younger, some more attractive, some less so. He came out of a reverie to hear Texel explaining that the WAAFery was on the other side of the village and that he did not think she should go unescorted in the dark.

Sid produced a slow wink to Taffy, Ken, Jock and Frank who had listened to the natter. It was not lost on Texel who always seemed to have his eyes everywhere, but he went on unperturbed. For some obscure reason he felt the need to justify his motive for offering escort and that his offer was based on the absolute in integrity, which only served to convince the assembled company that Tex thought a great deal of the WAAF Sergeant. How much it was impossible to discern. Texel was a pretty complicated character.

With the star having left the stage, weariness settled on the company, and Taffy it was who put it in a nutshell:

"I've got a head. I need a spot of kip."

"Likewise," said Ace, and there was no dissent, not even from Texel whose thoughts were elsewhere.

They were the last to leave the mess. Even Charlie, the barman had quietly closed the shutters and sidled out.

Chapter 3

OVER THE ALPS

Spring passed slowly into summer. For miles around the airfield nature's brilliant array of green hues beautified the scene. To the North the rich fields folded over a flowing rise in the topography into dense woodland. Here and there lay the brown remains of dank hayricks, depleted by animal feeding. Tall elms parading across the terrain picked out a pattern of little country lanes seemingly going nowhere but each having a purpose and destination. In the distance on a day of good visibility in a south westerly direction, Lincoln Cathedral stood up imposingly on the hill dominating the City of Lincoln though only to be perceived from the air over Holmdun airfield itself. In the village an earlier feast of swaying narcissi and dancing daffodils had decayed to leave only the stalks.

It was, for the most part, peaceful enough during the daytime, but at night the first Lancaster to bite the air would sunder the comparative quiet of earlier hours. With better weather the nightly disturbances grew more frequent as the Squadron winged eastwards. The battle of the Ruhr was under way with Essen, Krefeld, Elberfeld and Barmen, Gelsenkirchen and Bochum receiving Bomber Command's hammer blows. In general these targets were at no great distance, but by reason of the devious routes employed to fox the defences these operations were of sufficient duration in terms of flying hours to tax the strength and moral fibre of the crews. It was "attack", "attack", "press on regardless — your return is incidental" and there was a price to pay. Of the sixteen crews at Holmdun when Ace and his crew had joined the Squadron, only six remained although the total number had been maintained by replacements. Of the ten lost only two crews had completed a tour of operations and gone off elsewhere to instruct others. As to the rest the manner of their demise was unknown. One crew from 'A' flight were unlucky. They never returned from their 30th and last trip of the tour.

The demise of such an experienced crew might have struck fear in the hearts of those remaining to carry on the battle, but they grew to become cynically immune to the prospect of a funeral pyre in the sky, or to be blown to dust.

By the beginning of July, Ace Burnett and his crew had survived thirteen operations, a number that Taffy the wireless op was worried about. On that number they were catching up Sqn Ldr Denning and by the same token, Texel. Denny had eighteen on the board but he was on his third tour.

Ace and Texel were firm friends being frequently referred to as Castor and Pollux, the Heavenly Twins, although Sid once remarked when asked how Texel could best be described, that he was "A wanker with verbal diarrhoea".

Ace's crew usually went their own way. Taffy, Jock and Ken had built up a reserve of popsies in Lincoln. Frank, the quiet shy one wended his way to the same City but with less amorous intent. Sid, when the mood took him joined Ace and Texel, drinking freely enough to enhance Mess funds, or he would retire into a little shell of his own.

John and Marion were more often than not together enjoying a warm companionship that was seen to be permanent. They lunched together whenever possible wholly unaffected by Texel's continuing attempts to upset their composure. Indeed, at first whenever they entered the Mess together he would roar across the dining room with a "here come the lovebirds" warning. They had been initally embarrassed by the resulting grins and witticisms and by the stares of new crew members. Once John had threatened to knock Texel's bloody head off, but by and large, they discovered that the best defence lay in silence. With the passage of time the Mess accepted the liaison as a fait accompli. Only occasionally when Tex was in one of his blacker hangover moods when jealously leapt unguardedly from under his usual mask of indifference would he forget himself and fire off a caustic remark. Liking Marion as he clearly did, he resented John's ability to command Marion's attention. But there was no serious friction between the two men, which was just as well since in their youthful existence they were bound in common purpose. Sometimes when Marion had a domestic evening, John would join Ace, Texel and perhaps Sid in one of their little sessions of solid drinking, which did little harm and certainly ensured sound sleep, but his heart was not in it however much he contrived to enter into the spirit of the occasion. He had, in fact reached a point when without Marion's company he was restless.

It was after one such night that John and Ace strolled down towards the flights to see what the score was. Only the former had taken Marion's advice to draw a bicycle from stores, but he reserved it for off duty hours. Thus it was that the two were on shanks pony. A faint morning mist hung in the air giving promise of a warm sunny day. The air was heavy with fragrance making one want to draw in deep breaths, and to realise that there was a hell of a lot in life to live for.

Ace found Denny seated at his desk in earnest conversation with the engineering officer, while sprawled on rather than in battered chairs were a few 'B' flight pilots languidly exhaling clouds of tobacco smoke and making desultory natter. He nodded to the 'Lo Ace salutations and betook himself to his usual half perch on the low window ledge, there to expertly roll his own gasper. The engineering officer, business completed hopped it in haste, and the flight commander glanced around to see who was present. There was an unusual steely glint in his eyes suggesting that he had serious matters to convey to the gathered group, but his tone was level when he spoke.

"Have you seen that dead loss engineer of mine, Ace?"

Ace shifted his weight tentatively.

"I might know where he is. I'll go get him," but as he shifted full weight to the feet, a knock at the door preceded the figure of Texel accompanied by his fixed grin.

"Talk of the very devil," murmured Denny. "Put the wood in the hole."

"Morning Sir. Lovely day" burbled Texel. "Nice rich smell in here."

"That's because you are here." Denny was crispness itself. "Take a pew."

"I was thinking, if you don't want me for a while I'd like to pop out to dispersal."

"Think again," snapped Denny. "I've a bone to pick with all you lags." He glared around at the now silent group. "As your flight commander I have the dubious honour of being responsible for your sleeping quarters." He paused and then positively sniffed before proceeding. "I assumed that as the cream of Britain's youth you would contrive to keep your billets in a habitable state, but I took a gander after breakfast while you characters were still stuffing yourselves and found your quarters scarcely less dirty than a pigsty. The floors haven't seen a broom for months, there are dogends all over the place and in one hut there is a motor bike dripping oil, filled no doubt with petrol syphoned from some other poor blighter's tank." He glared around the company with quite startling severity. "And its got to stop forthwith. If the Group Captain decided on a snap inspection, who would carry the can back? You? Not bloodly likely. You're little tin gods, you can't easily be put on a charge, you know you're too badly needed." His blazing eyes targeted on Texel, rooting the latter to the spot. "Texel." Denny had worked up to a shout now. "I'm putting you in charge of 'B' flight NCO's accommodation, directly responsible to me. I don't care how its done, but do it. You could get some erks on jankers for all I care, but do it. Do you hear me?"

"Yes Sir," Texel replied weakly. "But there isn't a broom on the site."

"No brooms?. I'll have so many scattered around you'll trip over them, dream of them, that is if you've enough sensibility."

"Caw," murmured the poor flight engineer. "Joe again. OK Sir, shall be done. Do I get promotion?."

"You'll get a rise on the end of my boot if you don't wrap up that ropey humour and since there's a war on I hope you guys have clearer minds than habits." He waved a sign of dismissal at the engineer who exited like a dog after the hare, then relapsed quite suddenly into his customary smooth manner as easily as he had earlier risen to anger.

"Ace. I've had the Engineering officer in here as you saw. My kite Sugar is just off a minor inspection. I want you to take her up, give her a good run over and do a spot of air to sea firing. The rest of you can get in some bombing practice at Wainfleet. We may be top bombing squadron and we're going to remain so."

As the pilots drifted out, Denny stopped Ace.

"When you come in over the coast, keep your height. The last time you went thataway we received an acrimonious bitch from the so-called Senior Service."

"What about?" Ace's visage was in innocence the personification of a new born babe.

"Well I'll tell you. A low flying Lanc beat up a squad of naval cadets at Skegness, causing them to break ranks and prostrate themselves for fear of their lives. The squadron letters were reported, but not the number, so you were lucky."

"Damn bad discipline, poor show breaking ranks like that," Ace commented with bland innocence, shaking his head in disgust. "I thought the Navy was of sterner stuff."

"And I repeat the recalcitrant pilot was flying R Robert," Denny went on smoothly, "because you were the only one over there at the time. Now bugger off before I lose my temper again."

Ace scrammed. Denny watched the wide square shoulders and peculiar gait nudge through the doorway before permitting himself a slow smile. He remembered the time when the young New Zealander had first come through the flight office doorway. Then, although a complete sprog the latter had appeared to be quietly confident, and he was no different now. It was to be supposed that with experience had come some cunning and an added degree of daring. In continuing reflective mood Denny told himself that he ought to have been more severe over that Navy beat-up, but well, there was another side to it. There was little of the fighter boy's glamour to rub off on a bomber pilot. On ops he was obliged to slavishly follow the navigators instructions. From time to time he had to bank over, wing tips at the vertical, so that the gunners could search below for enemy fighters. Otherwise it was a long careful nursing of his Lancaster to the target followed by a perfectly straight run on to the aiming point however much flak was being pumped up from the ground. Then there was the long nervy run home in constant fear of enemy fighter attack, of collision and sometimes bad weather. And it was all in pitch black darkness.

It was for these reasons that the flight Commander had chosen to treat lightly Ace's deviation from strict rules. It was also in his mind that bomber crews had only a limited regard for the Navy, who, it seemed, invariably fired at the bombers setting out for Germany, or coming back, on a "fire first, ask questions afterwards" basis.

The young pilot was now one of the Squadron's top-liners. He was usually first home although this feat was not necessarily the test of success. Denny recalled the time when he, Denny, had had some misgivings that the early returns were due to some corner cutting by the navigator, or worse still, not going absolutely to the target, but an uneasy interview with Bert Apsley, the navigation leader left him in no doubt that suspicions were unfounded. In fact, Bert had waxed exceedingly angry. With hawklike nose high in the air, Bert had icily pointed out that all operational charts were backtracked and any undesirable features exposed. Bert had contrived to give the impression that only a stupid driver could possibly have conjured up such a supposition. The navigation leader's coup de grace was further supported by the crew's uncanny knack of producing aiming point photos under conditions that were far from conducive to good results. The rear gunner too, had achieved moments of glory, aided by the mid upper gunner. They had jointly shot down three enemy fighters which was a pretty good show for a night bomber whose tactics were defensive on account of inferior fire power. The main idea was to avoid fighters where possible, lose them rather than attack and if the bomber was attacked, evasive action was first priority, shooting down the foe second. In these circumstances, Jock the fearless Scot had managed to hit successfully, on the run, so to speak.

Denny broke off his musings as the telephone shrilled. It was much too noisy, bad for one's liver in the morning. He snatched at the instrument and tensed. The CO. was on the line. OPS WERE ON.

The western sky was an erubescent arc of molten light that seemed to flow right though the perspex canopy of Lancaster R for Robert. Five thousand feet below the lofty spur of Beachy Head stood out into the salmon flecked sea in dark outline, like a signpost. Although there was little ground for complacency Ace felt a sense almost of freedom as he positively basked in the last warmth of the sun slipping slowly in a half segment behind the serrated line of the horizon. Here he was, flying at 160 indicated, in perfectly stable air over the southern shore of England, while out on the port side the faint outline of the French coast was visible. It was a new experience to be heading south and John had earlier joked that he was not sure if he could find Beachy Head, the first turning point on the route. The usual route for months had been eastwards, thence to differing points on the Dutch coast and on to the Ruhr Valley, but on this occasion the C-in-C had taken an old rabbit out of the hat. Italy was to receive unwelcomed visitors, some 4 hours hence, TURIN the rendezvous and aiming point.

Briefing earlier in the day had been an eye opener, for as the target code word had been decoded and announced, the cheering crews had nearly raised the roof of the briefing room. To say that joyous abandon reigned would have been a masterly piece of understatement and there was a very good reason for this. An eyetie target was generally regarded as a veritable piece of cake. Even the prospect of a lengthy and tiring journey failed to dampen enthusiasm until it became obvious that there was a fly in the ointment. A fair part of the return trip across France would be undertaken in the early light of the following day and realisation of this produced some lessening of the joy. It was of course a calculated risk, the routeing being back across unoccupied France where in theory there should be no fighters. In practice of course, fighters would speed to take up battle positions, but such dispositions as there were, were likely to be more scattered and less concentrated. Thus it was a definite risk, for in daylight with its inferior defensive fire power, the Lancaster would be a sitting duck against purposeful attack. In any case the force of Lancasters would eventually have to turn northwards towards the homeland in to range of enemy patrols.

Ace was not now concerned with the return journey. Looking at the strategy of the attack, the weather over eastern France was expected to be no great shakes, but it would be clear on the other side of the Alps. According to the Met men a cold front lay across the route and although it was expected that the force would be well above the highest cloud at operational height, the expectation always had to be suspect as the forecasters had little enough by way of weather reports from enemy territory on which to base an accurate forecast. Thus it had to be said that rather than forecast, it was conjecture topped up with a modicum of fond hope. Besides, the Met men never claimed infallability, preferring to take refuge in the oft repeated truism that Meteorology was an inexact science.

As usual Ace was seeking to gain maximum height in the quickest possible time. However it was not as easy as all that. With a substantial bomb load and a full 2159 gallons of petrol on board and because it was a warmish evening, the 4 Rolls Royce Merlin engines were not so responsive, preferring ice cold temperatures for maximum efficiency. They needed coaxing, a kind of mechanical arm twisting.

The half sun fell suddenly beyond the horizon leaving just a reddish afterglow with the French coast looming only darkly as the mantle of night reached the ground first. It was at height, a half light that produced minatory shadows creating moments of anxiety, but there was nothing positive to disturb the steady climb for altitude. At the French coast, Ace turned on to the long leg to Lake Annecy on the near side of the Alps and was on the point of adjusting exactly to the navigators course when there was an urgent call from the rear.

"Rear gunner to Pilot," called Jock. "Lanc on the port side moving in towards us. Drop down quick — he's on our height."

The pilot's response was unthinking and immediate. He shoved the control column forward into a nosedown attitude. A black shadow floated over from port to starboard much too close for comfort.

"A bit late on his turn," commented Sid from the bombing compartment below the flight engineer's feet. "Unless of course John got it wrong." The navigator treated Sid's remark with contempt by maintaining total silence.

"He's turning now," said Ken, who felt it right to have another pair of eyes looking out.

"At least we know we've got friendly company and going the right way," replied Ace.

It was not long before they seemed to be alone in the sky. The night had swallowed up the other Lancaster. Down below the earth was as black as a hanging Judge's cap. It was on long trips like these that one realised just how big was the sky. It was also hard to accept that somewhere in the vicinity were 200 odd Lancasters.

Two hours later it was just as lonely without further indication of other bombers. Ace shifted his position for the umpteenth time. Sitting on his parachute for any length of time was a cross to bear, but to sit on it for a long time was like bearing the Cross of Lorraine — double trouble. Conversation had been desultory and had completely dried up since Sid had reported cloud below some half hour back. A half moon was in evidence, but only for a short spell till the aircraft ran into a veil of cloud, thin at first and then thickening sharply. Sudden vicious upcurrents of air bore R Robert aloft and then dropped her a couple of hundred feet. Ace had to put some effort into maintaining fluent control.

"Got to get above this Ken. Climbing revs 2650," Ace commanded. The four engines thundered under the surge of more power and there was a spasmodic cracking sound as ice particles smacked against the fuselage.

"You should see my gun barrels. Flame leaping between them." Jock had seen it all before but St. Elmo's fire never failed to fascinate or frighten him.

"Got some here," Ace replied as he blinked eyes in the glare of blue flame dancing along the windscreen. John peeped out from behind his curtain to ascertain what all the fuss was about. He promptly resumed position. A rapid glance gave him a momentary picture of the aircraft on fire as he reflected that Ace, who had had a Phoenix painted on the fuselage of R. Robert, had perhaps been unwise to buck mythology. At this precise moment John fondly hoped that if there was really going to be a fire, the Phoenix was going to rise from the ashes, with the crew intact. A violent flash of lightning did not help much either. Frontal cloud alright, thought the navigator, but Met had forecast cloud tops at 18,000 ft and here they were at 23,000 ft and still in cloud.

Slowly but surely the Lancaster was still beating gravity until the thick cloud thinned to a mist so that on occasions stars could be seen. Then they were in clear air. Ace throttled back to cruising revs at 2300, but maintained the additional height for they had yet to cross the Alps. John was not exactly happy. With all this cloud about it was unlikely that they would recognise Lake Annecy. He had hoped that moonlight would reflect on the water making it stand out against the earth's darker topography allowing him to fix their position, for long since they had passed out of Gee range and were flying on Dead Reckonning alone, which was OK as long as the windspeed and direction had not changed much. If those factors had changed, he was all too aware that an error of course would be magnified by increasing distance and time. There was little he could do but re-check his calculations, put on a brave face and certainly not communicate his fears at this stage. No need to worry the crew unduly. After what seemed like an eternity Sid called up.

"We're beyond the cloud approaching the Alps. Boy, look at that sight." Sid, usually phlegmatic and far from excitable seemed to feel some relief but whether it was unstated concern that the navigator might not know exactly where they were or from total boredom, Sid was not saying. A waxing half moon shed a haunting light on a barrier of snow capped peaks. There was an element of the hypnotic about the forward view through the bomb blister. It was great to be able to see the contours of the earth again. On the other hand the peaks looked dangerously menacing sticking up into the sky as if threatening to spike any aircraft that had the temerity to approach. Of a certainty, it was no place to be in a crippled aeroplane.

John had experienced some initial excitement as Sid made his sighting. It was a bit like a lost ship receiving a "Land ahoy" call from the top mast lookout. It waned a bit when he reflected that the Alps spanned a good many miles even into neutral Switzerland and they were not supposed to be in that locality. There was nothing else to be done but press on.

The mountains flattened — a sort of sinking into the ground. They were on to or more accurately over the plain of Lombardy.

"ETA 10 minutes," warned the navigator hopefully.

"OK John." Ace did not sound all that confident either, but some minutes later a red TI cascaded down, and there was instant relief.

"There's the marker." Sid confirmed the obvious. "We're a bit port of track John, maybe a couple of miles."

"Thanks Sid." John needed to know. He had not been far out in his calculations, but it could have been very different.

"How far to ETA John — it seems a good way ahead?" Ace had been stretching to peer through the windscreen and down but the front turret obstructed the view.

"I make it 5 minutes skipper," replied John cautiously.

"OK, but I'm pepping up the speed to 180knots and altering course 10 degrees to starboard."

"Right Ace. I'll plot it in."

The pilot turned on to the new course. He laid on extra revs just as the first red TI's received a fair and square backup. It looked as if Pathfinders had got the aiming point. A few searchlights waved about but to no definable pattern. Way down below some light flak hosed into the sky but for what purpose was anyone's guess for there were unlikely to be bombers at that low level. Ace felt quite elated for there did not seem to be significant defensive activity. It all looked to be a bit of a doddle. It was generally supposed that once the first bombs hit the deck, the eyeties would make a run for their burrows, but just at the moment they were being treated to little more than a brilliant firework display as Pathfinders checked that the reds were in the right place, before backing up with the greens. The markers spewed out now both red and green and they appeared to be pretty concentrated.

Sid dropped on to his stomach to watch the main concentration move into his bomb sight line. Bombs were beginning to fall on Turin identified by the flash of explosions, and now the city of Turin was laid bare in the light. The odd flak burst flashed but substantially below Ace's operational height.

"The natives are hostile," murmured Sid with heavy sarcasm. "Bomb doors open."

"Bomb doors open," replied Ace as he worked the release.

"Steady, steady," intoned Sid. "This is dead easy."

They made one of those steady run-ups to the target, that would, over a German target have been described as horribly steady. Straight and level R Robert flew, almost as if the aeroplane was glued to the atmosphere.

"Bombs gone. Hold steady for camera," Sid shouted.

"Turn on to 185 T for 5 minutes," said the navigator.

"Turning now on 185. Bomb doors closed." For all that he was on an Italian target Ace had the revs up to 3000. No point in taking chances. Get the hell out of here.

"Course 260T" the navigator called five minutes later.

"Right, course 260. Speed 165 indicated." It was a regular patter, instruction and confirmation. There was no room for error, not even over Italy. They were now at the half way mark. Turning for home was a great psychological boost. Behind, Jock had a great view of bombs crumpling on the city which was now lit up by photoflashes and fires brewing up from the incendiaries dropped with the high explosive bombs. What little opposition there had been had ceased. Occasionally the black form of a Lancaster moved across the rear gunner's vision in the afterglow, and then another and another.

What was abundantly clear was that the Italians had been surprised by the attack and even more clearly, had not the availability of early warning techniques.

As the glow from the target area faded, so did the sighting of other Lancasters and the chances were that for the remaining hours of night Ace and his crew would not see another. The route back followed a more southerly latitude than the route out.

Once again they breasted the Alps and crossed over the rain belt with rather less difficulty, being light of bomb load and the steadily reducing weight of fuel, hitting the coast near La Rochelle.

"Course 315 T. Lose height to 1000 feet," directed the navigator.

"OK John. Course 315 T. Speed 200 indicated." Ace added a warning. "Keep a good look out chaps. It's beginning to get light." Of course the gunners could see that. It was more a reminder to keep awake.

The idea was, if not to plunge, to get down to just above the drink so that there was less chance of being detected by German radar when they eventually had to pass near the Cherbourg penninsula.

Ace was tired, gradually being reduced to the status of an automation. His hands and feet corrected the aircraft's movement in the prevailing wind quite without direction from the mind. He was perched on his seat and yet without attachment to it. All across France a sense of alertness had remained sharply honed. Now as the French coast sank into the sea to the rear he fell into an attitude of thinking that danger was past, yet knowing all the time that danger was all the more poignant as the dawn's early light came up, but he could not rouse himself out of sheer fatigue. Then he became aware of several other Lancasters as he levelled out at about 500 feet, skirting through early morning mist. They were not too close, but close enough in the half light, so he braced himself. From the knowledge that they were no longer alone, loneliness evaporated as did the lethargy. Let the German fighters come — he really could not care less. He'd give them a run for their money, he mused but nosed down nearer the sea just in case.

"Hey Ace," called Jock from the rear turret. Get up a bit. I'm catching spray from the sea."

Ace grinned widely. "Thought you would like a morning dip." But he gained height a shade all the same for his eyelids were still encouraging sleep and the slightest miscalculation would dig the nose into the drink and a watery grave. Suddenly he was startled to see the parabolic course of a red Very cartridge half a mile to starboard. Danger was in the offing and the warning had come from another Lancaster. Four Lancasters moved into a loose formation on to Robert, forming an essentially defensive box pattern.

"Must be an enemy plane about," murmured Ken, the flight engineer.

"There he is," piped up young Frank from the mid upper turret in a voice that contrived to demonstrate iron adult control, but only served to accent the ambush of younger years. "On the starboard beam, JU 88. A mile away on a parallel course." Ace craned his neck to gaze over Ken's shoulder.

"Doesn't seem all that keen to get involved," he said laconically.

"Five of us has got him thinking," suggested Sid who by now had got up from his bomb position to man the front turret.

A burst of 303 gun fire fizzed out from one of the formating Lancaster's mid upper turret, taunting the enemy who was out of range, but there was no response.

"Navigator. I'm pushing the speed up to 220." R Robert forged ahead, but the other four Lancaster pilots opened the taps and reformated. They had got the message and approved. The sooner they got to the homeland coast, the better the chance of RAF fighter support.

Sid began to show some exasperation and mouthed accordingly.

"Come on you bastard — let's have you," but the fighter merely continued a policy of uninvited escort and was probably calling for reinforcements.

"Holy cow. What's he up to now?" Ace was rigid and staring ahead. "Open up Ken, full throttle. He's after a lone Lanc dead ahead. Stand by Sid, could be your party after all." Ken rammed the throttle wide open to full power and Robert leapt forward barely skimming the placid sea which flashed past at an incredible rate of knots.

"Fire off a Red, Taffy." Ace was wide awake now with sheer excitement. The red flare arched into the air with a muffled explosion as the wireless operator displayed a remarkable example of dedigitation.

"Hope the rear gunner spots the flare," murmured Ken. He did. The lone Lanc did a 180 ass about turn dropping from some 500 feet to skim the water towards the other friendly aircraft, while the JU88 overflew him unable to bring guns to bear because of too great an angle of deflection. The JU88's turn was too sharp. Sid blazed away from the front turret and bits flew off the tail. The lone Lancaster had turned again and was now formating. The JU88 banked away heading for the French coast.

"Blast — No guts the bastard," roared Sid who was doing the nearest thing to jumping up and down in the turret.

Ace was greatly amused. Instead of just smiling, he actually laughed and then turned it off quickly in case his crew thought he had gone bonkers. This was a new Sid, lapping up the prospect of battle and showing frustration at what turned out to be a mere fracas.

"Good show Sid. You bent him." Praise from Ace was brief but praise enough. It had to be plain sailing from now onwards and indeed it was. Start Point stood out into the sea way over to port and the line of the coast came up out of the sea. With Portland Bill to starboard R Robert crossed the English coast at Bridport. The navigator altered course for the final leg to Lincoln and home.

It was 7.00 hours when John pulled aside his office curtain to peer over the pilot's shoulder. Even at this incredibly early hour the sun warmed the cockpit. How strange, he thought, not to have to seek out the home base night flashing beacon to identify the airfield. There was Holmdun dead ahead seemingly without life. No other Lancaster was visible in the circuit.

"Home again jokers, and first," said Ace as he switched on RT. "Manger Robert to Bakewell. Are you receiving me?". He clicked over to receive.

"Bakewell to Robert. Loud and clear, Stand by." The WAAF was calling for patience.

"What the hell!" Ace was tired and anger came easily. He was first in the circuit and told to wait. "Sod 'em. We're going in. 20 Flap Ken."

"20 flap," echoed the flight engineer. He was not paid to argue the toss.

"Revs up." The pilot was always curt both on take-off and landing.

"Revs up." The reply was automatic. The constant speed propellors produced the Merlin whine.

"Hold it, Ace," warned Sid who had a wide downward vision through the blister. "They're changing the runway. Caravan's on the move. Looks like 30".

"Right Sid, thanks. What's the wind direction John?"

"About 320, Ace." The navigator with little else to do now had been listening and got the pilot's drift.

"That'll do. We'll judge it nicely." Ace turned from the downwind direction into a wide slow turn. With any luck he would be on the approach by the time he got the OK to land and not have to go round again.

"Wheels down Ken."

"Wheels down," echoed Ken. On came the wheels — locked — down green lights. The WAAF's voice floated up on RT, soft and consoling.

"Bakewell to Robert. Permission to land. Runway 30."

"OK sweetheart. Robert pancaking." Then to Ken, "Full flap."

"Full flap," replied Ken as he selected.

Lancaster Robert touched down sweetly less than 30 seconds after being given authority to land.

The navigator logged landing time. They had been in the air for 9 hours and 45 minutes. Much too long he thought, but for all that he had not had the time to scoff his chocolate flying ration or to drink the orange juice provided.

Chapter 4

AND AGAIN

The piece-of-cake TURIN op produced the unexpected. Every single crew expected to go out and return safely. It was that kind of trip — the spaghetti run, so it came as a shock to the squadron personnel to learn that the Wing Commander and his crew had failed to return. Although the failure of crews to return was an everyday event against which the survivors were largely inured, the loss of a dedicated and respected Squadron Commander was not an every day occurrence. It was a harsh thought that a man and his crew with such a wealth of experience behind them had finally kicked the bucket. It was like a ship losing its Captain overboard on the high seas, when although there were others capable of taking the helm, something of the unit's cohesion was lost. But the fact of his going was in accord with the law of averages. There had to come a day when his turn would come. It was a statistic that only 3 in 20 would survive a tour of operations over Germany. In the Wing Commander's case he had been the 1 of the 3 on his first tour and was two thirds of the way through a third when his luck ran out. No one knew the manner of his going, but since enemy activity had not been outstanding, it was generally thought that collision was the cause or even more probably, flying low over the sea on the way back, he had dug the nose into the sea in a moment of lost control by reason of fatigue.

The day after Turin was a Standdown. It was not all that unexpected because the crews involved had not got back until after sunup. After some hours of kip to recoup energy it was a time to make merry. To everyone's delight total standdown lasted a full 3 socially active days. There was a deal of conjecture as to the reasons, but it was generally accepted that the welcomed break was due to a more than middling moon coupled with good weather over Germany — conditions that would give the German fighters an opportunity to make hay with their superior fire power. Hence, on the fourth day, the atmosphere in 'B' flight office tended to joviality or just indifference.

The telephone shrilled out and Sqn Ldr Denning, a shade annoyed at having his office work interrupted, rammed the blower to his ear. Amid the ensuing silence the pilots present detectably offered each other a tentative glance.

"B. Flight Commander," said Denny. As he listened his eyes travelled round the assembled company with a look that expressed the view that something was on whether they liked it or not.

"Yes Sir, only 2 crews. One from 'A' flight and one from 'B' flight." The pregnant silence sustained itself. Something was cooking and that something was quite out of the common run. Denny pursed his lips in controlled surprise before asking:

"What time is briefing? Not here? At the Base station. I'd like to go Sir."

His particularly ungratifying look registered the bones of the Group Captain's refusal.

"Very good Sir, I'll send Burnett."

Replacing the blower with an air of resignation he was motionless for a few seconds wholly unaware that 'B' flight pilots could scarcely contain themselves. Something pretty special he thought, and why should crews take shaving kit? It could only mean they would not be returning immediately to the home station. Why was briefing at Base? He became aware of a dozen faces staring at him, displaying a suitable awareness of the need for uninterrupting politeness. I must look a bit of a clot, he thought, sitting here like a schoolmaster lost in the abstraction of a question that had a number of channels of enquiry.

"Ace," he said at last. "You have volunteered for the battle order." The buzz of conversation resumed, but instead of being inconsequential, it was pure conjecture. What the hell was going on?

"Big of me to volunteer," commented Ace with a sardonic grin.

"The rest of you can scatter — I know nothing. I would not tell you if I did. You know the rules. Whatever may seem to be on the face of it unusual, keep your traps shut. Right now hop it. Scram." The crews scrammed.

The sun beat down fiercely on the perspex cockpit which was perched like an afterthought on the Lancaster's squared oval fuselage. The rays bounced reflectively and penetrated refractively, turning the air in the cockpit into a hot fug which would have done justice to a Kew Gardens tropical hothouse. Ace sensibly clad only in shirt and battledress trousers felt little discomfort. A native of New Zealand's North Island with its semi-tropical climate he revelled in the warmth, the more so since such days in Lincolnshire were rare. Thus it was a pleasure for him to put his aircraft through the night flying test procedures.

He and his crew had taken off from their home station at Holmdun a half hour ago and, satisfied that all was in working order was preparing to land at the nearby Base station. He put R Robert into a vigorous split-arsed turn into the funnel of the runway approach, taking in as he did so the broad elongated view of the Lincolnshire countryside, which seemed to be like a painting in oils, easy on the eye and soporific. Calculated to make an impression on the all-seeing flight controller and other curious onlookers who might have noticed his squadron markings, not currently associated with this airfield, Ace floated R Robert down to a flawless 3 point touchdown just feet from the intersection of runway and perimeter track. The runway was not a runway in the accepted sense. It was just a general direction of landing to conform with the prevailing wind and even that was a dubious basis; for the wind sock hung limply. This famous airfield built many years before in the palmy days of peace was all grass and without the distinctive concrete usually associated with heavy bomber units. So far, during this war, it had been too busy to be vacated for the purpose of laying down concrete.

The crew gathered outside the rear door of their aeroplane to look on a distinctly unfamiliar sight. Instead of the prefabricated buildings on widely dispersed sites to which they had recently been accustomed, were three hangars of substantial proportions standing like sentinels in a seemingly straight line behind the control tower, with a backcloth of mellowed brick buildings and offices intersected by tree lined roads.

"Where's the red carpet?" asked Jock, in the haughty manner of a high Council official or other chairborne warrior dismayed at the lack of respect for his pompous dignity. "Don't they know the gen crew has arrived?"

"Afternoon siesta," suggested Sid.

It was soon apparent that although they were in a measure expected, they were certainly unheralded for no transport appeared to be sallying forth to pick them up, so they just sat on the grass and waited, not exactly with patience.

"Wonder what we're in for", mused Taffy aloud and somewhat miserably. He hated anything that deviated from an acceptable routine.

"Your guess is as good as mine, Taffy," responded John. "What is clear is that we'll not be returning to Holmdun tonight, or rather tomorrow morning. Why else would we have been told to bring shaving kit."

"No question of a diversion. The weather's bang on." Sid was confident on that score.

"Let's just wait and see," suggested Ace, a shade irritably. "Where is that bloody wagon?"

Sid was right, he had to be. It was siesta time. Tea was being poured.

"We'll walk," said Ace at last. His thought was that if the management took umbrage at their walking across what was presumed to be the runway, then they could bloody well lump it. It took them a good quarter of an hour to reach the main concourse. By that time Ace's transition from pilot to hiker had got him really worked up. A quickening of the pace boded ill for someone. He was not long in the control tower. His return was on a springheeled step, having dropped a few well chosen phrases upstairs, criticising the organisation or lack of it. Ace did not usually wax eloquent, but when he did it was telling, without regard to the rank and status of the recipient.

They found the briefing room without difficulty simply by following a signpost. Set amongst well selected flowering shrubs of varying fragrances, it had two stately birch trees standing guard before the entrance. Inside they came upon the personnel of 11 other crews, who were, except for the 'A' flight crew from Ace's squadron, not only strangers, but assumably their partners on the as yet unidentified operation. The most noticeable feature of the assembled group was the considerable spread of "gong" ribbons, indicating that this was a gathering of experienced aviators. The focal point of interest was the usual big topographical map, but unusually it had been extended.

"Crikey!" ejaculated John, whose eyes had naturally swivelled to that focal point. "Small wonder we need shaving kit and a fresh pair of pants wouldn't come amiss."

The normal coverage of eastern England and western Europe had been extended by taped on additions. A long piece of tape ran across the map and pinned at course alteration points. It ran southwards to Selsey Bill, from there to Fecamp on the French coast, then eastwards again on a long run across to Lake Annecy in the Haut-Savoie region.

"Ye Gods!" murmured Ace. "We went thataway 4 nights ago to Turin."

But it was the route beyond that was the mainspring of surprise and which had the whole company murmuring in subdued excitement. Again the route ran across the Alps pressing deeper into Italy than Turin to a target that seemed to be out in the wilds. Closer perusal revealed that the aiming point was definable only as a position in Latitude and Longitude, near Reggio, too insignificant to rate a map marking. The clear possibility was that there was to be a precision attack, probably at low level. This situation, if conjecture resolved itself into fact was likely to be a wholly new experience in times when heavy bomber tactics were of saturation attack from a decently high altitude, but it was the complement of the two final legs that precipitated the real excitement, for instead of then turning for home in a westerly direction, the tape ran south across the Italian coast by Genoa, on to Cap Corse on the northernmost point of Corsica and finally across the Mediterranean Sea to Algiers, in fact to a new continent. There was no route for the return journey and the shaving kit poser was resolved.

The buzz of general conversation was stilled as a youthful Wing Commander mounted the dais, motioning the crews to seats and requesting their earnest attention.

"Well chaps." He began in the customary "we are all buddies in this job" fashion. "Most of us, coming from different squadrons are strangers to each other as we have gathered together a group of senior crews for a special task. I'm Wing Commander Paisley and my brief is to control this operation at all stages. Sqn Ldr Akerman", he motioned to one side, "is my deputy in case I get the chop. We are the only heavies operating tonight." There was a communal gasp as the significance of what seemed just an afterthought penetrated the mental processes of the assembled company, for only 12 Lancasters going across the other side was all to the defensive advantage of the enemy. The Wing Commander went on encouragingly. "There will however be diversionary Mosquito attacks which will keep the enemy occupied and in any case the route has been carefully planned. The target is an immense electrical transformer station supplying a considerable part of Italy's war industry, and it is to be attacked at low level in two stages; first with bombs and then by both forward and rear guns; so let's make it good." After some further excited mutterings had subsided, he went on, "I shall illuminate the aiming point with orange indicators, although in the light of the almost full moon, we hope, we should all be able to identify visually. Then you will attack on my, or my deputy's orders. If you have not heard from us by Zero hour plus 10 you will press home the attack under your own steam from 1000 feet for bombing. On the gun firing run you need to be much lower, but you have freedom of action."

There was a spirited roar of acclamation from the gunners. For once they would be able to go on the attack, rather than just sit in their turrets, cold and miserable, only firing when attacked themselves.

The Wing Commander continued with his theme. "Now to the general features. Number one — labelled important — watch your fuel consumption for we are absolutely at maximum range. No. two — when the attack has been pressed home, gain height and in particular avoid Genoa. As a naval base it's bound to be reasonably well defended. You will land at Blida, near Algiers. All clear so far?" He gazed around enquiringly, but his presentation had been lucid and the sea of experienced faces seemed to register comprehensive understanding. He continued: "We fly out individually, each navigator plotting his own way along the scheduled route to rendezvous at point A which is 3 miles from the aiming point. In good visibility you should find point A which has been chosen as it's on a distinctive river bend. There you will orbit and await instruction, each pilot signifying arrival on VHF. In the event of poor visibility, once I have identified the orbital point I shall drop a red marker. Now to defences. There is believed to be an Italian fighter base in the vicinity from which only moderate . . . " His final words were drowned out by hoots of derision. He had to smile and left the rest of the sentence unsaid, but continued in cautionary vein. "But it is also known that there are German units in Italy to bolster Italian morale and so, the customary vigilance MUST be exercised. No trip is a piece of cake until it's completed and as I'm sure you all have the same view it could be reasonably said that that is the reason we have survived so far. Any questions?"

"Yes Sir, what about landing facilities at Blida?" The young Flying Officer who stood to pose the question had a point.

"Good question and I had intended to brief pilots separately. Some of you might have had the idea Blida was in the desert. However, as we understand it Blida is an old French Air Force station, now run by the RAF of course, with a single runway capable of taking transport Dakotas. I do not know the length of the runway, but I imagine Bomber Command HQ has looked into the problem. It must be remembered however that there is likely to be little wind and high air temperature, so don't overshoot or bend the kites because maintenance facilities for Lancasters will be limited." The Flying Officer sat down.

As the Wing Co. stepped down, the Base navigation leader detailed the route, followed then by the Intelligence representative who talked briefly about defended areas and the effect on the Italians if this particular electrical installation was destroyed. The crews had heard it all before. A good deal of such assessments had to be pure conjecture. They did, however, pay careful attention to the Met man despite the stick he often got. He was confident enough. A weak front persisted on the west side of the Alps but this was thought to be weakening all the time. As a result there should be no problems en route. There was however, a possibliity of an occasional thunderstorm in the target area, but, he stressed, only a possibility. The alternative in the target area would be patches of mist or fog. The briefing ended.

John began to lay in the route on his Mercator chart, measuring up distances along each leg in nautical miles. The track bearings and distances he entered on the log form. With the aid of a Dalton computer he applied the wind velocities forecast and came up with the courses "true" to be flown to achieve correct tracking along the route. He then checked that his calculated time on each leg matched the times laid down in the planning of the operation. Then he double-checked everything. It all took a long time, but it was an established pattern of working that became automatic and required absolutely accurate calculations. All the calculations hinged on the accuracy of the winds forecast by the Met men and the Met men were at a distinct disadvantage, not being able to get actual reports from Europe. A few reports came in from high flying Mosquito aeroplanes but these could only be on an "if-they-were-there" basis. John reflected that the Met man's lot was not a happy one, for he received little adulation for a good forecast and was reviled for a bad one. Once in the air, John and the other navigators would be ground fixing their positions as often as possible to calculate the actual wind speeds and directions. If the calculated wind velocities agreed with the forecast velocities, then the flight plan was correct at that particular stage requiring no alterations of course. If on the other hand it was proved that the forecast winds were wrong, then the flight plan was probably wrong from start to finish, which meant that the navigators would be constantly correcting and indeed anticipating some factors according to the actual weather pattern experienced.

Ace waited for John to complete the flight plan and then together they strolled the very short distance to the mess in the wake of the rest of the crew who had sloped off at the termination of main briefing.

"Long trip, Ace" said John. "Should not be too much of a problem though."

"Mmm. Like the Wing Co. said they're all a shaky do. You can just as easily lose an engine over Italy as over Germany. I always remember that only fools and birds fly and birds don't fly at night."

John smiled. Ace seemed to be the very embodiment of caution.

Lancaster R Robert turned from the perimeter track on to the flying field that though amply covered with grass despite fairly constant traffic, was underneath hard baked and wholly unrelenting. Ace gunned the kite into alignment with the caravan, the brakes hissing, while by the caravan itself stood the usual group of sightseers. There seemed to be rather more than usual. Perhaps a little bird had whispered that something special was on and they would have noticed the different squadron markings. There were of course personnel in the armament section who knew that the bomb load was unusual comprising 500 pound bombs and incendiaries instead of the 4000 pound cookie and incendiaries.

Ace made his final cockpit check, head well down to avoid the still considerable dazzle from the slowly setting sun in the westerly quarter. He thought how much more pleasurable it was to take off in daylight, when the hazards, although by no means dispersed, were greatly minimised. At least one could see the airfield boundaries and the trees looming at the far end some 15 degrees to port. What's more, he would not need to concentrate on what was at night a very narrow channel of flares through which to guide R Robert on take-off. The essential thing was to line up with the caravan and set off.

"Standby for take-off," he gritted into the intercom mouthpiece which was strapped into the oxygen mask. He eased the throttles forward tentatively middling for even power, holding the brakes full on. Ken, as always followed up Ace's spreadeagled fingers in the forward movement and the four Merlins pulsed with increasing urgency. Brakes released, the Lancaster moved forward, slowly at first, bumping more than somewhat on the uneven turf. On Ace's instructions Ken slammed the throttles wide open to 3000 revs and 14 pounds of boost. Halfway across the field R Robert bumped hard against a rising flow in the terrain and was momentarily airborne, but only for a second or two. She hit the ground again with a shudder. To John, the navigator, the bombs appeared to creak ominously in the belly beneath him, while in the rear turret Jock swore. Even Ace had begun to anticipate the possibility of cleaving a path through the boundary hedgerows that were rapidly approaching at some 100 mph, until suddenly, the bumping dissolved as Robert crawled protestingly upwards and clear. Jeez, thought Ace as beads of sweat dripped from his forehead, short run and little or no wind to assist the lift. I'd hate to take-off in this direction at night in this calm condition. He called to Ken with a series of sharp commands.

"Wheels up. Flaps up. 2650 revs." Ken operated the essential functions, confirming at each step.

Ace continued to climb, going into a wide circuit and only a few moments later the navigator came on to intercom to remind the pilot that he would not be able to continue the roundabout progress for much longer.

"Turn on to 198 degrees true in two and a half minutes," he advised. "Tell me when you are on course."

"Thanks John, 198 T." He checked the distant reading compass and turned on 360 degrees in an attempt to bring his aircraft back over the centre of the field within the two and a half minutes. It was a matter of judgement and Ace brought R Robert over the northern tip of the field just as the navigator said:

"Should be set course now."

"On course navigator, 198 T Right now." He was happy to have judged it just right.

"Thanks Ace. Well done." You had to give the drivers a bit of encouragement now and again, not too often in case they got above themselves.

All 12 Lancasters got away within the same number of minutes climbing steadily into the pale sky, in a loose gaggle, hardly a formation, heading southwards towards the coastal promontory of Selsey Bill. From time to time each Lancaster drew apart, before, behind and abreast as each navigator got a fix position from the G. Box, recalculated the wind velocity and direction, and applied the result to calculate a new course. But not all altered course at the same time. It all depended on the speed of the navigator's revisions.

Some fifty minutes from setting course, the squadron roared over Selsey at about 12000 feet, still climbing and turning towards the French coast.

It was still warm in the cockpit despite the now rapid fall of the sun below a serrated horizon. Ace eased his oxygen mask which was adhering stickily to the face, tracing out a roughly circular black mark that made him look like a Maori warrior in warpaint.

Down below the sea was dead calm but looking colder now as shadow leapt across its surface. Out to port two Lancs appeared to have drifted away a couple of miles, which reminded Ace that the sky was a bloody great bit of space. In due course they would creep closer again as course revisions were applied.

The French coast eventually leapt up darkly in the receding light, for although at height the wide arc of the sun's afterglow was still in evidence, at ground level twilight had almost merged land and sea.

Now enemy warning signals would be flashing out to distant night fighter stations, hopefully too far away, but whatever the activity in that direction the Lancasters roared on, their outlines merging into contrasting textures of darkness, coming into prominence as each floated up and down in mild pockets of air or banked onto corrected headings.

On and on they ploughed over the wide open countryside now unidentifiable except as a continuance of total shadow. Down there in the shadow, French eyes would have looked up knowing that the RAF was out again, knowing too that it was another step forward towards their liberation. In return from above, in a miasma of thought transference, consciously or unconsciously the aircrews extended their sympathies to those in thrall, before turning back to the immediate task, aware at all times they might suddenly have to react to a sudden stream of cannon fire by violent evasive action. The silence was interminable — it always was. The roar of engines silenced everything into a neutral background of normality. Up above the moon was waxing, strongly spreading its inanimate eerie glow.

At long last, out of the silence came the navigator's voice in casual questioning:

"Any sign of frontal cloud, Sid?"

Sid who had the best view down and through the bomb blister seemed to be weighing it up, for it was some few moments before he replied:

"Seems to be some stratoform cloud below, but quite broken I would say. Could be clearer ahead." It was difficult sometimes to identify cloud in darkness.

"Thanks Sid. Looks as if Met were right, weak front petering out. We should be coming up to Lake Annecy in 20 minutes. Might just see it this time. Give me a call."

"OK, John, will do."

Some 25 minutes later Jock came on the air from the tail remoteness.

"We've just passed over the lake, navigator. I can see the glint of the moon on the surface. We're probably 2 miles to starboard."

"Are you sure its Annecy, Jock. Is it the right shape?"

"Shoor I'm shoor," replied Jock in an aggrieved tone. "Have you ever known me dish up duff gen?"

"OK, Jock. Calm down. Good show. Take a drift reading on it will you."

The navigator breathed again. Jock was pretty good at map reading for a rear gunner. They were only about 2 miles port of track which is what he would have expected for the winds were light, and earlier fixes had given him winds that were blowing along the tail from the port side and then later from starboard. With this variation in both velocity and direction the aeroplane could have been blown to one side of the track and then the other, but being light would have minimised any error. And now by good fortune, the man in the moon with his cynical grimace had come up trumps, so to speak, right at the critical moment. You had to have some good luck and this was it.

Quickly John hammered a slight alteration of course and asked the pilot for a reduction in speed from 165 to 160 since they were a little ahead of schedule, adding the unnecessary remark that they were coming up to the Alps.

"You don't say," said Sid with heavy sarcasm. "Since I can see them plainly, it proves I'm not asleep." In fact Sid was positively drinking in the scene. The wild barrier of snow capped peaks looming ahead was an awesome sight, glistening in the moon at the tops, but it crossed his mind, as it had on the Turin trip a few nights ago that it was not an area on which to crash land. That would be curtains all the way.

Ace was thinking much the same, a sort of mental telepathy, but that implied a certain distance and Sid was only a couple of yards away. He was thinking of a Stirling pilot, who, having engine trouble coming back from an operation in Italy, had flown through the range rather than over it and returned to tell the tale. The thought gave him instant comfort for in the first place the Lancaster had a greater ceiling and would in any case fly adequately on three engines.

Once clear of the Alps, the pilot began to lose height for passage across the Lombardy plain. For hours now he'd seen nothing of the other Lancasters, nor had his crew, but this caused no anxiety. It was not uncommon in the big sky to complete a whole operation without sight of a friendly machine, except in the induced light of the target area.

Sid roused himself to confirm the apparent accuracy of the navigator's projections by producing a pinpoint position on the ground, adding sarcastically that with or without the navigator's assistance he could map read all the way to the aiming point, and so he ought to be able. The moon picked up the river and its bends. At 2000 feet, flaws in the blackout could be ascertained, although what the odd light represented there was no way of telling. Thus Ace pushed R Robert along confidently, while all the time now the gunners scanned the darker side of the sky. There had to be no careless optimism. And then as Zero hour approached, a red flare burst prominently illuminating a particular bend in the river. It was without doubt the orbital point. They had arrived and smack on time.

"Gosh!" murmured Ace. "I've forgotten to listen in on VHF." Rapidly he selected the channel button just in time to hear Wing Co. Paisley calling his deputy. When the brief acknowledgement had been accepted, Ace pressed the transmission button:

"Hullo Oxtail, Tintern Robert. Rendezvous."

"Good show, Robert. Continue to orbit." The Wing Co's voice came over substantially cut glass on VHF, which made Ace smile a bit. It was probably an affectation to instil confidence.

A series of voices confirmed arrival and it seemed that all 12 aircraft had arrived safely. Then there was radio silence as eleven Lancasters orbited, just dark phantomlike shapes steadily turning in a fairly wide circle to keep clear of each other, although occasionally there was a glint of light from moonlight on cockpit perspex and suppressed flame from the engine exhaust manifolds; while the leader went off to identify the aiming point. It was like a deadly game of ring o' roses except that none wanted to fall down, but it was not long, perhaps five minutes, before the Wing Co. called "Target identified — stand by." Stand by they did, still orbiting, waiting for enemy fighters but hoping they would stay away. The ground below was like a dead planet.

An orange flare gushed out its incandescent waterfall of sheer beauty and the leader began calling the Lancasters in, in quick succession, during which time the leader and probably his deputy as well backed up the original flare with more. Violent flashes indicated the passage of the aircraft over the power station now clearly visible. Buildings began to crumble in big clouds of smoke and fires started up. There were flashes of blue flame all over the place.

Then the squadron swept around in a wide circle to come screaming in over the crippled installation at little more than rooftop level, fore guns blazing and then the rear. Again blue flashes emanated from vital parts not otherwise destroyed by bombs. To say the least, the gunners were happy. There was a complete lack of opposition, the attack achieving the merit of total surprise. Not a searchlight flickered on and not a ground gun blazed in anger. There was no doubt that it was the planned target, but presumably the Italians had not considered it vulnerable, so far from England and so relatively small. The attack was none too soon, for Ace, coming in last on his second run noted that a thickening haze was creeping insiduously across the ground. A half hour later on target would have presented identification problems.

Boring away from the target on to the southerly course ordered by the navigator, Jock had the final say as he unleashed the spitting power of his four guns. They were on the way to a point on the coast a few miles East of Genoa. All together they had all been in the target area for about twenty minutes.

"Boy Oh Boy!" quoth Sid, who had made the most of his short burst of unusual gunnery activity. "Pity we couldn't blaze a trail all the way to the coast."

"Good idea," said Jock enthusiastically.

Their remarks and hopes were an invitation and a temptation to the skipper who momentarily caught the mood, but common sense prevailed.

"Sorry chaps. No dice," he replied. "Save your ammo. We may need it. In any case you'll soon be out of range. We go up to 5000 feet. There's pretty high ground ahead."

The gunners didn't argue. Ace was the boss. He knew what he was doing, they thought. And of course he did. Light of the bomb load he was climbing fast to avoid a range of mountains that ran up to 3000 feet plus in some places. Once at 5000 feet he called for cruising revs and Ken obliged. Next stop Algiers, he hoped, or rather Blida nearby. It was now very hazy below making the forward and downward visibility piss poor, as Sid described it, presumably to pre-empt any criticism from the navigator if he could not come up with a pin-point position. The moonlight played teasingly on the fog neither helping nor exactly hindering. As they approached the coast the highlands stood starkly above the fog like craters on the moon, but none were positively identifiable.

John came on intercom to warn of imminent arrival at the coast and to present the pilot with a new course for Cap Corse, when startlingly a finger of light bathed Robert in something like broad daylight. Half blinded by the light's intensity, Ace got his head down and threw the Lancaster in to violent starboard evasive action. With the searchlight still on him and joined by others it was a minute or two before he realised that he had probably gone the wrong way. He should have taken evasive action to port, away from Genoa into whose defensive edge he had strayed. Just for a moment he felt that by some strange trick Essen had been transported to Italy, but wherever he was he knew he had to get weaving. He threw the Lancaster into a dive, all the time conscious of the hills roundabout, pulled out into a fast climb, then a port dive, and again a climb. The searchlights followed easily. At this height his manoeuvrcability was limited. He felt like an unwary fly caught on a flypaper. And then all hell was let loose. Long curling trails of tracer homed in on Robert, pouring up and around, seemingly slow travelling from below but accelerating as they got nearer. Sharply against the stressed metal of the fuselage wings and engine cowlings, nasty bits of hot metal twanged like the rapid fire of Jock's guns. Ace cursed long and loud as the emergency declared itself. There was only one way out. Full power, Ken.

John, behind his curtain saw nothing. He did not want to. He could hear it. That was more than enough. His limbs turned shamelessly to water as the notion that he was on the precipice of death and life struck him. At any moment he anticipated being turned incontinently into a missile, or rather a part of it in the shape of a flaming torch falling in a slow gyratory fashion towards the deck, unstoppable like a falling leaf in an autumn gale. But he was still alive and kicking and the Lancaster was leaping away now. They really must be nearly over the sea by now when gunfire would be unable to reach out on its destructive purpose.

Quite suddenly the rattle of shrapnel ceased, and the searchlights to the rear flickered disappointingly out.

"Anybody hurt?" Ace asked anxiously as he gasped painfully for breath. With quiet relief he heard almost the correct number of streams of invective on the intercom.

"What about you John?" he asked as he noticed a lack of response from the gen man. But the navigator's ears were temporarily closed as he stared wide-eyed at his instrument panel. It was almost completely shattered. However that was not what most concerned him for it was clear that what had caused the destruction must have come from behind and he was in no hurry to look. Courage and the power of human curiosity eventually won. He glanced round and nearly had kittens. Right behind his head was a large gash in the fuselage. The shrapnel must have grazed his helmet by a coat of paint. Then he remembered when it had happened, although he had not been altogether aware of the reason for the crashing sound. It had occurred when Ace was throwing the Lancaster around which action deposited most of his, John's navigational instruments on the floor and he had bent to retrieve them. God. The mere act of bending down had saved his life, so far.

"I'm alright, Ace," he said. "Nearly bought it. My panel is a write-off."

"Keep calm," was all the pilot said. He had his own worries. Time would tell whether or not the engines had taken too much stick.

"There's a hole in the perspex by your side." Ken motioned to a hole in the cockpit canopy.

"I thought it was getting bloody draughty in here. Normal cruising revs. Let's take stock. Check up the oil temperatures.

We've taken a hammering and it's a safe bet we've got engine damage."

"They're OK at the moment, Ace, but we could still have a coolant leak," replied Ken. He would be watching his panel like a hawk from now on.

"What happened, John? We must have stooged over the outskirts of Genoa." Ace had begun to think about the inquest.

"Can't say, Ace, unless the wind speed and direction has altered sharply. Been running on DR from the target. No positive means of fixing ground position due to the fog."

Ace did not reply, feeling that conjecture was useless at this point. His navigator would probably come up with the answer later, but whatever the answer, it would represent another lesson learned the hard way, to be firmly logged into the memory bank as future protection from the hazards, if there was a future of course. They still had a long way to go, a whole sea to cross.

John was really puzzled, almost to the point of irritation. He rechecked his calculations. They appeared to be OK. He was fairly certain that Ace had steered the correct course, for it was part of his, John's drill to check it on his own repeater. The DR compass could be wrong. But why? It was a pretty reliable piece of equipment and it had been alright out to the target. There was always a chance of desynchronisation on account of its electromagnetic design, but that normally only occurred after violent evasive action when it was possible for the gyro to topple and give a false reading. But no evasive action had been necessary until they had strayed over Genoa. The only other possibility was demagnetisation produced by outside magnetic sources as produced in thunderstorms. That too was out of the question.

"Ace, would you check your DR compass against the standard compass, please," John had to research the possibilities. "Apply 4 degrees of variation."

"OK John. It'll take a moment or two." The standard compass was not exactly in an easily readable position, being tucked away under the dash.

"I've got 5 degrees of difference," advised Ace. "Can't make it out."

"Neither can I," replied John. "I suggest though you use the standard magnetic compass as far as Cap Corse and see how it works out."

"OK John. We'll give it a try." The pilot deferred to the navigator's wisdom. Cap Corse loomed up in the dawn, a thin pencil line at first about which a thin morning mist hung, perhaps the prophesy of a hot Mediterranean summer day and indeed the sun was now obligingly in evidence. No other friendly aeroplanes were visible, which was a little worrying because there were German fighters down there somewhere. R Robert and crew were on their own for better or worse.

It was then that Ken spoke up, breaking a silence that had persevered from soon after vacating Italian airspace. As might have been expected there was no elation in his voice. Rather was it in the tone of sad inevitability.

"Don't like the look of the starboard outer Ace. Oil temperature's climbing." Ace said nothing. Ken, a trained engine fitter before he had remustered to aircrew would tell him when the critical point was reached. In the meantime he would use all available power. It would not do any harm to gain a bit of height as a safety precaution. There was still a long way to go from Cap Corse. The navigator came on to advise what was in theory the final course to Algiers, advising Ace to use the standard magnetic compass. The pilot altered course and agreed the procedure. It was not easy to fly by this compass since the needle swung considerably, but it was the best thing to do.

It was not long before Ken said: "It's no good, Ace. We'll have to feather the starboard outer engine."

Ace nodded. He reached forward for the outboard throttle. Ken pressed the feathering button to stop the windmilling action, while Ace adjusted the remaining three engine revs to balance the now uneven pull, reflecting as he did so that while the Lanc flew pretty well on three engines there could be more trouble in the offing, with a fair bit of sea to span. Already to his ears, the port inner did not sound too good, but perhaps it was his imagination. He was tired — perhaps that was it. It was more hope than logic.

Underneath the Mediterranean stretched out, the line of the horizon just about merging into the paler blue of the sky. It was calm enough, or it seemed so, but at 5000 feet you could not be completely sure. If it came to ditching the kite and manning the dinghy at least they would not have to face the experience of conditions common to the North Sea and English Channel. For all that it was cold comfort. Ace who had the possibility firmly in mind could not whip up enthusiasm for putting regularly practised dinghy drill into real action, for air/sea rescue services hereabouts were likely to be non-existent.

Corsica receded to the rear and none too soon for that Island was enemy territory and no member of the crew wished to adopt prisoner-of-war status. The sun came up maturely in the East lacing the sea with shades of blue. Not a ship clove a furrow or trailed a wash. It was getting very warm in the cockpit. The wearing of battledress was not any help.

The port inner really was running rough now and the pilot was now inclined to accept the view that if they reached Algiers they would not be merely lucky but incredibly so. The engine was vibrating as if a number of loose bits were being churned around. As yet, the flight engineer had made no comment, but he must have had an awareness of the particular problem. To make matters worse, both pilot and flight engineer were aware of the discouragingly high fuel consumption, although it was not desperate. The landing procedure, if it got that far, would call for lobbing the aircraft in to land without any possibility of overshoot. Ace hoped the navigator would succeed in plotting the shortest distance between the two relevant points, that is from Cap Corse to Blida, but whatever his personal worries, there was no call to alarm the crew unnecessarily at this stage. His concern might however have been evident to the navigator when the pilot called for a revised ETA.

No other member of the crew spoke. If they were worried no one admitted it. There was tiredness of course and consequential danger. Aware of the danger the pilot passed a grimy hand over face, now free of the oxygen mask, gouging knuckles into heavy eyes as if to tear out slumber.

After what seemed like an eternity, in the bomb blister Sid rubbed his own eyes and rubbed them again. What seemed like a patch of cloud swam into vision. He blinked and refocussed. It was still there in an otherwise cloudless sky.

"That's funny," he said. "Why one solitary cloud and we're heading directly towards it. Can you see it, Ace?"

"No Sid. I can't. Hang on a minute though. I've got it. It can't be cloud in these stable conditions. Smoke perhaps. John, repeat your ETA."

"30 minutes." The navigator hoped he was right. There were enough doubtful factors.

"Could be smoke," Sid said ruminantly. "But if it is it's a bloody big fire."

And that was what it was, for quite soon the coastline loomed obliquely against the sea with the high terrain rising on either side of the Bay of Algiers, and there was a now towering column of smoke in the dock area. A sense of excitement ran through Robert's crew, but even as it bubbled up so it died, as the port inner engine coughed explosively and lost power.

"Feather port inner," rapped out Ace. The flight engineer was ready. He'd been waiting for the event. The engine windmilled and finally stopped. The pilot pushed up the revs on the remaining two engines not in complete balance, for the port outboard engine tended to pull more than the starboard inner and some juggling with the engine revs was necessary. The best that could be said of the situation was that there was an engine on each side and the worst that with increased revs to maintain level flight the petrol was being soaked away rapidly. R Robert staggered over the bay at about 2000 feet.

"Ship blown up in the harbour," was Sid's immediate intelligence, but Ace was not interested. It might have been a diversion in the normal course but he had his problems still. The starboard inner was beginning to vibrate most uncomfortably, and Ken stood at the ready.

"Shall I feather, Ace?" he asked.

"No, leave it a minute Ken. What's that airfield on the port side Sid? Can you see it?"

"It's not Blida." This from Sid who was obviously on the ball. "Must be Maison Blanche."

"God dammed Yankee field." The navigator spoke up.

"That'll do," said the pilot. "Fasten belts and pray like hell. Come out from the front, Sid. Ken, watch that engine. We'll have to feather in a few moments. I don't want to be stuck with a sudden dud engine on the approach."

'Righto, Ace." Sid was unflappable but the pilot's commonsense instruction could be a life saver. He climbed up between the flight engineer's legs, pushed past the navigator, patted Taffy, the wireless op on the shoulder and removed himself over the main spar to the bunk just forward from the mid upper gunner's position. There he took up his favourite horizontal position. Ace turned carefully to port in an arc on to the fringes of the airfield and switched on R/T.

"Maison Blanche from Lancaster Robert. Emergency landing instructions please." There was no reply, so Ace tried again, but without success. "OK chaps, we're going in."

"We've got to feather, Ace. That engine will go on fire in a moment." Now Ken was worried.

"OK. Feather," he said. He'd completed a wide circle and was lined up with the runway for landing. The engine would have to be stopped now, leaving only the port outer engine to maintain flight. With luck, if his approach judgement was good they might make it to the runway.

"Fire off a red, Taffy," the pilot called urgently. The red cartridge plopped out trailing a curve of smoke and red fire.

Ken feathered the engine. Ace pushed the revs up to 2650 on the outboard engine which immediately slewed the Lancaster fearfully to starboard, and the pilot had to put on full left rudder to compensate.

The red Very cartridge must have had some effect. A Dakota on finals tucked up its wheels to rejoin the circuit. Another Dak, just having landed and taxying casually, put on a spurt to clear the runway. What appeared to be two fire tenders and 2 blood wagons were speeding round the perimeter from the control area. If control had not received Ace's R/T call, they had obviously seen the emergency red and were reacting with speed.

Ace guided his faithful Robert into finals, fully aware of the limitations imposed on him by circumstance. If he adjudged the approach badly and ended up short of the runway, there could be a nasty accident, and a comparable situation would arise if he lobbed down too far along the runway, for he did not have the power to overshoot. There were other uncertainties too. The wheels were down but the locked down signal had not registered, nor was he certain that there was braking power. It was no easy task lining up with the runway. The single outboard engine had to have sufficient power to keep the aeroplane airborne but it pulled the Lancaster hard to starboard because of its position on the outer section of the wing so Ace had on full left rudder to compensate.

He also needed to throttle in bursts to maintain a reasonably accurate approach, dovetailed into use of that full opposite rudder. It looked good. He would make it if fuel lasted out but it was touch and go for the tanks registered nil capacity. The Lancaster lost height rapidly in the final stage, bumping down hard some thirty yards from the beginning of the runway, and with a last despairing cough the fourth engine died. Ace fought for a straight run with brakes squealing protest and then with speed safely under control he ran the Lancaster off the runway to avoid obstructing the landing of other aeroplanes, coming finally to a full stop. There the Lancaster would have to stay until towed on to the main concourse.

Not one of the crew moved. Each basked in an aura of total relief. Even the sun's now hot rays beating mercilessly on the fuselage and perspex cockpit, turning the interior into a tropical hot house, failed to provoke the smallest protest. The navigator logged 10 hours and 55 minutes airborne. That was enough time to induce utter weariness and severely cramped limbs. No one noted the arrival of blood waggons and firetender together with a jeep. From the jeep a voice with a drawl from the southern USA projected itself upwards.

"Is you all at home? Anyone hurt?"

Ace stared sightlessly forward until another voice crept into the channels of his grey matter. He wearily opened a little window at his side and peered out. Two American army men came into cloudy view. Seeing movement of the helmeted pilot's head one of the Americans called up again:

"Shore had us worried, you bozos did, when you didn't answer. Thought this flying box had ghosts or sumpun."

Ace managed a wave and a sickly grin although the lingo had not penetrated.

"Looks like some guy's bin usin' a pea shootah on you alls," a voice persisted. Without comment Ace unfastened safety straps and moved jerkily and painfully from his seat to the floor. His legs were cramped, his feet with only barely perceptible feeling. Putting feet to ground, he was wary like an unecstatic bather testing the water with a toe. His body was clammy with sweat in the thick battledress fabric and his posterior felt as if it had been flogged. With difficulty he surmounted the main spar and stumbled to the rear door, willing to be lead by his crew who were equally weary but for the most part had the shortest distance to travel. Someone managed to fix the short ladder and they all dropped more than climbed through the gap, metaphorically kissing terra firma as they did so.

Somewhat hypnotically their eyes were drawn, not all at once, but without conscious delay along the length of the fuselage, along the wings and engine cowlings. Up on the fuselage, by the cockpit were depicted 39 bombs and 3 swastikas, indicating respectively the number of operations over enemy territory undertaken by R Robert and three enemy fighters shot down in the process. Fourteen of the bombs and the three swastikas had been painted up since Ace and his crew had commenced operations several months ago. Now the 40th bomb could be added, but only just, for one look at the state of the Lancaster told the story. All along the 69 foot fuselage were groups of jagged holes in pepperpot pattern. All along the underbelly bomb doors and on the engine cowlings, and along the wings were jagged holes. It was something of a miracle the engines had survived as long as they did, a miracle that the flak along the wings hadn't blown the petrol tanks. It had to be assumed that some of the flak had been at extreme range with less consequential damage.

One of the Americans climbed lazily from the jeep, hitched up his trousers a peg, tongued a piece of chewing gum from a tooth cavity and ventured brief comment:

"Some ship," he said.

"You've said a mouthful," replied Ace, and added pointedly, "Was."

The other American, unlike his southern States companion was a Goddam Yankee, pure and simple. He threw Ace a puzzled look.

"Wher yuh from, hey? Didn't know the RAF had ships like this heah."

"From England," put in Sid. "Ever heard of it?"

"Sure thing." The American put on a sardonic grin. "That's the 49th State of the good ole US of A, ain't it."

"Not bloody likely. Didn't know the US of A was involved in this war." Sid was beginning to enjoy himself. He'd almost forgotten how hot it was in battle-dress blue.

It was the other American who came on the line next.

"You all boys ain't so smart. Evah heard tell o' Pearl Harbour."

"Sounds like a decent spot for fishing," quipped John.

They all laughed. There was, generally speaking, a common understanding between the British and Americans that accepted a fair amount of playful rivalry without any accompanying animosity. Indeed there was probably more animosity between some of the Americans who were still involved in the Civil War.

"How come yuh heah?" The Southerner continued the questioning. "Got lost or sumpun?"

"Lost? Lost?" John drew his noticeably medium stature up to a maximum. "Man is never lost, particularly in the RAF. This isn't a B17. We know our way around."

"We were en route for Blida," Ace volunteered quickly, feeling that perhaps the friendly rivalry could get out of hand.

"Yuh usually fly on one motor?" queried the Yank. "You boys gave us a heat."

"Not as a general rule. Gave ourselves a fright too," replied Ace and then lost interest in the chitchat, for he was hungry and bloody hot too. "Do you have a mess or feeding place on this establishment? I'm starved."

"We sho have. Climb on the blood waggon and we'll lead yuh in. You'll have to go see the RAF liaison guy. This is an all American unit."

As the blood waggon followed the jeep and trailed by the fire tender, the driver cast a quizzical look at Ace.

"You ain't a limey, huh?" It was not exactly a question the way he spoke it, but an answer was desired nevertheless.

"Nope," said Ace. "I'm from New Zealand. God's own country".

"Oh yeh!" It was not a question this time but it expressed doubt. Probably the driver had never heard of it, but it did not bother him overmuch. "Well, glad to know you brother, all of you".

They were disembarked at a small stone built building on the admin site, which had over the door the RAF crest. Hot and fairly shimmering from the heat they flowed into a room with a few chairs, and it was suddenly surprisingly cool.

"Home from home," said Jock. "Where's the orderly room? Want to see if I'm promoted yet."

They were sort of welcomed by a bored looking Flight Lieutenant, whose stock rose in the eyes of his visitors when he soberly announced that he had arranged for their breakfast, and Taffy could not resist commenting that he really had not expected such good service from the RAF. The Flt Lt smiled wanly at this back-handed compliment, accepting it in the spirit given.

"I've still to arrange transport, but that's no problem here. Americans don't like walking, so there's plenty. While you are scoffing, I'll notify Blida if you will just give me pilot's name and aeroplane identification. Judging by the flap you caused, I take it the kite is unserviceable," and when Ace nodded he went on, "Your landing on one engine was a shock to the Yanks. They haven't got a four engined kite capable of a single engined landing."

"Too right," said Ace.

"Well I did not personally see you land, but it's been a talking point since you arrived."

"Just as well you didn't. Like me you'd nearly have had a baby," replied Ace.

"Bad as that". Ace nodded assent. "Well, keep your pews. Just write down the gen I want while I arrange transport to the mess." He disappeared through a door to reappear only a couple of minutes later to find himself staring at seven sergeants asleep.

Breakfast was a humdinger and the crew did it justice, tired as they were. It had to be assumed that the breakfast they were given was the normal American standard, and not in any way to be compared with the frugality of an English breakfast in wartime. It did not compare with a peace time English breakfast either. There was just too much of it for comfort. They had first, orange juice and a choice from single-meal cereal packets, followed by half a dozen rashers of crispy curly bacon each with as many fried eggs as desired. The third course turned out to be flapjacks awash in maple syrup, and the whole was lubricated by coffee ad lib and a pint of milk each. It was all supremely enjoyable but it also had to be endured for food was pressed on the crew as if they had been found starving in the desert, and common courtesy called for valiant effort from each one of them.

Further endurance had to come, for it was a fair few miles to Blida. The RAF sent one of the standard tarpaulin covered heavy trucks to convey the crew from Maison Blanche to Blida and the journey proved to be less than satisfying. The Algerian roads left a lot to be desired. The vehicle or perhaps the driver seemed to have the knack of selecting every conceivable rut, crevice and bump on the dusty road. The air trapped under the tarpaulin was frying hot and for most of the journey Ace and his crew were spitting arid dust over the tailboard. It is said that all good things come to an end, well so do the bad ones. Journey's end was a relief. The white stone buildings of the old French aerodrome fairly shimmered in the late morning heat, but within, the monotonous swirl of fans effected a dampening down of humidity to a bearable level. In one of these buildings the crew were invited for debriefing which was a formality to be endured. It transpired, however, that their homebased group in Lincoln had not been notified that they had reached the flight plan destination.

Ace and the crew accepted this statement with a nonchalance born of the commonplace. Quite clearly the RAF had demonstrated and indeed exported its talent for organised administrative chaos from England to North Africa. However, in one particular matter it had excelled itself by prematurely dispatching a signal to England to the effect that Sgt Burnett and his crew were overdue and posted missing. John and Sid in particular, blew their tops as they all drank in the possible outcome of this bit of super-intelligence. Very soon now, if the matter was not put right pretty sharpish, next-of-kin would be receiving telegrams baldly stating "The Air Ministry regrets . . .," unless of course there was a similar balls-up at the other end.

The pilot knew what he had to do. He took himself off at a fair level of knots to find Wg Cdr Paisley. It was some consolation to learn that the Winco had blown his top and fired off a few well chosen rockets in the appropriate administration quarter, though it was doubtful whether his complaint would have any more effect than slopping over a couple of teacups.

A night's sleep cooled a few hot tempers. Tomorrow was another day. On the morrow the composite mind of the crews was on the trip as yet unscheduled back to England, but for Ace and his crew the possibility of flying R Robert back was a remote one. Two fitters, who had done some time on Merlins were dispatched to Maison Blanche to assess whether Robert was a patchup job or not. Certainly, if it was decided the aeroplane needed engine changes the crew could resign themselves to a holiday on the Mediterranean until a Transport Command aeroplane going to England had space for seven passengers.

Taking the most optimistic view R Robert could not be serviceable for a week.

Providentially, the days went by. A week passed without news of a return to England, a situation that could not have been happily acceptable to the C-in-C, Bomber Command, since he was effectively short of a complete bomber squadron. What was surprising and scarcely credible was the reason for the delay. While the North African skies were devoid of even the smallest cloud, drop of rain or breath of wind, it turned out that the weather in England was bad or at least too bad to justify the risk of deploying aeroplanes from a distant base without a suitably important target to bomb *en route*.

Somewhat belatedly the crews had been issued with tropical uniforms which was a blessing. During the daytime they lazed around in the messes or sleeping quarters conforming with the noonday siesta pattern, thus disabusing the time-honoured adage that "Mad dogs and Englishmen go out in the noonday sun". They smoked cheap issued cigarettes or played cards or read out-of-date papers. There was just nothing better to do.

The evenings provided more satisfaction, for with the blistering solar eye on the wane, transport was provided for nearly 90 men to a well chosen spot on the Mediterranean for a swim, well away from Algiers where pollution from the dirty washing tainted the sea. There, at this special little location, the crews wallowed in warm water. Nearby was an establishment, nominally a cafe which dispensed eggs fried in olive oil, the sole choice on the menu. The only snag was the lack of fresh water and more importantly the lack of a good pint of ale, Algerian red wine being a poor substitute, seemingly only suitable for petrol lighters. After a prolonged soaking, the crews sped back towards Blida through country side monopolised for as far as the eye could see by grape vines. Here and there as the sun began to sink, they passed through Arab villages where the population turned out en masse to view the cavalcade. The spectators were not exactly enthusiastic. It was more a matter of curiosity. At one place, the natives seemed positively to be ill-disposed towards airmen, indicating their displeasure by spitting on the vehicles as they passed through. The crews thought it was all a bit funny at first, but one does not spit upon an Englishman and expect him to turn the other cheek. He may accept a punch on the nose if merited, but when it was a matter of being spat upon by filthy natives, he begins, albeit slowly to see varying shades of pink, turning to red. Even then natural reserve compels him to half turn the other cheek, dismissing retaliation as unworthy. If he is spat at twice, his purpose and power knows no bounds. The Englishman always wins the final confrontation.

Thus it was that upon the second night they passed through the village, the boys were, if not exactly ready, wary and taking up defensive positions. For all the preparedness, one extremely large gob managed to achieve a quite remarkable trajectory into one of the trucks, as a result of which the epithets were loud and long. On the third night the crews went on red alert and rose as one to show their mettle in the matter of expectorant power. A profuse flow of saliva drenched the enemy line, the latter retreating in total dissarray. As the week unfolded itself the crews got the whole thing to a fine art. The enemy were not routed but the battle was becoming one-sided. Skilfully taking into account the variable factors, principal amongst which were the speed of the vehicles and a light wind, the crews got right on target. Particularly, the navigators were expert, skilled in the art of allowing for drift until finally the enemy retreated sullenly into their hovels. Once again the British, together with the Commonwealth, won the final battle.

Once during that week Ace and his crew, strangely together in social matters, walked into the little town of Blida. It was of course a case of "mad dogs and Englishmen" and a New Zealander, for the sun was hot and the air seemed even more so. The town was a peculiar blend of French and Arab. In what might have been regarded as the main square, although it was rectangular, French white stone built dwellings and houses of business that seemed to be entirely respectable, provided the main interest. There was however limited activity. Only a few people seemed to be about, but their journeys were short, presumably because in the heat it was better to be within than without, and in any case it was probably siesta time. Those that were around appeared to be cosmopolitan. One or two obvious Frenchmen and women rubbed shoulders with a sprinkling of American GIs and British servicemen, while the odd pair of Moslem women mooched about warily, faces hidden behind yashmaks. Not least of the limited humanity in view were Arab shoe shine boys trained to parade a form of salesmanship in respect of which unrelenting persistence was a principal element. There were also one or two urchins who had clearly dispensed with shoe-shining and its attendant labour, in favour of the potentially lucrative practice of selling their sisters' bodies to any interested party. These were children of ten to twelve years old, most revoltingly forward and persistent, aware far too early in life of the importance of sex and its application in the most degradingly lustful manner. After one bout of dedicated importuning by one of these street arabs, Jock the rear gunner who was of puritanical stock, aimed a kick at one of the offenders and hissed:

"Piss off, you dirty little buggers". It was doubtful whether they understood English, and even less, English with a Scots accent.

"That's it. Kick his ass, Jock", insisted Sid, while the rest of the crew laughed in quinary chorus, with Frank the mid upper gunner demonstrating his unworldliness by colouring up a brick red. The urchins pissed off.

At a second glance the curious mixture of French and Arab cafes dispersed within the square exhibited a less than wholesome aspect, particularly those in the tenancy of the latter. Dark dingy interiors gave an obscure impression of menace and latent devilry. One had the feeling that incautious ingress might attract a silent but fatal knife between the shoulder blades, expertly executed behind darkly hanging curtains, for it was quite clear from some of the looks focussed, that some of the populace were not over-friendly. Perhaps they were still trying to make up their minds whether Vichy French, the conquered, or the Allies, the victors, were the side to come down on. Ace and his crew decided not to be incautious and retraced their steps towards the more solidly acceptable confines of Blida Airfield. It was a relief to leave the town behind them.

By the seventh day all the crews were infinitely bored with the monotonous round of eating, drinking less than was customary. Even the swimming had palled. The novelty of easy living after living dangerously in the skies was wearing thin. Sid was inclined to be morose. He was normally taciturn, but his present mood was even more so. Perhaps it was the sun that had got to him, regularly leaping into the sky at dawn, burning its way through the day towards sundown but being reluctant to finally fall below the horizon and slipping away so suddenly that it was pitch dark before one could look around. Perhaps Sid was worried that the false and premature signal "missing in action" had reached his wife before being amended, or that his wife would worry that his regular letters had ceased. The crew had not known until very recently that Sid was indeed married and it was a mystery to them why Sid had, under the circumstances, opted to dice with death in the air. After all, it was his own choice for only volunteers were accepted into aircrew. If he was worried, there was no way he could reassure her from N. Africa. There was a third possibility. He could have received one of those infamous "Dear John" letters written by a local well-wisher, only too anxious to inform him that his wife was carrying on at home with another man. It was all speculation and with Sid there was no way of knowing. In all matters private, he kept to himself.

John had similar feelings and it showed. Instead of doing his suffering in silence like Sid, he got really irritable. He was missing Marion and wondering whether she knew the score, and one night he lost control. He awoke to realise suddenly that the blankets on his bed were being carefully removed by what had to be a thieving arab. He sat up with a jerk, grabbed his revolver and let off a round at a now rapidly receding shape. He was somewhat mollified to hear a shout of pain indicating that the bullet had found the target, but the arab managed to remove himself into the shadows and disappear, as silently as he'd arrived. There was a bit of a hoo-hah the next day. The Station Commander informed the navigator that it was not the done thing, but there was a trace of a smile accompanying the censure. It was all confirmed by a notice on Daily Routine Orders to the effect that "The indiscriminate shooting of arabs must cease forthwith".

Taffy and Jock, although mercifully not entangled by serious affairs of the heart, began to be more on edge with each other simply because of their respective Welsh and Scottish descent. Frank and Ken were the least affected, content to be relieved of the tension of battle. Ace clearly missed English ale and said so repeatedly, but since he was already 7000 miles from his homeland when in England, a thousand miles in another direction was no skin off his nose.

On the eighth day there was news. Briefing would take place at 17.30. Wing Co Paisley took it upon himself to travel to Maison Blanche to fly the patched-up R Robert back to Blida and it was a great relief when the Wing Co told Ace his kite was airworthy. Airworthy it might be, but it did not look like it, for little attempt had been made to do a proper repair on the fuselage. Some sort of smoothing out process had been exercised but you could see where the rents had been. It was a tribute to the ground staff that airworthiness had been achieved at all, since they had had to work throughout the heat of the days. But as Ace commented, he did not give a damn if the kite was draughty as long as the fans kept turning.

The crews assembled at the appointed hour in a building that closely resembled a temporary cinema judging by the arrangement of chairs and benches. There were no tables and after some traditional bitching the navigators repaired to the floor with their charts to be immediately regaled with cries of "get off your knees". It was a right comedy. It was unusual to note that the target had already been marked up on the map. It had to be assumed that the local command did not think it necessary to overdo the secrecy angle, simply because the target was again Italian. The general briefing got under way in a somewhat disjointed manner from which it was ascertained that Leghorn, the Italian naval base was to be blessed with Bomber Command's single squadron attack, the latter proceeding there after on a westerly track reciprocal to that followed on the route outwards. The pattern unfolded gave the crews little cause for raised body temperatures or pulse rates and the consensus of opinion was that since it was a long grind home, the sooner they got mobile the better. Perhaps the most significant part of the commonplace briefing was that of the Intelligence Officer who said that the last time Leghorn was bombed was by the US Air Force which reported heavy flak. He added that the RAF would place this report in more moderate proportions. A ghost of a smile crossed his face as his audience raised a roar of derisive laughter. The further intelligence he added was that the Germans were known to have a few fighters in Corsica, but the warning failed to lower the state of euphoria. The whole trip looked like a piece of cake. Wing Co Paisley wound up with tactics and procedure:

"Take off in any order, nearest to the runway first and so on. Engines are not to be started up until the previous aircraft is approaching take-off. There will be no run-ups for the soundest of reasons. The air temperature will still be high and you all know Merlins do not take kindly to the heat. So pilots must taxy immediately the engines are running. That's all chaps. See you in England".

The crews filed out leaving the navigators to complete flight plan calculations. By now John had accustomed himself to the martyrdom of housemaid's knee and changed to full stretch on his stomach. Everything seemed to be alright. Light variable winds would mean course the same as track — well, more or less — at least to start with. More positive winds would have to be calculated the further west they got. Time now for the last meal on N. African soil. He could not be happier.

It was 21.10 hours, twenty minutes prior to take-off time when the rest of Ace's crew took their first gander at R Robert since the traumatic landing at Maison Blanche. It looked pretty battle scarred, but was in one piece.

"For Pete's sake, don't touch it, John," warned Ace as the navigator tentatively fingered a rough patch on the fuselage near the rear entrance door.

"It's red hot", the navigator replied, sucking his fingers soothingly.

It was too hot to board the aeroplane prematurely, so they all sat on the grass. It was also too hot to don "mae wests' or battle dress blouses. John took out his pipe, filled it from a well worn pouch and puffed vigorously for a few seconds to create a bluish cloud of smoke separating into perfect successive rings that seemed to hang suspended in the heat. From a recumbent position near at hand Sid took a long draw on a fag and murmured:-

"For gawd sake, John, what are you smoking?"

"That's my business, Sid", replied the navigator.

"Yeh?. Well, how do you dry it?"

John just grinned and puffed away happily, totally relaxed. It really was half way towards being pleasant lying in the shade cast be the Lancaster's massive airframe. Barely a sound disturbed the air, nor was there a breath of wind. It was as if there was an established evening siesta as well as one at mid-day. With any luck, he thought, in 9 hours they would be home, almost at the extremity of another continent. But it was too good to last. The minutes were ticking away. Ace perused his watch, reluctantly heaved himself into a vertical position and said:-

"Right jokers. Let's have you. Rise and shine." He sounded like a physical training instructor bidding his victims prepare for a pre-breakfast bout of calisthenics. An hour before he had been uplifted at the thought of caressing the old kite into the air on route to home base where he could at last get a few pints of respectable ale, but now the thought of entering a kite that had been boiled and roasted in the hot sun all day was one of rather less enthusiasm. He wished with all his heart that take-off could have been retarded a couple of hours and he was not mollified by the knowledge that strategic considerations determined the time schedule.

The jokers stubbed out cigarettes and climbed into the rear door. All along the line of parked Lancasters other crews finally synchronised watches ready to get weaving.

R Robert's crew had just got settled into their respective positions on board when the first engine of the Wing Co's Lancaster smote the air and, just as soon as the fourth engine had fired and was ticking over, the chocks were wipped away to allow taxying towards the beginning of the runway. Watched now by a small group of RAF men semi-permanently stationed in North Africa who were probably conjuring up envious thoughts of Blighty, Wing Co swung onto the runway. With scarcely a pause, his Lancaster put on power and moved away, at the same time throwing up a swirling cloud of dust that temporarily engulfed the tail section. It seemed as if the aeroplane would never get airborne, but eventually the battle between drag and lift was won by lift right at the far end of the runway. Then the second Lancaster moved into position for take-off but unlike the

Wing Co, the pilot paused for a moment or two, which was not at all surprising.

"Just look at that cloud of dust," remarked Ken. "Wouldn't like to take-off until it's clear." Ace made no comment. He was third in line and pre-occupied with hand signals to the mechanic down below patiently manning the starter-ack. Quickly he called "contact" at the same time raising a thumb in confirmation of his call. The four engines sprang comfortingly to life in turn, coughing at first before settling down into idling rotation. Ace breathed out. The Merlins sounded pretty good. He hoped the engine fitters had done as good a job as they sounded. It was to be profoundly hoped that there were no loose bits of metal scudding around inside the cowlings. Rapidly he turned Robert for the short taxy to the start of the runway, swinging then into line for take-off with a controlled burst of engine power. It was only then that the significance of Ken's remark, only half heard, struck him, for a pall of dust hung over the runway with some persistence, but there was nothing for it. He'd have to go by the feel of it. No way could he afford to idle on the runway with oil temperatures climbing. Ken echoed his concern:

"Temperatures climbing, Ace. Better get off the deck as soon as possible." Ace just nodded. He eased forward the throttles with rather more initial pressure than was his habit. The tone of the engines rose sharply to a comforting whine, suggesting as yet unclaimed boost. With brakes off R Robert moved forward slowly into a dust storm. For a few moments Ace was blind and then they were in the clear just as the wheels were on the point of leaving terra firma.

"Climbing power, Ken. 2650 revs."

"OK Skip."

"Wheels up."

"Wheels up," echoed Ken.

"Flaps up."

"Flaps up. All systems go." Ken was pleased to see the temperatures holding. The pilot did a rate 1 turn to port following the customary left hand circuit since his seat was on the port side of the aircraft and was able to view the dust cloud that was increasing in volume and intensity. The leading edge of the cloud was drifting very slowly towards Blida. The bystanders had scarpered doubtless regarding discretion as the better part of valour.

"See that cloud of dust, Sid", asked Ace. "Looks like the locals will have sand in their shoes."

"Reminds me of a song," advised John. "Sand in my shoes, sand from Havana."

"I don't fancy we're popular with the natives," said Sid with a short laugh.

R Robert crossed the Bay of Algiers at an altitude of no more than 2000 feet, its pilot exuding all the wariness commonly employed when crossing an enemy coastline. Although it was not exactly that, one could be sure that the telephone lines would be signalling to the enemy that a force of bombers was leaving North Africa in a northerly direction, for there were those in Algiers who did not find favour with allied forces. What was more, Ace and his crew had frequently been fired on by the Royal Navy and he was taking no chances, remaining on full alert. He took the view that if AA gunners were a bit short on experience in the all important matter of aircraft recognition, they might just assume the 12 bombers were the enemy and react on the basis of shoot first and ask questions afterwards, the more so since Lancasters were scarcely commonplace in the North African theatre of operations. Happily there were no untoward incidents.

The coast receded slowly to the rear as Ace coaxed Robert into a very slow steady climb, and slow it had to be for it was soon obvious that the prospect of gaining an operational height of 20,000 feet was unlikely to be achieved, or at best only after a prolonged struggle. The Merlin engines clearly did not like the hot air temperature and were registering protest. But where there's a will there is a way. By means of slowing the rate of climb together with an occasional levelling off and with the added bonus of air cooling at the adiabatic lapse rate at increased height, the engines began to settle into something like normal efficiency as the aeroplane pounded on into twilight with the sun slipping rapidly over the horizon.

John made his second intrusion onto intercom when Robert was within half an hour from Corsica:

"Can we sling out a flame float, Ace?" he asked hopefully. "I'd like Jock to get me a drift reading."

The pilot hesitated and John, being aware of sound reasons for this went on: "Forecasters were vague about the winds. Dusty was not my idea of a comprehensive forecast."

The pilot still hesitated. As skipper he had to weigh up the requirements of navigation against the possibility of exposing his aeroplane's approximate position in an area that was near to enemy occupied territory, but it was Jock's announcement that tipped the scales.

"Flame floats going down all over the place", he advised.

"OK John. Ask Taffy to throw one out down the chute."

Taffy responded while Jock in the rear turret was only too eager to be involved in any action, however minimal, that provided some relief from dull monotony. Furthermore it gave him in his lonely tail location the opportunity to find out if the crew up front were still around.

"Nil drift, John" he said at last and that's bang on. Shall I come up front and show you how to really navigate?"

"Thank's for the first, Jock, no bloody fear to the second. We want to get to England, not Russia."

"Och. There's gratitude for you. Ungrateful Sassenach."

Sid called up in due course to say that they were passing over Cape Corse, just a shadowy outline against the different shade of water, some 16000 feet below, and a few seconds later the navigator came up with the change of course for Leghorn. He was more confident now that he had confirmation of correct tracking. The winds forecast had been classed as light and variable — a navigator's nightmare. In theory, light and variable wind speeds and directions should average out to achieve course equal to track, but if the variable factor operated consistently from one segment of the compass, that neutral course/track ratio was made a nonsense of. In this instance, fortunately the variable factor was constantly variable so a neutral course was working out well.

Ace acknowledged the alteration of course. He had rather less confidence than the navigator, but for quite different reasons. Just ahead or so it seemed in the gathering darkness was what appeared to be an unbroken layer of cloud at a lower level of altitude. If it did not break there was little chance of their identifying Leghorn from height for the Squadron did not have the Pathfinder's Force target determining technique from above cloud. The plan as it stood was based on a cloud free target illuminated by ground markers, and was different from the attack on the electrical transformer station in so far as there was no orbiting point and the aeroplanes would not be "called in" to bomb. As soon as the markers had identified the target, each pilot would aim for the markers in his own time. All this ran through Ace's mind, but he consoled himself with the added thought that fruitless speculation was useless at this stage. He would play it by ear, so to speak. With that comforting decision, he eased his posterior and rechecked that he had not deviated from the navigator's stated course. He grinned to himself when he realised that John could not check him on his repeater compass, since that was one of the things that had not been repaired.

Zero hour approached. The cloud was thinning into a patchy formation and the pilot permitted himself a low but essentially tuneless rendering of "Waltzing Matilda", forgetting he had failed to switch off his intercom.

"Um. Nice, Ace. You'll be singing next," suggested Sid.

"I thought of it, Sid, but desisted".

"Thank gawd for that. I wondered who was doing the heavy breathing act".

"Eight minutes to Zero hour", the navigator intoned and sat back in his chair, confidence oozing from him, certain too that the opposition would be insignificant.

The pilot, however, was in the habit of ignoring common conjecture that an Italian target was a piece of duff and proceeded to settle himself to rapidly run over the possibilities. He remembered only too well the trip out and the doddle it was expected to be, and proved not to be. He had no intention of losing sight of the fact that although the Italian navy might not have the stomach to put to sea, they would certainly have a few heavy guns around. He squirmed a little, experiencing the momentary spinal chill that always preceded a run up to target.

Five minutes later out of the night and from the even blacker darkness below, an orange flame burst at perhaps 2000 feet identifying the port itself in the two dimensions of sea and land. Seconds later two further flares added more orange daylight, more or less in the same area. It was Leghorn alright without a doubt. Immediately a dozen searchlights flickered on to flash upwards probingly, springing from pinpoints at ground level to sharp pencils of light widening with height. There appeared to be no controlled radar directed searchlights with the bluish tint like the Germans employed, but rather standard jobs aimlessly jerking about.

"They are windy already," observed Ken as he tried hard to determine if there was an organised search pattern.

"Yeh. Give me a nice smooth run up, Ace," Sid requested. "Bomb doors open".

"Bomb doors open," replied Ace and suited the action to the words.

"They'll need new pants when this lot reaches the ground." Sid was never happier than on a bombing run, which it is to be supposed natural enough since bombing was his principal function, but perhaps it was partly because he could take up his favourite horizontal position, except that in this circumstance he was required to lay on the stomach instead of his back.

Streams of light tracer were now arcing upwards with more hope than any judgement and hopelessly out of range of the high flying Lancasters. For a moment a long searchlight beam chanced on R Robert, but for some obscure reason failed to latch on. Thus it was that Ace, prepared to take the aeroplane into evasive contortions, found it unnecessary to vary his smooth straight and level approach. A few seconds later a heavy flak shell burst dead ahead with a vicious wink and with a moving trail of smoke emanating from it, but the pilot still held the course while Sid watched the naval base run up the line of the bombsight.

"Keep her steady, Ace," cautioned the bomb aimer.

"What the hell do you think I'm doing," gritted Ace. "We're flying as smooth as silk."

Sid's toneless "Bombs gone — keep her steady for photo" came quickly and as an anti-climax, for it was only when the opposition was fierce that the bombing run seemed to be so abominably long and so horribly steady.

As soon as Ace had turned westerly on to the navigator's course for home, he called up the rear gunner:-

"What's it look like, Jock?"

"Bombs in the right place alright. Not a lot of fire. Seems pretty concentrated."

"Understandable, Jock. We're not carrying incendiaries — just 500 lb H.Es," Ace reminded the rear gunner.

They were on their way home, towards the Alps, over the Alps, across the width of France to England, land of home and beauty.

R Robert droned rhythmically across the English coast by Beachy Head, after a long monotonous stooge that called for solid endurance and relentless vigil. All that was left was the straight leg of the route to Lincoln. The crew could now relax partially, but safety could not be wholly assumed, for there was always a possibility of an enemy intruder on their tail. Total relaxation would only come when the aeroplane was back in their Holmdun dispersal with wheels stilled and engines cut.

John, head in his hands, withdrew bloodshot eyes from his Mercator chart and yawned widely. It really was a piece of cake from here. He could indulge in a spell of masterly inactivity. As he stretched his legs to reduce muscular stiffness, he felt some sympathy for his driver, who, sitting up forward in the cockpit, could not entertain such spontaneous relaxation. Ace would be cramped in muscle with feet stiffly on the rudder bar and hands now less sensitively on the control column. He would also be very tired indeed after 8 solid hours at the controls and with still a half hour to ETA. Of a sudden the navigator felt quite guilty: he really must justify his flying pay, measly as it was. He reached forward to the G. Box, lined up the strobes and got a fix. He re-measured the distance to base and recalculated ETA. No change. In any case — what the hell — it would not matter now if the timing was a couple of minutes out, but a sudden thought struck him:

"Ace, are we supposed to land at Base or Holmdun?" he asked.

"Damned if I know," replied the pilot, relieved to hear a voice on the intercom if only to jerk him into wakefulness. "But we're going right home. I want my own pit to sleep in," he added with a small degree of belligerence.

"Me too," echoed the navigator.

"Your own, I hope", said the rear gunner.

"Where else, you Scotch idiot". There was just a touch of irritation.

"Och. Heard you got a WAAF Sgt on tag. You might want to sleep in the WAAFery".

"What if I do. Belt up, addlehead."

If the conversation was not exactly brilliant, it served at least to keep everyone awake.

The sun was well up as they came up to Lincoln and the inherently neutral topography looked distinctly exciting, with its varied greens and browns, so unlike Algeria which, apart from the vineyards, looked arid. Over to starboard running on a parallel course was another Lancaster. One of our lot, thought the pilot. And there ahead was Holmdun looking absolutely deserted in terms of humanity as it normally would be at 6.30 hours. If the squadron had been dicing last night they were certainly back now, the aeroplanes dispersed all round the airfield.

Ace switched on R/T and called:-

"Manger Robert to Bakewell. Are you receiving me?" It should have sounded like that but Ace garbled rather than spoke clearly. It should have been intelligible to control down below, for the R/T operators were pretty well used to their pilot's voices in any guise, but if the dawn chorus had not succeeded in chirruping the operator into wakefulness, neither could Ace at first go.

"Bakewell. This is Manger Robert". This time Ace's diction was more pure even if it had a pronounced antipodean inflexion and it was beginning to sound as if he meant it. There was no answer and now devoid of patience the pilot thumbed the button:

"Wakey, Wakey, Bakewell. Dedigitate. Get your bloody fingers out". Even that failed to elicit any response. "Prepare for landing, jokers. We're going in, but I'll have the whole bloody place awake first". He rammed the nose down and throttled forward. Robert roared over the perimeter at about 30 feet, thrashing over the tower at well over 200 knots, finally pulling up in a sharp climbing turn into the downwind leg. He was well and truly awake now and so would everyone else be.

"Flaps 20", he called. Ken responded. Ace got the revs up.

"Wheels down", called Ace and turned into the wind lining up with the distant runway, "Full flap. Radiators closed". It was all standard pattern. Two green lights glowed on the cockpit panel indicating wheels down. The pilot noted the WAAFery moving into proximity as Robert lost height and with a quick grin he gave the engines 3 sharp bursts of power. With full flap on John was now calling the indicated airspeed 120 .. 120 ... 115 ... 110 ... 110 ... 105 ... 100 ... The wheels glanced on the concrete runway with tyres squealing slightly as Ace corrected against a crosswind. He let Robert roll gently to the intersection and turned towards the perimeter track. There was still no one about and none to marshal him into dispersal. Cut engines was his final command.

"8.28 hours of flying", John informed the crew for their individual log books and promptly closed down his log.

Over in the WAAFery a Sergeant WAAF stirred from a fitful sleep as she became conscious of 3 bursts of engine power, and then the distant crackle of Merlin engines. But it could not be. The squadron had been on standdown. What was the time? She looked at her watch. 6.30. And then the earlier engine sound reincarnated itself on her now complete wakefulness. It was Ace's signal, that secret arrangement she had made with the pilot to signal a safe return of John and indeed all the crew. Even John did not know of the arrangement. Praise be to God. Out of the dawn had come deliverance.

There had been rumours. At first Ace and his crew were posted missing. Then it was said that the signal had been countermanded, but no one knew for sure. Marion closed her eyes as glowing happiness coursed through her young body. It was like taking a double brandy to ease the numbing chill of an Arctic winter. He was safe. That was all that mattered. Momentarily she researched her emotions. Why should she feel like this? Was she truly in love? It was new to her experience. She drifted into the deep unconsciousness of the utterly exhausted after eight nights of little sleep and patterns of chaotic dreams.

Chapter 5

TEXEL AGAIN

The sun shone down out of a pale blue cloudless sky. John reflected that he might be still in North Africa, for although the air temperature was well below N African norms, it was pretty warm for Lincolnshire. The countryside was silent, tranquil and beautiful. The leaves on the trees rustled faintly in a light breeze while gleams of sunshine played hide and seek amongst the branches. After N Africa with its monotonous expanse of grape vines, where, he felt, if the vines could be swept away, there would have been nothing left, here in Lincolnshire he felt and saw with wondrous pleasure the flowing undulation of small fields spanning far over the rise to the north in a varied panorama — a field of green, then a light brown square of lately mown grass and then another field in a different shade of green with a haycock in one corner, newly stacked. Further again was a small farmhouse with its slate tiled roof shimmering in the reflective heat of the sun, with a splash of white as a farmer moved across the doorway of the milking shed, and then all around in a wider circle the pattern was roughly repeated. John had looked and seen it all before, but never before had he appreciated the scenery. His pulses quickened with an obscure surge of emotion as if some of the strength of the land was being sucked into his being, implanting in him the will to try as best he could to preserve this country in his small way, and that he thought, was what this war was all about — the preservation of civilisation and the land on which humans were raised and fostered or reared.

Slowly he walked up the lane from the billets, breathing in deeply the heavy fragrance of shrubs and new mown hay, listening to the steady buzz of insects all vying for supremacy over each other. Odd he thought, humans are doing the self-same thing, but it was good to be alive anyway.

The comparative coolness of the Sergeants Mess enveloped him pleasurably, the more so since it was empty except for the kitchen. It looked rather as if the squadron had also been out dicing with death and were now sleeping off the effects, re-charging batteries, or just waiting for the Tannoy to boom out a call to action. On the other hand aircrews were notoriously late risers, particularly after a night on the booze. He poked his head into the dining room from which emanated a variegated medley of sounds; the clinking of eating irons being laid out for lunch, the glug of water being poured, the scraping of repositioned chairs and a subdued clatter of cooking utensils from the kitchen beyond.

"Hello Nora," John said to one of the waitresses and without waiting for a reply sheered off into the ante room to see whether anyone else had condescended to appear, totally unaware of the effect his brief head-in-the-dining-room-doorway had created. Nora had turned white as a ghost as if she had in fact perceived an apparition. She was generally regarded to be a pretty attractive Miss, but if would-be admirers had seen her at this moment they would have been stunned by a vision of open-mouthed idiocy and small wonder, for she had been told that Ace Burnett and his crew were missing. She also knew that crews posted missing never came back and yet suddenly a ghost had risen before her. It was very frightening. When she had first arrived at Holmdun it was her first posting to an operational station and she had been horrified to hear the casual, seemingly heartless mention of "they bought it last night," or "they went for a burton," or "they've had their chips," but gradually, painfully she had come to accept that surviving crewmen could ill afford to ponder morbidly on past history, however recent. So it was that she was shocked to see a member of a crew who should not have come back.

There was no one in either the main or smaller ante rooms. John experienced an irrational pang of disappointment that Marion was not around and then more sensibly concluded that she would be on duty anyway. There was an easy way to find out. He retraced his way to the hall and snatched the blower.

"Watch office please," he requested, and a click registered immediate contact. "That you Marion? You heard we were back?" For a few moments he listened to her golden tones and finally asked, "Any Gen? Nothing on tonight? Not yet. OK. I'll be in the mess." He replaced the phone mechanically, realising that he was impatient to see her, but then he had never been away so long. It had to be a case of absence making the heart grow fonder. Marion was one of those women that few other women would forget and even fewer men ignore. In a contrived effort to control impatience he threw himself into an easy chair and took up the Daily Telegraph with the intention of making inroads on the crossword puzzle while it was still virgin, but he was unable to concentrate. Even the Daily Mirror's Jane he quizzed with notable indifference before nodding off as insufficient sleep caught up.

A voice from the back of beyond startled him into a small degree of wakefulness:

"Well lookee who's here — the lost navigator. Where you been? Thought you'd put some nice WAAF in the family way and bogged off AWOL." The navigator dimly beheld the shape of Texel standing before him, tap room eyes bleakly watching with more than a trace of enquiry.

"My name's not Hanson," John replied and added, "For which I thank my lucky stars. Now scram. I'm trying to get a bit of sleep."

"Aw c'mon Johnny boy," soothed Texel. "Come have a drink and tell Uncle Tex all about it."

"Who is paying?"

"Well I am, or I wouldn't have asked. Now would I?" Texel was quite hurt at the implication that he could be mean with his pocket money.

"Not so I'd notice it, but I'll come," replied John and prised himself out of the chair with difficulty, thinking as he did so that Texel's bar conversation although singularly barren of topics remotely on an intellectual plane, was nevertheless often enlightening where knowledge of recent history was called for. Texel had essentially the nose of a woman when it came to accumulating the snippets of squadron gen and currently John stood in need of news about the squadrons activities during the past week.

"Where the hell you been?" asked Texel again as he ordered two pints at the bar. As well as having the curiosity of the fairer sex, he also had their impatience, particularly on this occasion when for once, he was apparently uninformed, but before John could make suitable reply, Ace's familiar drawl sounded from the doorway:

"Relaxing in sunny Mediterranean climes by permission of the Air Ministry, as a reward for devotion to duty. Make it three pints, Tex. I've got a real thirst on."

"Yes. Texel's paying. Make the most of it," advised John.

"OK, if you insist. I'm easy." Ace capitulated without a fight as he caught the navigator's tone and accompanying look of bland innocence. "And take your hand out of my pocket. I'm flat broke."

"God with friends like you who needs enemies," Texel ruefully remarked. "C'mon, don't keep me in suspense. Where you bin?"

"I told you. We been bathing in the Med — Algiers boy — hell of a spot, little good ale, just sour red wine. I was often reduced to craving a glass of clear cool water, but there was none of that either, leastways none that was fit to drink." The pilot smacked his lips at the prospect of a foaming pint of Ale and grabbed the pint that Texel seemed reluctant to pass along. With almost indecent haste he took one hefty gulp and downed it in one. "Gee that's good. Can feel my blood coursing again."

"Well if you were anything of a buddy you would have had the decency to bring home a few bottles so we could judge the quality for ourselves." Texel was tentative rather than admonishing, for he could not accept that Ace would let such an opportunity slip by, with no customs around to poke their noses in.

"Don't panic, Tex," put in John. "We've brought some bottles of wine and a few bottles of scotch. Lost some of the wine though — exploded under pressure at operational height."

"What? Lead me to them." Tex was half mollified.

"It'll keep," replied Ace curtly.

"Ah that's better. I knew you boys wouldn't forget the best engineer of the best crew on the Squadron."

"Balls. You want to get your knees brown." One single pint had not loosened Ace.

"You're not kidding are you?" Texel was still not sure that Ace and John were not feeding him a line. "You really bin to Algiers. Lucky old sods."

"It's no line Tex," advised John. "We've been sunning it up. Couldn't get back because of bad weather on route."

"You can say that again. Weather's been dud here at times." Texel seemed to be convinced at last and then went on a little wryly, "We thought you boys had had it, got the chopper, met the grim reaper. There was a rumour you made it, but nobody knew where, and then it seemed it was all duff gen. Denny sniffed around for a while and got nowhere. Yards and yards of security and red tape. In fact, that reminds me. I'm a quid to the good. I bet Denny you were OK. As I told him the evil finger will never be on you." Texel paused for a moment, carefully controlling some rare emotion and then admitted, "I bin drinkin' myself sick. I was in a hell of a quandary. Couldn't decide whether I was drinking to your survival or topping up a prayer for souls departed."

"Oh Tex," murmured Ace with an exaggerated look of abandonment. "I didn't know you cared."

All three laughed for it seemed that Ace had struck the right note, finding it within his scope to turn sobering thoughts into nonsense. He was back on his home ground again and proceeded to give the Flt Engineer chapter and verse in his customary clipped fashion, finally adding laconically that he had had to pancake on a single outboard engine which left the engineer open mouthed in frank disbelief.

"Struth. You're kidding me," he said.

"No line Tex," said John evenly and his voice indicated sincerity inspired by absolute acceptance that his own life and those of the rest of the crew had been preserved by outstanding pilot skill, albeit topped up with a shade of luck of the good variety. He remembered with a shiver how even the fourth engine had packed up on touchdown through lack of fuel. It had been a close run thing. It was clear that Texel had got the message, strength 5, for he could not find anything to say for a while but then finally got around to producing essential current news. "While you bin livin' it up on the Med, we've been getting east of the Wash — couple of times. Been out once myself, and while I think of it, when a new crew comes from OTU, pilots and navs go second dickey with experienced crews for a couple of trips to give 'em some idea what it's all about. So you can settle your mind to having an extra bod with you on your next stooge."

"Clutters up the kite a bit," was Ace's rejoinder. His permanent frown was more pronounced than ever.

"Sure does. We took one pilot three nights back. Denny made him sit on the step by the W.Op until we were well under way. Then he came up and sat in my seat. Didn't know where to park myself. Everytime I wanted a looksee I had to practically kidney punch him, and here, just listen to this." Tex was now in full flow at the centre of the stage. He made a pretence of spitting before continuing: "Talk of insufferable clots — this guy was one of the wonder boys — such a goddammed good driver that when he got his wings out in Canada and a commission, stayed on as an instructor. It seems that on account of his extended experience he thought he was the cat's whiskers, you know, 'there's bugger all you bloody NCO's can teach me.'" Texel's customary grin was wholly absent as he continued, for once deadly serious and somewhat distastefully: "We had one of those quiet trips — you know the form — kites going down all around, hell of a lot of searchlights and flak but nothing too near." He paused again and the look he passed around was positively combustible. "Well the long and the short of it is that when we landed and I had completed the formality of kissing the ground in dispersal, this bod cocks up his snoot and says, 'Well if that's all ops are I don't know why I joined.' You could have knocked me down with a feather. I just could not believe what I was hearing." Texel was almost gasping for breath and in truth as well as spellbinding himself, he had the consolation that both pilot and navigator were practically open-mouthed in astonishment. Ace shifted his weight to the other foot, snatched up the second beer thoughtfully provided by John and downed a top half. It was a moment during which Texel would normally have revelled, his auditory literally hanging on his words, but for once he was not playing to the gallery. He was deadly serious.

"I can't believe that. You must be joking," said John.

"It's as true as I'm standing here," the flight engineer replied. "You should've seen Denny's face. It was positively pitying. At first I thought Denny was going to hit this bod, but he turned away as if he hadn't heard. I just gave him one of my hideous looks reserved only for unmitigated clots and then told him that if he didn't get wise to himself pretty smartly the evil finger would be on him at a very early date, and believe it or not, this bod ups and threatens to put me on a charge for insolence to an officer. God, I could've poked him right in the eye but desisted when Denny waved me away. Instead, I said 'say your prayers, Sir,' and walked away."

"Who is this character?" asked Ace, worried that perhaps he might be saddled with him on the next op.

"Who *was* this character, you mean, Ace old boy? The following morning the guy cavorts in to the flight office and complains to Denny about my impertinence. Denny told him to go and find something more useful to do, and that was just his polite way of putting it. But now I come to the climax of my story. The guy was on the battle order that night with his own crew to the same target and one of our aircraft is missing. RIP."

"God," exclaimed John. "Pretty tough on the crew. Never had a chance from the moment they crewed up." It was clear that Ace and Texel had the same sympathetic thought for there was a short silence while they chewed over the navigator's remark.

The sound of steps in the open doorway broke the silence. John turned expectantly, feeling the shoe leather thicken under his feet. It was indeed Marion. He had known, had felt her presence. As she hitched her cap onto a peg, John thought how unbelieveably lovely she looked.

"Hullo boys," she greeted them musically. "You're unusually quiet. Anything wrong?"

"Just shop," said Ace.

"Thanks Ace, you know for what," she said.

Ace just grinned, while John sought her eyes in mute questioning.

"Why don't you kiss her Johnny boy," suggested Texel roguishly. "She's been starved for over a week."

No one could accuse Marion of aggressive feminism, but she gave Texel such a sharp stab in the ribs that the latter nearly drank his pint twice over.

"Vixen," he said. "To think that I've lavished my affections on such a virago."

Marion accepted a sherry from Ace and they all drank in the mood of quiet celebration. Now Sergeants were beginning to filter in for lunch and judging from the rising clamour in the dining room the food was coming up on schedule. The dining room was by no means full which was perfectly normal after a night of ops. Those present were the ever hungry while those still to come preferred to arrive at the last minute before termination, causing dissatisfaction amongst the catering staff, who being perpetually short-handed had then to cope with many demands for immediate attention, often to the chant of "Why are we waiting?" Ace, Tex, Marion and John decided to be on time.

A new waitress served the soup nervously, occasionally slopping overfull dishes on to the cloth. Her nervousness was not improved by Texel who suggested that the concoction looked like "oil being poured on troubled waters," and for his pains got a lapfull. Ace did a spell of soup identification while John spooned away mechanically, his eyes cautiously on Marion, who sat opposite him.

"Just look at our two lovebirds." Texel whispered loudly to Ace. "Look at the light in their eyes. Makes me want to puke."

"Do you mind? I would like to enjoy my meal." Marion was not at all pleased.

"Well I'm willing to bet we don't see you two for the rest of the day," quoth Texel. "No doubt you'll be navigating to some cosy little nook to make up for lost time. It's haymaking time, so haystacks are in fashion. Nice and warm too I'm told."

"Thanks for the tip," replied John as he strove to silence the engineer who was even now on the sharp end of a withering look from Marion. "Raise your mind above the gutter, nondescript. I used to think you were a decent chap, but apparently appearances are truly deceptive. As a matter of fact we're going cycling and doubtless we'll pass innumerable haystacks."

"Well just keep cycling, love. You must know what these navigators are like. All with one track minds and an eye on the aiming point."

"It's a pity you and Ace don't get a bit of healthy exercise to get your blood circulating and the alcohol out of your systems," she replied.

The rejoinder more than half wiped the smiles off the faces of both Texel and Ace. The latter kicked Tex under the table. Button your lip bud was the implication. A woman should always have the last word. Happily for both of them Sid arrived to nod pleasantly at the company before taking his seat. He too peered suspiciously at the soup and called over his shoulder:

"What's this Angie? Mucous soup?"

John spluttered and nearly had seconds.

"Have a heart Sid," he plaintively suggested. "I've finished mine."

Angie, one of the regular waitresses disliked being hurried. She was accustomed to adverse comments on the fare provided, but as the mere distributor she could scarcely be faulted. With this comforting thought she normally had not the need to make excuses, but she had a teeny bit of a crush on Sid, the strong silent type of her dreams, and accordingly murmured huskily in some sympathy:

"It's better than it looks, Sergeant. We've served the same for seven days and nobody's been carried out, yet." Sid looked back over his shoulder as if to ascertain whether she was being funny peculiar or funny ha ha, but Angie had moved away strategically so dispelling the opportunity for further investigation. Sid bowed the head to tackle the soup with the inbred caution of his crewmates. It was not too bad, just innocuous, could be chicken, could be anything.

"Where are the rest of the boys, Sid?" asked Ace. "I want a word."

"Oh. They'll be in shortly, but Taffy is in a right binding mood. I left Jock trying to pacify him if you can imagine the scene — Jock trying to pacify Taffy is like heaping coals on a roaring fire." Sid could not restrain quiet amusement. "It seems that Taffy was in the mess earlier trying to ring a popsie in Lincoln and got the brush off. Had a date the night we set off for North Africa and she thinks he deliberately stood her up. Anyway the air in the billet was red hot when I left — enough to singe one's flying boots. I beat a retreat."

"Must have been pretty interesting in Welsh," suggested Ace.

"Worse than that. I reckon the grass round the billet has withered for 10 yards."

"Being one of the female species, perhaps I'd better get a move on and exit before Taffy arrives," suggested Marion, with an accompanying little laugh that was more like the tinkling of a silver bell.

"I shouldn't worry," said John. "He won't come near us in that fiery Welsh mood." His tone was confident, but one has only to speak of the devil and in he comes. There was a mild commotion in the hall which superimposed itself on the subdued conversation of the diners. Then the glass panelled door crashed back on to its hinges with a violence sufficient to shatter the glass to minute fragments.

"Here comes boyo," said Sid unnecessarily.

Taffy stalked into the room closely followed by Jock who threw a knowing wink at Ace and company. To the rear were Frank and Ken clearly revelling in the celtic cuffuffle.

"What cher Taff. What's she done? Shot you down in flames eh?" asked Texel in his hear-me-all voice.

"Wrap up you has-been non flying engineer," was the stinging retort laced with sheer venom, that is, if it could be identified, for Taffy was high on the "Land of my Fathers" lingo and was close to needing a translator. Taffy glared around the room like an animal at bay and then strode purposely towards the far vacant corner, his lips still moving silently. Certainly, a trim little pair of ears in Lincoln would be well and truly burning.

"Didn't realise that Taffy was going steady," mused the navigator.

"Steady my foot. His vanity has taken a tumble," replied Sid.

As the main course began to put in an appearance Texel mused aloud:

"If that's what love does, I'm glad I've no female encumbrances. There was one once," he continued while contriving to gaze soulfully at Marion, "but she threw me off like a top boot, laid my heart bare and trampled it underfoot. Ah me."

"You're too adolescent to love or be loved Texel," Marion advised. "Grow up a bit and you'll get caught running after some woman, I've no doubt."

"Well, I tell you. If I looked as dewy-eyed as that love-sick swain of yours, old girl, I'd be so disgusted with myself I'd commit hari-kari."

"You look stupid enough in the normal course," cut in John while Texel paused for breath, "so you might as well commit suicide now in the interests of posterity." He added acidly. "Anything that would put a stop to your constant inane drivel would be an infinitely worthy act. We might even accord you a martyr's funeral."

"Boys, boys," chided Marion in the manner of a mother hen and the contretemps ended abruptly. She could be quietly formidable and capable of exerting control in mixed company.

The main course turned out to be the roast beef of old England, but judging by the persistent champing of jaws and a sudden lowering of the general conversational murmur, it might well have been designated the old roast beef of England, and for sure the recipe for Yorkshire pudding did not emanate from that County. However, valiant efforts that were only successful by dint of iron will power and healthy molars won the day and the dish was generally disposed of. Then the sweet appeared.

"Glory be. What ever is this?" Sid had every reason to be puzzled. It was, so Angie informed Sid, trifle, and whatever the ingredients were, the kitchen cooks had certainly trifled with it. Such a pity really. The food probably started off as good provisions, but when one considered the staff recruitment policy, it was not altogether surprising that some of the table offerings were, well, dubious. If you were a clerk in civvy street you might be trained as an engine fitter; if you were a butcher you ended up in the Orderly Room; if you were a carpenter, it was logical that you could supply one lot of chips as easily as the other, so you became a cook. It had to be some brilliant master plan to defeat the enemy in the long term, however many home casualties there were in the interim period.

Ace leaned away from the table into a stiff upright position to allow food to pass more easily from gullet to stomach and produced from battledress pocket a packet of cigarettes. Normally he rolled his own but he had not said no to a service issue in North Africa. He proffered the packet with such a rapid sweeping action that the packet was restored to the pocket before anyone could take material advantage of his generosity.

"Cheap round," he said thankfully and lit up.

Texel fixed him with a dirty look which had no effect so the flight engineer had to delve into his own resources somewhat ruefully. Senior Service were a pretty decent weed and not to be refused.

"What's the programme for tonight?" asked Ace as he drew ecstatically on his cigarette.

"Well now. Let me put my brilliant brain to good use," replied Texel with typical immodesty.

"Can't get animation from a block of wood," reminded John, but Tex ignored the remark.

"Suppose we do something original. What about a crafty pint or two in the mess. I've been quite off beer since you boys bogged off to North Africa, for convalescence. Had to have one or two of course for to keep mess fund solvent." His look of bland innocence would have deceived many but not so the gathered company; least of all Marion who could give the lie to his statement, for she had perceived him tanking away at a level that barely allowed any degree of sobriety. She made no comment choosing instead to regard Texel with a straightened look of which the flight engineer was well aware. Marion knew that Texel had missed Ace's companionship much more than he would have been prepared to admit. Strange how the two hit it off so well, the one garrulous, jovial, moody in turn, the other generally quiet and deep thinking.

"Suits me. I'm easy," replied Ace. He too liked the little corner by the bar, where he and Texel had acquired a dubious reputation of being hard drinkers, a dangerous pastime perhaps for those who needed their wits about them to pursue dicey endeavours in the air. What their critics would not remember however, and critics never do, was that neither airman would go near the bar if there was the faintest possibility of being called to the battle order. Whats more their association was not a purely social one, for each had a lot to learn from the other and were doing so. Texel was an ex-Halton apprentice aircraft fitter remustered to Flight Engineer and he could teach Ace a hell of a lot about engines, and Ace always listened. On the other hand Ace was a first class bomber pilot who had taken the trouble to learn the theory of aero-dynamics as well as the practice of flying. Texel was learning too. The latter was mindful of the fact that there was always the possibility that he might have to take over the controls from Denny at short notice if Denny should suffer injury.

Marion was reflecting how odd it was that Ace never went on leave. Coming all the way from the antipodes, it was to be supposed that he would have the inclination to move around a bit and see the Old Country, or go off to London like so many of his Commonwealth compatriots. John had asked him to his own home, but Ace had declined courteously. Ace was adamant that he'd seen enough of the country from the air to last him a lifetime, and he could not be moved.

After coffee, Marion and John rose to leave. Nothing was said. It was just an eyeball to eyeball arrangement.

"Well so long soaks," said the navigator brightly.

"Don't do anything I wouldn't do," cautioned Sid with the trace of a smile.

"OK, Dad," said Marion sweetly.

They passed through the swingdoors. Only two pairs of eyes followed them. Ace's were comtemplative, Texel's sardonic, a kind of ungentlemanly stocktaking. Unhitching hats from pegs, Marion and John ambled out into summer sunshine. It was a grand day to be in the open air. Even in Lincolnshire it could be sometimes rather wonderful and the multitudinal insects sang the praises. The two walked, wheeling their bicycles towards the village, saying nothing. What was there to say that was important, for they were back together again after a week that had seemed like eternity. But there was more to it than that; there was an increasing as yet unspoken feeling of warmth in a relationship that had so far gone no further than being one of very close friends with similar interests.

"Will you meet me at 1500 hours at the WAAFery?" Marion asked.

"Will do. Bye for Now." It seemed to be a brusque farewell but he could hardly wait. John watched her jump with becoming grace onto her bike and ride sedately through the village. He reflected that he must be in love for he could not keep his eyes off her, and it showed, which was a bit disconcerting, especially when Texel, who missed nothing, was around. It was a thought both gratifying and alarming. He was aware that Marion carried the power to generate sexual awareness but no way would she give herself to a lover before having him sign on the dotted line. But what could he, John offer her? Perhaps a short and merry life with no future. Surely she would not go for that. It was possible that no such similar thoughts had entered her mind and yet, somehow he was intuitively certain that her thinking had embraced the possibilities.

Chapter 6

BACK FROM LEAVE

Three weeks later, in the cool of evening the local bus from Lincoln pulled up with a squeal of brakes outside the "Old Cow" to disgorge it's predominantly "boys in blue" load of passengers. A few perhaps had been into Lincoln for a few hours break before going on night duty or shift. Fewer were returning from furlough. One of the latter was John, back from his 6 weekly spell of 7 days leave and for him it was a relief to breathe fresh air after bumping along in a coach thick with cigarette smoke. He was tired too, after an arduous journey by train which had been both crowded and late. He and Marion had arranged to take leave at the same time, although they had not spent the time together. The navigator had gone to his home in the west country while Marion had gone to hers in Norfolk. When the matter was first discussed they were unanimous in agreeing that visits to home were a clear duty. It was also in their minds that if they took leave at the same time, they would be apart for a minimum of time. Once again John had asked Ace to go with him, but the latter, while showing clear appreciation of the offer, had declined on the grounds that there would be nothing more restful than remaining on station without having to face the call to ops. Cheaper too.

To the navigator, the prospect of seven days had been at first invigorating, but the outcome had not lived up to the promise. True his folk had treated him, as they always did, as a conquering hero returned, an attitude that was both understandable and wholly discomfitting. On the other hand, old friends were mostly away in the forces and the local was devoid of anyone with whom he could achieve more than a passing interest. Then towards the end of the week there had occurred an unlooked for occasion while walking down the High Street which totally ruined his leave. Out of uniform he was suddenly accosted by a harsh female who demanded to know why he was not in the Army. With jabbing bony finger the old dear kept repeating her question, which attracted a number of sympathetic glances and poisonous stares. Pale with anger, the navigator was on the point of issuing a stinging retort or two that rushed involuntarily to his lips, but with iron control that he was not aware he possessed, he flung away the offending claw stretched out to him as if it was leprous, and marched on.

Bloody cheek, he thought. Stupid cow, and the others who'd mutely supported her. Probably conscientious objectors anyway. Sod them all. He could not assuage his anger; he considered it bad enough to have it suggested that he ought to be in the Army, a brown job, but to be accused of dodging the column was tantamount to slander. With seething contempt it occurred to him to wonder how so many people could be so narrow minded and how so many people were thick enough to base criticism on purely surface observations. The rough comfortable texture of an expensive pre-war sports coat turned into sackcloth on his shoulders. He was tempted to rush home, don uniform and parade up and down the street just for the hell of it, with the hope of meeting the hag again. He even toyed with the idea of getting digits ready for a super two-fingered salute. But as rapidly as anger had flooded over him, it subsided leaving mere distaste. Perhaps, he mused, the old girl had lost a son in the War, although she had not mouthed the fact, and was a fair way towards being deranged. Whatever the reason, he decided to be charitable and forget the unpleasantness.

Now, happily back from leave amongst civilised people joined together in common cause for King and Country, amongst people who really knew the meaning of living simply because their life expectancy was precarious, and usually brief, he relaxed. The least pleasant aspects of leave paled into insignificance. He trundled his travelling case down the lane breathing the air ecstatically, losing quickly earlier weariness. He was effectively back home. Dumping case unceremoniously on his bed, he retraced his steps up the lane and turned away from the village this time towards the communal site and, of course, the Sergeants Mess. Without a doubt Ace would be thereabouts, propping up the bar, probably with others, for ops seemed not to be on, judging by the inactivity around the Lancaster dispersals which were in sight of bus passengers coming from Lincoln.

As John gained the path to the Mess he remembered how glad he had been that Ace had not accompanied him on leave, because for all Ace's controlled stance, the pilot would not have accepted the jibe of cowardice lightly and might well have proceeded to take the little market town apart. What was more, it would have been a thoroughly shaky do for Ace to have been so involved after having travelled half way across the earth to fight for the Mother Country.

With some dexterity he flung his forage cap on to a vacant peg like a ring and hook board champion, perceiving as he did so Ace and Texel in earnest session, while to the left in the main ante room the aircrew there had all the appearance of being wholly relaxed. Clearly ops were not on. As usual, Texel, pint in hand was holding forth to Ace who seemed content to listen or at least appear so while one elbow on the bar took the weight off his pins.

"Well look at whose here," quoth Texel. "The passionate paramour himself. Didn't you bring your betrothed." John shook hands with both, but fixed Texel with a straight glare.

"For the information of you besotted, glassy eyed boozers, the lady in question is not betrothed as far as I know, nor have I seen her for 7 whole days, which fact is implied to the contrary by your remarks, Texel." John was patience itself so it had to be assumed that leave had done him some good. Texel though, looked astounded and burst into a guffaw of derision. Rocking unsteadily on his feet, he declared:

"Come off it Johnny boy. I wasn't born yesterday. You two fiddled your leave together without telling anyone, but I have my spies, and now when confronted with the obvious you declare you haven't been shacking up. Well I don't believe it."

"You can think what you like, but I'm pretty sure Marion wouldn't like your insinuations." John remained calm.

"It's not Marion I would blame. It would be you, old son." Texel displayed just a faint tendency to retreat, for he really did not wish to incur the real wrath of the WAAF sergeant in case she gave up darning his socks. "Actually we thought you'd fizzed off to get spliced. Aint zat so Ace?"

"We had casually mentioned the possibility," said Ace carefully.

"Well I'm still a bachelor," confirmed John with a tolerant grin. "So I don't owe you for a pint. I'll have a pint."

"Right, a pint for lover boy." Texel gave the order and continued: "You mean you're not churched yet." The engineer was nothing if not persistent.

"Change the record Tex. You were in earnest conversation when I came in. What's the gen?" He knew the ploy would work, for as long as Texel had a subject, any subject, he was happy to natter.

"Officers, smooth types. It seems the policy has been to commission pilots and navigators straight from training. That's why we're getting sprogs arriving with a single thin ring. Been going on for some time, I gather."

"So those of us NCO's on active squadrons have been forgotten," replied John.

"That's about it, old son, but I expect you and Ace will be up before a commissioning board before long. You notice of course that there's no consideration for flight engineers who carry the burden of ops on their shoulders."

"Poof" scoffed John. "All flight engineers do is watch a few gauges and lineshoot the rest of the time. All piss and wind."

"Crude bastard of a navigator you got Ace," suggested Texel.

"I'm not interested," Ace made one of his rare interjections. "Little to commend it — higher mess bills to start with."

"Better Pension for dependants." Texel had obviously given the subject some thought. "Better prospects for civvy street, if you ever get that far. Big rank and a row of gongs must be an advantage."

"Not so sure." John was unimpressed. "Its likely that those who remained as civilians will get all the promotion they need during wartime and more than a head start over demobbed servicemen, you know, the kind who would say that they keep the country going while we're having a bloody good time."

"You can't believe that." Even Texel was doubtful of the validity of John's contention.

"But I do. I never had much faith in the 'land fit for heroes' dictum. The same things were said during the Great War, but never came to pass. History always repeats itself and of that I am absolutely certain. Mind you I don't expect preferential treatment — just a fair crack of the whip."

"Do you know, Ace, you have got a prospective MP for a navigator." Texel was almost serious.

"Rubbish." John was adamant. "Job for deadbeats. No good for anyone with drive." Even Ace was nodding at that and accordingly replenished the drinks.

"John and I are due for uplift to Flight Sergeant. This is an early celebration," he said.

"I rather cotton to a crown above three stripes," said John. "Gives the impression of bags of service in."

"I'm more interested in extra beer money." Ace had an anticipatory gleam in his eyes.

"Well if the truth is known," put in Texel helpfully, "they probably know in the orderly room if you really are due. I should nip in and find out."

"Good idea. You can be useful sometimes Tex." Ace was really being complimentary.

They mouthed drinks silently until John asked casually:

"Seen Marion yet?"

Texel grinned widely with gravestone teeth prominent in line abreast.

"I wondered how long it would take you to get around to asking," he said. "Still we're willing to be obliging, aren't we, Ace. She left a message to say she would be in the Mess at 19.30 hours. Mind you I told her my conscience would not allow me to be a party to passing love messages for clandestine meetings. Can't think why she took such a dim view. Nearly pinned my ears back." Texel drew himself up expanding his chest a full quarter inch oozing magnanimity. "However I bear no ill will. I feel your impatience and my kind heart prompts me to deliver the message as requested."

"Thanks Tex," said John simply. "For your great sacrifice and in view of the happy gist of the message, I'll stand you half a pint."

"Half a pint?" His grin snapped into a thin straight line. "Mean bastards, you navigators."

"I'm looking after your health, Tex," replied John with a poker face.

"What's wrong with my health? I'm A1 all the way."

"Shocking complaint you've got," pursued the navigator. "I'd be really worried if it was me."

"What's he getting at Ace?" Texel was beginning to wonder.

"Simple diagnosis. You have Verbal Diarrhorea, but drink up. Get your mouth in the mug and you're cured, at least temporarily." Tex choked down what had quietly materialised as a pint instead of a half and was speechless, while John added, "You're slipping Tex. Never known you choke over a beer before."

"Not as much as you are, old son." Tex thrust aside discomposure and continued: "I may well be ailing, but at least I'm master of my own soul, undominated and uncontaminated by the fairer sex."

"I was not aware I was dominated. After all I'm quite prepared to slum it in your company, when the mood takes me." John had really begun to enjoy himself, but Texel, like an old woman wanted the last word:

"Any rate, you're a changed man. You rarely come to the 'Old Cow' these days and the ivories are turning yellow for lack of use."

John scratched his head signifying a degree of contemplation. It was true he was tending to be unsociable in the accepted sense, but he was not aware that his absence would matter too much to Texel and Ace. "But I'll tell you what. Next standdown I'll tickle the ivories in the pub, if you like, OK?"

"Suits us," replied Texel, speaking unasked for Ace as well, although the latter confirmed with a nod. On a further more positive note fresh pints emerged from the cubby hole and at that moment Marion came through the outer door, threw her hat on a peg and moved to the bar. Moved was perhaps an inadequate description. She just flowed in gracefully.

"Hullo boys," she said quietly.

"Lo Marion." John pre-empted salutations from the other two. "Texel said you would not be in until 19.30. Did you enjoy leave?" The flight engineer nudged Ace meaningly, but Marion, like any woman, did not fail to notice and was unabashed, uncaring too.

"Fine, John, just fine. Put my feet up and it was nice to see the folk again. Wonderful to get away from the noise of aeroplanes and the perpetual panic of ops."

"I suppose," said Texel, ever anxious to get his oar in, "this little bit of play acting is for our benefit, designed to throw us off the scent. You two don't look as if you have been parted for a whole week, since you don't look especially joyful at being reunited. On the other hand you both look love sick and moony eyed."

"I realise the import of your insinuations." Marion said evenly, but with an expression of arctic fraternity, "but you are quite wrong as usual. I spent a perfectly respectable 7 days and since you've harped on the subject before, I have to tell you that there are innumerable haystacks on our farm and I have not been coaxed into any one of them."

"Wrong again," groaned Texel in mock despair. "I believe you, love, but thousands wouldn't."

Ace, who had been standing there motionless with a slightly sardonic grin brought the colloquy to a belly flop:

"Like a sherry Marion?" he offered.

"Not just now, Ace, but thank you."

Ace may have belly flopped Texel for a moment but it was transitory.

"Can't you see she's only thirsting for her lover," he said.

"Belt up Tex." Even Ace had had enough. "Let's go feed our faces."

Left to themselves Marion and John passed through the doors into the main ante room, pausing then for brief salutations with several crew members restfully pouring over magazines and then moved towards another pair of doors leading to the smaller writing room. Leslie Harman, a Canadian pilot who had got some service in and a member of 'A' flight said drily, "I'll put up a notice 'don't disturb Johnny'. What say bo."

"If you please. Most kind of you," replied John drily.

The writing room was sparsely but adequately furnished with 3 small tables with accompanying high backed chairs, while along two walls easy chairs were ranged. Above, several unshaded lamp bulbs hung uncertainly from the ceiling. In one corner was a piano, rarely used except when there was a party on, in which case it was wheeled into the adjoining room, or if for a dance it was propelled into the dining hall. With restricted use and the occasional act of removal the tuning left a great deal to be desired. Today the piano was silent and all home correspondence completed, deferred or not envisaged, for there was no one present. Marion and John sank into easy chairs and relaxed.

"I'm glad to be back," said John after a while, "despite the going over we get from that Texel," he added ruefully. "Civvy Street seemed to be another world, strange and even uninviting. I did not know what to do, all my old friends like us away in the Services. I tacked about like a boat without a skipper. To put it bluntly I missed you very badly." He went on quickly to tell her about his experience with the old woman.

He sensed rather than saw her soft brown eyes upon him and he dare not allow himself to be drawn by their powerful magnetism. Hesitantly, he continued, conscious of a desire to open his heart, yet not knowing how to put his innermost thoughts eloquently.

"The break did give me the opportunity to think — about us," he said at last. Now he could not resist her eyes and as he looked at her courage came to the fore safe in the knowledge that she was aware of his pent-up emotion, although she gave no positive sign immediately. After a moment or two she said:

"Yes John." It was an invitation to share confidences.

"It's like this," John went on, "until I went on leave, away from service routine and away from you, I just didn't realise how much you have become a part of my life, sharing in a measure my fears and joys. I was aware of being terribly lonely and, looking back, it struck me quite forcibly how selfishly I've leaned on you, expecting you to give me your spare time without the smallest consideration of your own possible interests. It shames me when I think that there must have been times you'd have preferred to be alone, especially after a long spell of duty."

"If there were John," she interjected, "I think I could have found excuses, but I haven't had that need. I've always been happy to share your company." Marion's hand crept over the side of the chair to grasp his hand and when she spoke again her voice was low but vibrant. She had about her a most becoming look of serenity. "I must confess I have experienced heart searching, something quite outside my control. I'm in love with you John and my heart is ruling my head absolutely."

"That's just it. I love you too and in so doing I'm being extremely foolish. We just cannot blind ourselves to what goes on on this operational station. Ops and love don't mix. Unless I'm very lucky indeed, there's no future for us. Who knows, I am baring my heart to you tonight and tomorrow I may be hurled unprepared into judgement."

"Don't John." She was almost weeping. "One must always look to the future however uncertain it seems."

"I'm sorry Marion love, it's just a stark reality. We all joke about it. Ace says there's no future and harks on what duties we'll be called upon to perform in other places — pole star polishing or harping, and you must know our percentage survival rate is minimal." He could not go on for a moment aware that he was not marshalling his thoughts too well, and then proceeded hopefully. "It wouldn't have mattered so much if we'd remained just good friends, but now there's a new dimension. If I don't come back one night it would be terrible for you because you could never be sure whether I'd bought it or ended up languishing in a prisoner-of-war camp."

Apart from a trembling of her lower lip, Marion seemed to have control of her feelings now and her response, was framed evenly.

"I know we have to talk about these things John, and I suppose it is as good a time as any. You are not the kind to have a girl in every port, so to speak. I know you are entirely sincere and I like that. I've watched you, read your moods of contemplation or, if you like, exercised woman's intuition, but you really are trying too hard to be cruel to be kind."

"It's the decent thing, I hope." Whether Marion thought so or not she gave no sign and proceeded:

"I have considered our situation too. I have never told you much of myself and you have been careful not to pry. I must tell you now I was more or less engaged to a Naval Officer whom I haven't seen since the outbreak of war — somehow or other our paths have not crossed mainly because he operates on a far station. But, we've always had what is commonly known as an understanding. We grew up together. Our families would approve our marriage. It's only recently that I've come to the conclusion that there was little enough basis for maintaining the tie. Had we met more often, there may have been, but I doubt it. Consequently I have written to him along those lines. The letter will probably take ages to reach him, but I suspect he will not be too upset, even though I have said outright that I love another."

John clasped both her hands, took a swift look around to make sure that no one was looking through the glass doors, and kissed her lingeringly. When he came up for air and was able to breathe again, he said:

"You honour me greatly. I'm very happy, but — I'm still concerned."

"I don't know why you worry so much, John. We're only two of thousands caught up in the effects of this horrible war."

But John was still worried, whatever she said or made light of.

"So long as you fully understand the odds, I'll not worry so much, but I repeat, the odds are stacked against us. You may or may not have seen some of the widows of married men who have been interviewed by the Adjutant and given their men's belongings. They come out swollen eyed with weeping, their lives crushed and broken so very suddenly. Then there are those who do not live out around the station receiving the dreaded telegram 'The Air Ministry regrets...' They may never know what happened to their husbands, whether scattered like dust in the atmosphere or went into the agonising pain of being fried alive in an aerial coffin."

If the navigator thought he clinched his argument in warning her in an as gentlemanly way as possible that he was a sort of pariah she would do well to ditch forthwith, he was mistaken for she said quite sharply now:

"Don't be melodramatic, dear. You paint a vivid picture, largely true of course, but provided you give me your sole love and affection I shall be happy. If I love you, as I do, then in my book there are few obstacles. To me, a woman, the important thing is to be loved and to love. So I live only for the present. In essence I follow generally the attitude of men at war and if fate decrees only a few weeks of real happiness then I accept them wholeheartedly. Besides," she added on a lighter note, "Texel says the evil finger will never be on you."

"P'shaw. Texel. But darling..."

"Please let me finish. For your own confidence, it is remarkable how often Texel has been right. It's silly I know, but he does have either an eye to the future or his ravings are unbelieveably coincidental to events. As I said, I do not myself dwell on the future, except as regards one particular problem." She paused and John sensed that what she was about to add was going to be hard going and he could not interrupt. "You know I'm a few years older than you, or if you don't I'm prepared to own up now. It probably matters little to you now, but if it comes to marriage I'd have to consider the risk of your tiring of me in the future. In the maelstrom of war, emotions are sharpened, but would it be different after the war with a change to humdrum living. After living so precariously, would you not have too much time to watch me ageing more quickly than you. I might find it difficult to hold your interest."

John practically scoffed.

"I've no fear on that score. You'll always be beautiful to me not only in appearance, but in your inner self." He was elated that she had considered their relationship in depth and grateful for her courage too. He continued: "I'm something of a creature of habit anyway, a one-woman man and I don't change easily, but in the face of your plain-speaking I feel positively inferior."

"Don't be silly John. It does not really take courage to state facts, or it shouldn't if they are important."

"That's true enough. I know that you have helped me to weather this tour of ops so far and you have the knack of saying the right things at the right time. You soothe when I'm irritable and when weariness is a drug you are here to sharpen me up. I know too that you nearly always wait up for our return from ops. Ace slipped up and let the cat out of the bag with his aerial signal. Also I sometimes see the tiredness in your eyes. God, how I wish we could now return to peace and sanity."

The WAAF Sergeant said nothing. It was the aftermath of too much bottled up feeling, now released. Outwardly she had now the cold serenity of a marble Venus, but she wanted to reach out and smooth the young prematurely ageing face with a gentle caress. She longed to entwine her fingers in his wiry red hair, but she dare not in the Mess. Once she let go, there could be no retreat-she might break down completely and that would not do either's morale much good.

"Johnny." She called him out of abstraction softly, but it was a moment or two before his eyes re-focussed. "It's a question of carry on regardless as we are at present. Then if we come to a mutual acceptance that our lives are irrevocably inseparable, let us receive this blessing and act upon it. Personally I am optimistic about the future, whatever Ace or anyone else says."

"Woman's intuition again?" John's smile was creeping back.

"Take me home John please. I don't want supper. I'm just very tired but very happy." She held out both hands for him to draw her to her feet. Rigidly he forced himself to resist clasping her hard to him, altogether very conscious of the glass doors through which anyone might peer, at any time. The threatened and promised notice hung on the door handle, saying "Do not disturb — private audience." Fortunately there was no grinning audience nor was there any sign of the terrible twins, Ace and Tex.

Chapter 7

RECOGNITION AND PROMOTION

Denny did an unusual thing. He rose to his feet from behind office desk, brushing aside as he did so a column of cigarette smoke that hung centrally in the air. It seemed to be the prelude to an anouncement, for he then cleared his throat to claim undivided attention. The little group of 'B' Flight pilots ceased to natter, the faces exhibiting some mild surprise for Denny had no pretensions as a platform orator in the first place, and in the second he rarely moved his posterior from the chair except to leave the office on business.

"Before we figure out the day's programme, I have an announcement to make. F.Sgt Burnett RNZAF has been awarded the DFM and it is my pleasure and privilege to offer congratulations. His navigator has been Mentioned in Despatches and you can tell him Ace that his F.Sgt rank has come through as well as yours."

Ace Burnett who was nonchalantly rolling a gasper was stunned to the extent that his tongue, half way along the adhesive edge of the cigarette paper came to a sudden halt. Unbelieving he allowed Denny to practically paralyse his hand in an iron grip. If he had been told that the war was over, he could not have been more shaken. He was unable to reply and so Denny went on: "You don't say much. In fact you are a prime example of antipodean modesty, but your valiant efforts have not gone unrecognised. On the N. African trip in particular, in an almost impossible situation you put your kite down on one duff engine, which by all the rules was unfliable." 'B' flight pilots crowded round to voice their acclamation for DFM's were not awarded frequently while the flight Commander added as an afterthought: "The new Wing Commander wants to see you together with your navigator at 1100 hours."

Ace found some excuse to lumber out of the office into the sunshine. He was in the situation of not knowing whether he was on his ass or elbow. It was simply a case of automatic limb reaction strangely divorced from torpid mental processes. Quite suddenly the two human agencies combined to make him realise that instead of heading towards the navigation section he had gone the wrong way and was confronted by the forbidding appearance of the camouflaged bomb dump. At once he retraced his steps, drew in new breath — it would not do to be late in the Wing Co's office.

"Ye Gods," he murmured aloud in pure soliloquy. "It's all very well being handed out a gong, but what had he done to merit it? He had merely co-operated with man's instinctive sense of self-preservation. What about the unfortunate bods who'd been a shade less lucky, perhaps just a matter of getting a shell or two nearer their aircraft's vulnerable spots? Who could tell what heroic deeds had preceded their eclipse, masked by darkness — deeds that would never be recognised and recorded in the annals of the RAF, with only epitaphs as rewards." At the navigation centre he found John midst a group of other gen men, all studying charts of recent operations. Ace walked up to Bert Apsley, the navigation leader who was industrially engaged in marking up newly reported flak positions.

"Hello Sir, Busy?" Ace contrived to be mildly interested to allow Bert time to complete his effort.

"Always busy, us navigators." Bert was as hearty as his underlings when it came to promoting his gen section. "To what do we owe this privileged visit? Have a weed."

"Not just now, thanks. Can you spare John? Wing Co. wants to see us at 1100 hours and we're short on time."

"Well I suppose Wing Co takes precedence," Bert replied with a quiet smile. No trouble I trust."

"No Sir. No trouble." Ace did not enlarge. That was his way. Wait for the event before opening your trap.

"Crikey," ejaculated John, who, perceiving Ace's shambling form had moved into earshot. "I haven't shaved this morning. Does it look too bad?" Bert winked at Ace. "Awful," he said. "You've had it in a big way, particularly since the new Wing Co's a stickler for hygiene."

"Oh I don't suppose he'll notice that bit of fluff." Ace seemed confident enough as he ran a horny hand over the navigator's face. "Can't feel a thing."

"A mere fledgling," Bert put in condescendingly. "But you had better get mobile, and good luck." The navigation Leader might have known what it was all about but he was not saying a dicky bird either.

The Wing Co's office was an inner sanctum via the Adjutant's office and they paused at the door marked, "Adjutant, Knock before entry." In response to their request for attention came one single word — "Come." Within the office they came to attention with a reasonably well organised salute. Although their timing was scarcely precise, there was in their attitude the mark of respect, for the Officer commonly known as Adj who sat before them with an ease accomplished over many years in the RAF, was held in high esteem by the whole Squadron.

Flt Lt Preston was one of the Great War's RFC flyers, who had retired later in peacetime and again called to the colours during the present emergency. He was in his mid forties and seemed somewhat ancient to the young men of the Squadron. His head was topped by an iron grey mat of hair that had little thinned with the passage of years. He had that charming and tentatively understanding expression that was the personification of a true Officer and Gentleman. Pen in hand with a pile of "leave" passes before him awaiting signature he looked up with a welcoming smile.

"We're to see the Wing Commander at 1100 hours, Sir," ventured Ace.

"Ah yes. Take a pew. Wing Co's on the blower. Shouldn't be too long. May I offer my sincere congratulations on your award, Burnett."

"Thank you Sir," replied Ace while looking straight over the adjutant's shoulder. He was more than slightly discomfited for the words came from a man who was positively an air pioneer. Likewise he was aware of John's head now turned towards him in startled enquiry. A bell tinkled softly in the next room.

"I'll wheel you in," said Adj rising to his feet with the agility and ease of a man thirty years younger. He opened the inner door.

"F.Sgts Burnett and Howard, Sir," he announced and withdrew, softly closing the door behind him. The pair managed a pretty snappy salute. Wing Co looked up from his desk to say, "At ease chaps."

They relaxed gladly, but not wholly, for though the CO was said to be a pretty good sort, he was altogether impressive, both in bearing and somewhat stern remoteness. The Wing Co leaned back in his chair surveying first Ace then John with what can only be described as a steely look that was disconcerting, but when he spoke the voice was deep toned and well modulated like that of a senior academic.

"Burnett I am commanded to announce that HM King George has graciously approved the award of an immediate DFM. My congratulations. Jolly good show." John's eyes opened wide as the purport of the Adj's remark in the outer office clarified, but his attention reverted quickly as the CO's eyes swivelled onto him. "Howard, you have been Mentioned in Despatches for your excellent support of your skipper throughout your tour so far."

103

John gulped while the CO's eyes moved back to Ace. "I have further to tell you that you have both been recommended for a Commission in the General Duties branch. I take it you have no objections to becoming Officers, for as senior crew here on the Squadron in terms of number of operations completed, this matter is long overdue." He obviously took it that there were no objections for he went on smoothly, "At all times whether in or out of uniform, you will uphold the traditions and spirit of the service as officers and gentlemen, being at all times an example to other ranks, thereby gaining their total respect." He leaned forward to pick up his pen, a clear indication that the interview was concluded and need not be prolonged. He added in confirmation, "Good luck chaps. That's all." His tone was finally of brusque dismissal, so Ace and John came again smartly to attention in uncommon unison and about-turned to leave.

"Phew", said John as they gained the outside of the building. He ran a finger round dank collar to ease the constriction, not entirely due to the warmth of the day. "Why couldn't you warn me Ace. You must have known or at least suspected what it was all about. I realise now that the Adj let the cat out of the bag but I didn't grasp it at the time." But the navigator was not really sore. Clapping Ace on his broad back he said simply, "Wizard show. Time you were recognised." The pilot waved a faint hand indicating that the matter had been more than well aired, but he knew that it was not yet concluded by any means. He would be expected to stand drinks pretty well all round in the Sergeants Mess which would be a depressingly expensive occasion. Then sometime in the very near future it would cost a fortune again when his commission came through, and that would not be too far in the future the way the Wing Co. had spoken. In theory he ought to be interviewed by the Group Captain and then finally by OC Base, but it rather looked as if these latter interviews, if they did materialise, would be a matter of rubber stamping.

As they walked back briskly to the flight offices Ace reflected that the one thing standing out in his thoughts with a kind of choking pride was the regard in which his crew beheld him. True they berated him for dicey landings if he put his Lancaster down with anything more than the slightest bump, but that was all in fun. The lack of any real criticism implied there was no need for laudatory expression. He was glad to be good in their eyes. They walked in silence from the admin site to the flight offices, each with his own thoughts, where John left the pilot to gain the navigation centre. Bert Apsley would want to know the score. So would the other gen men.

All was normal again in the flight office when Ace shambled in. The subdued murmur was as consistent as the atmospheric fug. Then the phone rang softly and the flight Commander fastened onto it with a satisfied smile. True to his word he had had the instrument changed. The ring was no longer likely to make one jump a foot — it was almost a buzz. But if the ring of the phone was softened it did not follow that the message received was of easy acceptance. For a moment Sqn Ldr Denning listened. Then with increasing attentiveness poised pen dipped to scribble on his pad.

"Yes Sir, I can manage 9 serviceable aircraft with one in reserve." The murmur of voices ceased and one could have heard a pin drop. It was patently obvious that ops were on.

"OPS are on," he said needlessly as he replaced the telephone receiver. "Nine aircraft from this flight and ten from 'A', bless all our hearts." He swivelled in his chair to survey the wall board on which was recorded the state of the flight, with pilot's names, usual aircraft numbers and number of ops completed by each pilot and crew.

"Ace, I'd like you on the battle order for I want you to take a new pilot, Pilot Officer Bill Chatterforth as second dickey." He waved to the young officer resplendent in smartly cut new uniform that was a rare sight in the flight office, for apart from the flight Commander himself and Flt Lt Hills, the deputy, the rest were Sergeants in their grimy well-worn battledresses. Denny continued, "Give him all the griff you can. He can't know too much. For that matter neither can any of us. Terry, you can stand down as you have had a basinful lately. So it'll have to be Ace, Harry, Happy, Les, Don, Chas, David, George and Peter. You can all get weaving on night flying tests. Briefing is at 1730 hours."

There was no conversation now. The pilots merely nodded acceptance of their lot, while Plt Off Chatterforth half rose, uncertain whether he would be required to accompany F.Sgt Burnett on NFT. When Ace nodded to him he clambered fully to his feet with a keen agility that left the rest open-mouthed, for such virility in the morning was a bit much to expect. Pilots accustomed to nocturnal perambulations were scarcely wide awake until lunchtime.

"By the way Ace," Denny said with a grin. "You take your pick of Robert or my Sugar. Which ever you don't take will be in reserve in case we have last minute unserviceability."

"I'll take Robert." Ace was positive. "Your flight engineer reckons Sugar is only held together by bits of string and chewing gum he's pressed into the cracks."

105

"Texel talks out of the back of his neck," replied Denny. "But please yourself. Sugar has served me well and has seen some service."

"Again, Texel says it's all on the practice bombing range," said Ace with a disarming grin.

"I'll kick his ass when I see him. Now bugger off. I've got work to do too."

The pilots pushed off. The wheels were beginning to turn slowly, but the momentum of the day and night's programme would increase as the tendrils of Bomber Command HQ flicked out to each group, feeding them with full details of the plan of operation. Ace and his prodigy swung round the block towards the navigation centre to begin the process of collecting his crew. As they came to the control tower Ace saw Marion looking down from the wide open window of the watch office. In answer to her mute enquiry he made a thumbs down signal.

She grimaced unhappily before turning back to her work. She knew ops were on because, as watchkeeper, she was the medium through whom all the relevant detailed information was fed on the scrambler line from Group HQ. On this morning and every morning when ops were scheduled it was her hope that Ace and his crew would not be on the battle order, for it meant a sleepless night waiting for the pilot to call "permission to pancake" on return, always fearing the worst and experiencing untold relief when Ace's harsh voice grated on RT.

"Girl friend?" asked Bill Chatterforth tentatively. He was not just being nosey, but rather searching for something to say in the company of the taciturn senior pilot.

"Not mine," replied Ace. "My navigator's. Open and shut case. No intruders. Nice girl. Grim for her having a flyer for a boyfriend. Shouldn't be allowed really but you can't fool around with human nature." It was quite a speech for Ace who felt perhaps that as well as being openly informative, it would put the sprog at ease.

Ace collected the crew and soon they were on the truck out to dispersal, where Robert and other Lancasters stood starkly motionless awaiting the pleasure of the crews. Taffy, the w/op and Jock, the rear gunner were having a go at each other all the way out in the truck. So serious did their contretemps seem to Chatterforth that he looked really worried until Ace told him that the bloody celts arguments were as regular as Daily Routine Orders.

Once in the air, in a different world both detached and remote with the tall sky above, Ace thrilled to the moment as Robert responded easily to the controls. He throttled back to the point of stalling in straight and level flight, but all that occurred was a gentle drop instead of a rapid nose down action demonstrating how, aerodynamically, the Lancaster was almost perfect. He threw Robert into a series of alarming motions that were more suited to the manoeuverable Spitfire with which they sometimes practised defensive tactics. Then he went into a fast climbing left hand turn before straightening out, to go then into a stall turn. Next he put the aircraft into the peculiarly discomfiting corkscrew movement that was often successful in nullifying fighter attack, on this practice occasion causing some barely audible rumblings from the rear turret where Jock clearly considered that such contortions should be reserved for avoiding the enemy. At last, after his crew had checked out their equipment, the pilot headed back to Holmdun where he lobbed down to a flawless landing that the crew could not possibly complain about. It was, of course, more than his reputation was worth to drop in from ten feet with the new, keen young pilot on board.

With Robert stilled on the dispersal hard standing, the crew awaited the arrival of transport which would take them the mile and a half back to the crew room with martyred impatience. According to tradition, transport seemed never to be available when needed, but martyrdom was distracted by the arrival of the petrol bowser which backed very carefully into position for pumping in the designated fuel load for the forthcoming operation. While this was going on Ace strode off to meet F.Sgt Arrows, i/c maintenance, familiarly known as Rooty, who had emerged at a rapid pace from the dispersal hut, eager to enquire as to the state of the aircraft following the night flying test. Rooty was extremely thin, looking at all times as if he could do with a square meal, but what he lacked in stature was amply compensated for by prolonged bursts of energy. More than once he had been referred to by the little band of fitters and riggers under his control, as a coiled spring. Given the chance to propound, Rooty had only one real topic of conversation and that was Rolls Royce engines. His attitude suggested that the engines had been manufactured solely and exclusively for him to maintain. In all other respects he was a quiet chap of even temper with a ready smile that always reached the eyes. One thing was sure. He kept his men up to scratch without difficulty. Ace both liked Rooty and got on well with him.

"Any snags?" Rooty asked. His tone implied that nothing could be wrong.

"Nope, smooth as a baby's bottom, as usual," replied Ace. Rooty looked a mite embarrassed for Ace was rarely loquacious and these few words were praise indeed. It was one thing to have confidence in one's ability, another to have it confirmed.

"Oh these Lanc 1's with the pukka Merlins are peaches. Generally only have to take the cowlings off for major inspections. They tell me, over in 'A' flight they've got a couple of Mark 111's with Merlins manufactured by Packard and are having some teething troubles. Technically they're an improvement with the Stromberg carburettor and it probably won't take long to get the position in hand, but gimme the real Merlins everytime."

"In that case I'll have to look after Robert," replied Ace quietly. "She's going pretty well considering she got chewed up over Genoa, but as long as the fans keep turning, I'm easy."

"Good show, Ace. I don't forsee trouble. Must go now." With a quiet nod Rooty moved away, anxious to ascertain that all was well with the rest of 'B' flight kites, leaving Ace to reflect happily that one could not have a more capable and dedicated chap in charge. If one could start confidently on the ground, confidence accompanied one into the air. Responsibility for aircraft serviceability was an onerous burden, for seven men in each Lancaster were at risk. Particularly in the winter months the ground crews worked, often in the bitter easterly wind that came unobstructed across the predominately flat Lincolnshire countryside, clambering over ice cold metal with numbed fingers or balanced precariously on tubular trestles, wrestling with intricate engine parts. Even when their immediate tasks were completed, unless off duty, their only comfort was a draughty dispersal hut with the occasional wad and cup of char heated up on an inefficient stove of primitive design which gave out only grudging warmth. When the NAAFI van called it was practically a royal occasion. Without the glamour of flying, the ground crews were indisputably the unsung heroes of the RAF. Indeed if the motto of the RAF was just and proper for the service as a whole, it was amply displayed at ground level.

Ace was tempted to ask the bowser operator details of the petrol load if only to get some idea whether the proposed target was of long or short duration, but he desisted on the ground that it would put the man in a difficult quandary, and discarded conjecture. His crew, tired of waiting for transport were now reclining in a huddle on the grass just off the concrete apron, smoking dogends hastily snuffed out before take-off, while the navigator exceptionally puffed happily on a pipe.

"Any gen?" asked Sid, who had read Ace's first intention.

"Could be anywhere," replied Ace.

"Likely to be the Big City," suggested Jock.

"I doubt it," put in John. "Not enough hours of darkness this time of the year."

"Well, the newspapers have been blathering about razing Berlin to the ground." Jock was persistent. "Although they'd run a mile if we invited the press to join us. You'll see, it's the Big City or I'll rub Taffy's nose in the dirt in the morning."

"You'll what. I'd like to see you, you Scotch peasant."

"Jock could have something there," put in Ken, after some moments of thoughtful silence. "It's just the sort of move the C-in-C would make. Butch could be taking the view that Adolph won't expect us with all the advanced publicity."

"Aw nark it, Ken." Sid occasionally lapsed into the cockney of his forbears and was proving he had not nodded off in his usual relaxed horizontality. "The painter's no fool. I'll lay a fortnight's pay that the night we crawl into the air bound for Berlin, enemy fighters will be queued up waiting for us."

"Cheerful, aren't we." Frank the midupper gunner, who was still in trouble with his adolescent complexion, coloured up as he spoke and laughed quaveringly. His interjection, although barren of any constructive thought fell startlingly on a company highly suspicious of Air Marshall Harris' intentions.

The arrival of tardy transport cut short further speculation and promoted a ragged cheer which failed totally to impress the WAAF driver, who was of the general opinion that aircrew were a bunch of spoilt moaners. She wouldn't date any one of them, that was for sure. Back on site, some 134 names had been promulgated on the Battle Order and filtered out to significant locations; the flight offices, flying control and not least the mess kitchens. One might ask why the kitchens, but it should be recorded that each name qualified for fried eggs straight out of cackle berries and bacon, for pre-flying supper. No others were entitled to this luxury, nor would be served.

Late in the afternoon, at about 1700 hours the navigators foregathered for preliminary briefing, while pilots and other crew members reported to their respective sections. This arrangement was designed to brief crew members on the particular detail relevant to their tasks ahead and to allow navigators maximum working space without the hubbub caused by mass gathering that was not conducive to concentration on charts and attendant calculations. John was pretty well the last navigator to arrive for he had briefly lingered at the watch office for a few words, the conversation being conducted between the navigator on terra firma and Marion from the upstairs window. He was quite calm. Whatever else Marion had achieved during their recent heart to heart talk, she had succeeded in quelling his fears for her. In any case, this was just another op, just another number on the ladder to achieving the magical number 30. He would, like all the crew members, experience some pre-flight nerves, but once in the air with wheels tucked up, continuous solid work would produce clear thinking and conquer tension.

He was struck at once by a silence that sustained itself, a silence not wholly on account of relatively small numbers present, but partly because Bert Apsley was in the process of route marking on the big chart. Unusually the route was across northern Holland and looked like ending up in the Baltic. Of a certainty it was not a Ruhr valley target.

A voice broke the silence at last:

"You're not kidding us Sir?"

"No joke chaps, Hamburg it is. It's a long time since you've gone thataway. Most of the trip is over sea, so you haven't got much to bind about," said Bert. And of course he was right. They would get a fair distance before attracting enemy fighters. It was not an overlong trip, about the same distance as a Ruhr target with the added advantage that if radar navigation equipment packed up, there was a fair chance of fixing position at the enemy coastline. It was a bit of an anti-climax, for most had been expecting the Big City.

The tracking planned was devious, designed as usual to deceive the enemy as to the ultimate objective. The first phase would provide no clues although German radar would indicate where the bomber stream was at any particular time, for the route crossed the Dutch coast at Texel Island, a point common enough to a projected attack on Emden, Bremen, Osnabruck, Hannover, Luneburg or Berlin. At that point the Germans would be alive to the possibility of an attack on Berlin, but at that time would not know where to concentrate night fighters. Even when the bomber force was well into Germany there was no way that the ultimate target could be assumed, for even if the force was heading direct towards a particular target, this could be a feint merely. It was all a matter of tactics.

Bert Apsley wrote the forecast wind velocities on the board, having got a preview from Met who would later provide total weather conditions expected over the route. This was enough for the navigators to go on with. For the timing on each leg of the route, the forecast winds would be assumed to be flawlessly correct, but any deviation would stretch the navigators to further rapid calculations in the air, calculations that would mean alteration of course to maintain the planned track and variation in aircraft speed to maintain the standard timing at each turning point. Actual flight conditions nearly always called for revision of the wind velocities, courses and timing, produced by obtaining a fixed ground position over which the aircraft passed and applying the triangle of velocities principle.

John had by now laid in the tracks and measured up against points of the compass. With dividers he measured the distances per leg. Applying the forecast wind velocities and directions with the aid of a Dalton computer he calculated the courses the aircraft would have to follow to maintain essential tracking, and the airspeed to fly at in order to achieve a groundspeed that would be right for the timing per leg. All detail he entered into his log. These actions were the initial solid basis from which all else would follow.

A voice from nearby cut in on John's cogitations:

"What wind are you using for the climb, John?" For a moment he made no reply as the answer was not as pat as would be supposed by a layman. The forecast winds were provided for heights of 2000, 5000, 10000, 15000 and 20000 feet, and were often from differing directions at the different heights, the wind speeds usually increasing with increased height. Since it would take time to reach operational height with a hefty bomb load, an average wind would have to suffice and it was the skill of deciding that determined whether or not one got a good start.

George Stokes, the questioner had only three trips on the board and was therefore regarded as definitely inexperienced, a sprog in service terminology.

"Oh I should say 295/45 knots would fit the bill, wouldn't you." John said at last, ending on an interrogative note calculated modestly to give the new boy the comfortable feeling that his own advice was being sought.

"Yes, I think so." He was not at all sure, but it would give him something to think about, something to learn too. "Would you also check your tracks and distances with me?" George further requested, explaining that he would like to get a good start in case the G. Box failed to operate.

John laughed softly, encouragingly and replied in helpful fashion:

"Sure thing. Have a look at my log, but just watch your pilot maintains the right course at all times. As good as my driver is, I have one eye on the repeater compass pretty well all the time." George checked the calculations and lifted his head happily. A lot of the tension had disappeared already.

"We seem to agree," he said.

"Can't both be wrong," replied John. "We seem to have finished before the shower arrive and that's what I always aim for."

At that moment the briefing room door crashed open and shivered on ill-fitting hinges. The shower, that is to say, pilot's and crew members other than navigators had arrived. There was instant pandemonium. Chairs scraped noisily on bare boards. A navigator's trestle table collapsed with a resounding crash as the legs folded up, followed by less than charitable remarks on the parentage of the perpetrators from the navigator victim, whose neatly arranged maps, charts and operation equipment were deposited on the dusty floor to be necessarily reclaimed quickly before being ruined by heavy feet.

"The roughs are here," said John, doing a Texel in a voice loud enough to surmount the general clamour. George Stokes grinned acknowledgement while a roar of disapproval swept the room.

"Pipe down, pipsqueak."

"Get knotted, navigator."

"Wrap up, Lothario." John's fame was now assured. He had a bird on station and a sergeant at that, but it failed to put him out of countenance.

"What generous comments," he replied blandly and Sid cuffed him playfully across the back of the head.

"Who are you calling a rough? You navigators are getting too cocky by half."

"Sit down, pinpointer," replied John with a grin. Sid was alright. He could take a joke.

John thumbed his nose at Taffy in order to forestall any remarks from the Welsh quarter, grinned at Jock who maintained a celtic silence and seemed to be far away in thought, glanced at Frank who always exhibited a pasty look at briefing and finally waved to Ken, Ace and Bill Chatterforth who had only lately arrived together.

Gradually the crews settled down in slipshod order around their own Navigator's table and then all came to attention as the Wing Commander hurried in accompanied by Groupie and the specialist section leaders.

"Sit down, chaps," he said and beckonned Bert Apsley to uncover the route.

All eyes were on the route. Most of the crew members were too far from the map on the wall to the rear of the platform, but all were able to see that the target was not far enough east to be Berlin. There was a noticeable lessening of the tension. The Press had a lot to answer for. From their chairborne situations in Fleet Street they had been hustling up a threatening posture on paper. "Berlin will be bombed" they had kept repeating. It was alright in their book or rather their paper. It was quite another matter to create an atmosphere in which C-in-C Bomber Command might have been challenged to go along with a venture which during the summer months embraced difficulties of which the Press had little or no knowledge. Fortunately, Butch Harris was of sterner stuff, the true commander, with a mind of his own and a mind for his boys, or old lags in the terminology. Nevertheless Press action had rubbed off on the crews unfairly.

"It's Hamburg," Wing Co. said, and a faint smile hovered around rather thin lips. A man of ops himself as the row of gong ribbons on his chest demonstrated, he readily understood the crew's thoughts and fears, particularly since except for himself, a career officer, the aircrews were almost to a man, civilians in uniform and all volunteers. He went on: "As your new Wing Commander, I want to tell you that it has always been my policy to draw attention to the senior crew in terms of number of operations completed, and so I say F.Sgt Burnett and crew will lead the Squadron tonight." This caused a bit of a flutter although most present seemed to sense the reason behind the Wing Co's stance, which boiled down to "if a non-commissioned officer can get as far as he has, so can you all." "Now, we have not been to Hamburg for some while and it might be quite a surprise to the Germans. So give 'em hell. Every single attack shortens the war and that's what we all want. Pathfinders will drop red target indicators. The master bomber will assess and order back-up with greens. As usual, unless otherwise instructed, bomb the densest concentration of markers. Pilots must remember to switch to VHF 15 minutes before zero hour and ensure that you are not selected to transmit. Bad form to blot out Master Bomber. Would merit MHDOIF award at the very least."

Wing Co. had a sense of humour it seemed for the suggested award was the "most highly derogatory order of the irremoveable finger." With this serious witticism, he sat down to easy laughter. A bespectacled, studious looking intelligence officer started a bit nervously to explain how important the city of Hamburg was in terms of industrial production. With increasing confidence he even managed the trace of a smile when howls of laughter greeted the statement that it was thought that numerous additional flak positions had been installed around the city. He proceeded then like a Dutch uncle to say that an accurate disposition of enemy fighters en route was not known, except that Texel Island itself had been reinforced. The IO sat down suddenly, seemingly pleased with his performance.

The Met man was quietly confident, which made it, in the eyes of the crews, highly suspicious. Similarly bespectacled, but infinitely more weedy than his predecessor, he gave the impression that his forecast was infallible as he tapped the synoptic chart like a school master making a point before dense pupils. His head turned back from the chart to his audience and back again with metronomic regularity as he propounded the view that whilst there was a layer of cloud cover over central Germany, it would in no way affect aircraft at their operational height and went so far as to suggest in his wisdom that it might afford some protection from the enemy, a remark that was treated with profound scepticism in total silence. With this pearl of wisdom he turned a baleful eye on the auditory, and continued in full flow:

"The target is expected to be clear, ideal conditions for a ground marking attack." Once again he gave the impression of expecting a cheer from the assembled company, but of course he was not to know that the crews would prefer cloud all the way *and* over the target provided that Pathfinder's force could successfully mark the aiming point. In the end he sat down a trifle disconsolately with the feeling that somewhere along the line he had boobed.

The specialist leaders took their turn mainly for the benefit of the whole crews, for they had already briefed in detail their own men and main briefing was concluded. It was now time for relaxation, followed later by flying supper, followed by ultimate take-off.

"Jock got it wrong again," said Taffy in the mood of stirring up the Scotsman a bit.

"Och. I'm nearly always right, mon. No one's perfect."

"Bloody lineshooter," replied Taffy, keen as always to best his celtic colleague.

"Still a shaky do," mused Sid. "Lots of fighter bases in the area."

"It's always dicey east of the Wash." It was Ace's usual remark designed to remind his crew that every trip could be a killer.

Frank said nothing, but looked as pale as usual. He had the air of being a forgettable sort of character, but he was proficient, of that there was no doubt. Ace had never known Frank to panic.

Ken was miles away, probably thinking of a popsie in Lincoln who might be expecting him and was going to be disappointed.

John smoked his pipe, thinking all the time of Marion.

The intercom crackled sharply as Robert's navigator switched his face mask microphone to the "on" position. Above the heavy background roar of the four motors synchronised to cruising revs that easily penetrated the earphones and only partially muffled by enclosure within leather helmet, his voice came clearly:

"12 minutes to ETA Texel Island."

"OK John," Ace replied and went on critically, "you've left it a bit late to warn me."

"Sorry Ace. Been having trouble with winds. They are lighter than forecast."

"Right Taffy, start windowing in ten minutes." Taffy acknowledged with a grunt and being a Welsh grunt it was no improvement on the English variety. He was not all that keen on shoving metal strips down the shute, for though it was a new but essential chore to confuse German radar, it was also a cold and very draughty job.

"We won't see the coast," Sid advised from the front. "Ten tenths cloud below."

"No problem," put in John confidently. "We're no more than a mile to starboard of track and that's probably due to pilot error." He grinned into his mask, prepared to listen to one of the biting rejoinders Ace was quite capable of spitting out between gritted teeth, but all that came back was "shit."

"ETA Texel now," said the navigator after a while. "Alter course 095 T."

"OK navigator. 095 true. Right jokers. Prop your lids open. We're dicing with death. No talking except for official business." There was no reply and none was necessary. Each member of the crew reacted in his own way with greater attention to his own responsibility. From the rear turret Jock audibly blew on the microphone, testing for continuing serviceability, and keyed himself up to ensure instant response to sudden danger from Germans with Iron Cross ambitions. For the next few hours anything might happen and if it did unexpectedly, then the outlook was grim for nearly always an attacking fighter had the advantage of seeing his quarry first because the four engine exhaust manifolds of the bomber were a dead give-away. So the gunners had to see a marauding fighter first as a result of which they were ever watchful. From time to time Ace banked over to starboard and port in turn, but always giving due warning to allow the gunners to look below the Lancaster, its most vulnerable spot.

"About those winds John," said Ace. "I thought Met forecast steady winds."

"He did. Trouble is that direction is nearly down the line of track and it doesn't need much of a directional shift to whip us off track, either way. But don't worry. Everything's under control."

"Good lad." Ace saw the problem and was content.

Outside the Lancaster, the celestial ceiling revolved around the Pole Star, while inside, in the cockpit, the instrument panel with its multiplicity of luminous dials was like a reduced arc of the heavens. The pilot's eyes moved from the panel out through the perspex, while sitting beside him in the flight engineer's seat, the second dickey's eyes were peering out to starboard. Ken the flight engineer was busily logging his oil pressure and temperature readings. Of the crew of seven plus one, only two were not keeping watch without for the vicious silhouette of a fighter. These were the w/op and the navigator. It could be said that the w/op was also on watch but in his case it was a radio listening watch, whereas the navigator, behind the blackout curtain that separated cockpit from his office, was too absorbed in checking and re-checking calculations and chart measurements.

Again Ace banked his Lancaster over to port, for a moment standing on the wingtip while quiet young Frank had a good look-see down below. Then he banked starboard so that the mid upper could scan the other segment of downward vision. To Frank, it always seemed to be an action comparable to looking for a needle in a haystack, but there was always the chance he might get a sighting of the needle and it might be a life saver. There were vague shadows, too many vague shadows that often had him poised ready to mouth warning, but so far so good. No dark phantom stood out in the gloom. It was an exercise that had to be repeated frequently.

Time passed by. It was pretty quiet if one could disregard the powerful throbbing motors against which there was little insulation. Just now and again on each side, in the distance, odd searchlights waved about apparently aimlessly, and it had to be supposed that the odd Lancaster had wandered off track, unless of course the activity was caused by intruding Mosquito diversionary tactics.

Position B, just a latitude and longitude position on the Mercator chart, and pretty well due south of Hamburg came up seemingly quickly, and up to now the German defences would have been unaware of the ultimate objective, since in general terms the bomber force had continued easterly.

"Position B. Ace, now," advised the navigator. "Turn port on to 359 true." Ace acknowledged and turned with great care through 90 degrees. It was a particularly dangerous moment, for he could easily collide with an aircraft that had left it a bit late to turn since altogether there were several hundred Lancasters on or about the same height although in theory spaced out by timing steps. The navigator watched the DR compass needle hunt round the dial and stabilise correctly. Satisfied then that the pilot had not misheard the instruction, John turned to the task of rechecking ETA target. Now the German defence would be pretty certain of the aiming point for the force was now pointing directly at Hamburg.

Ace jerked forward suddenly as his eyes chanced on what seemed like a darker shadow ahead, but a momentary blink dispelled the phantom, and then suddenly the Lancaster rocked about like a boat in a storm as it caught the slipstream from an aircraft ahead. He had been right after all, but the other could not be seen. It was a moment that although frightening was also consoling for it indicated that they were not alone in the sky and what's more they appeared to be in the right place. It could of course be a fighter ahead but the strength of the slipstream demonstrated otherwise.

Down in the bomb compartment below the pilot's feet on rudder bar, Sid sprawled full length on his stomach, and was very wide awake indeed and to prove it he came on the intercom:

"Cloud below has dispersed," he confidently stated. "Looks as if Met forecast is pretty good." Ace acknowledged this intelligence and was glad to know that Sid was alert. In early days of training Sid had shown frequent signs of surrendering to the tendency to sleep when in the horizontal position. It had to be assumed that the wallowing motion of the aircraft produced a situation like getting a baby to sleep by rocking the cradle. Now, Sid's night eyes, fed on a diet of carrots, were valuable.

"Ten minutes to ETA," warned the navigator and the crew braced up even more. While below and ahead all seemed to be quiet, once the Germans were absolutely sure of the aiming point and when Pathfinders began their search for the exact aiming point, the sky would light up.

"Corkscrew port Go. Go," came a frenzied call from the rear gunner 63 feet to the rear of the cockpit. There seemed to be too little time for the initial warning scarcely preceded the Go command, but Ace responded like an automaton throwing Robert into the violently uncomfortable manoeuvre, diving, banking, turning and climbing in rapid succession, while the staccato bark of Jock's 303 guns vibrated down the fuselage accompanied by a strong odour of cordite. The enemy was frustrated. Total surprise had been lost. The fighter could not bring guns to bear because of the violent jinking of the prey. Now only through extreme patience and perseverence could the enemy pilot hope to outwit the extraordinary manoevreability of the Lancaster, and then only if Ace made a tactical error. At long last came the gunner's breathless comfort:

"OK, Ace. He's buggered off to look for an easier target. It was a JU88." The pilot resumed course without comment. Ahead searchlights were now flickering into the sky and the sharp wink of heavy flak bursts were to be seen. Then as Ace switched on VHF, a bit late because of the recent diversion, the Reds were down, brilliant waterfalls of colour.

"Two minutes to ETA," intoned the navigator.

"Bomb doors open," Sid requested.

"Bomb doors open," repeated Ace. "All eyes out. That fighter must still be around."

"There go the Greens," said Sid excitedly. "Left, left, left... steady." Ace slewed the Lancaster to port and then the sky opened up. Up came the heavy flak shells, flashing and smoking past. It was now to all intents and purposes daylight and there was Hamburg with the wide river and estuary to the sea.

"Can't miss this one," said Sid to no one in particular and then to Ace:

"Right a bit. Steady. Keep it there. Just right. Steady..."

"Bamber from Marmalade," came the Master Bomber's voice, "Bomb the Greens, I say again, Bomb the Greens."

"Keep it steady, Ace," complained the bomb aimer as the Lancaster rocked from the blast of an exploding shell nearby.

"Steady... steady. Bombs gone. Steady for photoflash."

"Course 295 true," called John.

"Bomb doors closed," said the pilot. "3000 revs, Bill. Let's get the hell out of here." Bill Chatterforth had reacted instantaneously to thrust the throttles forward. At maximum speed the Lancaster was on course to cross the coast north east of the Frisian Islands.

From the rear turret, Jock as always had the best view of the target area after bombing and he was ecstatic:

"The place is alight," he volunteered. "Looks like a wizard prang." Out to starboard a gush of flame lit the sky like an aeroplane exploding.

"Kite shot down," suggested the second dickey.

"Could be," replied Ace. "Could be a scarecrew. Jerry's fond of using 'em to frighten us."

There were a few odd searchlights waving about on the coast and out to sea a ship threw up some light flak, wholly ineffective at their operational height, but they were still within easy range of enemy fighters. Constant vigil was vital. The Lancaster was back on cruising revs now with an air speed of 165 indicated as far as point C, the Lat/Long DR position in the North Sea, and the final turning point, whereafter it would be a straight course back to Holmdun.

"Turn on to 265 true now," instructed the navigator. Ace acknowledged, adding, "I'm going to lose height very slowly and pushing speed up to 170, OK?" It had to be OK. Skipper said so, but it would mean new calculations, so John set to work again.

"ETA revised. 0345," he advised the pilot a few minutes later. It was a summer night. At 20000 feet the faint glow of the sun had barely fallen entirely below the horizon in the West before the same faint glow of oncoming dawn was visible in the East, to the rear. It helped a bit for there was a better chance of picking up an intrepid enemy fighter venturing out to sea in the wake of the bomber stream. At 03.30, heading for the Wash, the friendly aerodrome beacons winking the two letter morse characteristic were a sight for sore eyes. Lancaster Robert crossed the English coast just north of the Wash and it was not long before Ace was pressing the transmission button:

"Manger Robert to Bakewell. How do you read me?"

"Bakewell to Robert. Strength 5. Clear to land." The WAAF's voice was pure Honey.

"We're first back by the look of it," Ace said to Bill Chatterforth. Ace turned downwind, viewing the fairy light flarepath and began to issue orders to Ken, who had retrieved his normal position beside the pilot, while Bill Chatterforth took up position on the step by the wireless operator.

"Flaps 20," and Ken put down twenty degrees of flap. As a result the speed dropped to about 150.

"Revs up." The constant speed propeller controls were advanced with a resulting whine from the engines.

"Wheels down," Ace continued.

"Wheels down," echoed the flight engineer. They were now on the penultimate leg, and about to turn on to the runway.

"Radiators Closed," Ace rapped out.

"OK, closed," repeated Ken. Two green lights came on on the instrument panel.

"Wheels locks down," confirmed the flight engineer. The landing strip, as always, looked very narrow from the far approach.

"Full flap," called Ace.

"Full flap." Confirmation of the order was part of the absolute discipline and Ken put down the lever, while Ace juggled with the trimming tabs for the glide.

"Speed 130 . . 130 . . 125 . . 120 . ." John was calling the airspeed to allow the pilot complete concentration on judging the approach in the darkness towards the landing flares.

"Speed 115 . . 110 . . 105 . . 100 . ." John's voice went up a sharp. "105 . . 100 . . 100."

"Cut thottles." Ace's command was peremptory. The Lancaster hovered and floated for a hundred yards until there was a faint bump as the main wheels and tail wheel kissed the concrete in complete accord.

"Super landing Ace," Jock was quick to voice disapproval but equally to give praise, as usual. It was part of his patter. He never missed.

Now in the circuit, navigation lights on, other Lancasters were queued up for instructions to land, and in the mess with only one light on to keep her company, Marion who had heard the first aircraft in the circuit had phoned and got the message. Ace Burnett and crew were home. John was safe.

The debriefing room had its usual complement of persons, ready and waiting for returning crews. Present were Groupie, Wing Co., Bert Apsley and other specialist leaders together with Intelligence officers and a couple of WAAFs armed with a tea urn, cocoa and a number of mugs.

"Good trip Burnett?" Wing Co. was all smiles.

"Yes Sir. Successful I should say."

"Right, I'd better not hold you up. I expect you are all pretty tired." They took seats in front of a waiting Intelligence officer.

"Well how did it go?" he asked. It was the standard opening gambit.

"Pretty well," replied Ace. "Markers concentrated and target alight." There was a whole series of questions. Any fighter attacks? What position? Time? Flak strength? etc. The crew in turn put their oar in. Jock mentioned one particular mighty fire blossoming out. And then briefing was over as far as they were concerned. Being first home, they had not had to queue. As they left, other crews were drifting in, all dog tired. It was nearly a mile and a half to the mess, which, although the big transport bearing them thence had screamed round two bends at a fair rate of knots, seemed like ten and a half miles. Fatigue had really set in. Breakfast and bed.

Chapter 8

COMMISSIONING AND ALL THAT

Ace addressed the drinks handed over the bar without apparent request while Texel projected one of his long enquiring glances first to John and then to Marion.

"When are you two getting married?" he asked. "You really ought to make it legal."

"Play it again, Sam. You really ought to change the record." John was pretty quick off the mark, but Marion was more hesitant:

"I don't know Tex," she replied directly to his question, unembarrassed and without surprise. She might just as easily have been replying to a request for the time of the bus into Lincoln. "What make's you think it's our intention?" Texel grinned. His round baby face contorted into a grin was more like a leer.

"Well," he said, "with such a wonderful romance surely it can only come to a logical conclusion, unless that doubtful lothario of yours is leading you on."

"Why?" Interrogation was short enough to subdue the flight engineer if only for a brief moment until he could think up a suitable answer.

"You'll have to give us notice so we can save up for the celebration."

"We'll tell you in good time." Marion could not be really angry, for Texel went to great pains to stir up trouble to confirm that he was a bad lot. It never quite came off simply because he was not a bad character at all, but for some obscure reason he got a kick out of seeming so.

"I say you should watch that navigator. Probably roll you into bed on the promise of marriage and then ditch you." Texel never knew when to stop, and this time Marion really did put the freeze on and there was a stony glint in her eyes which boded trouble with a capital T.

"Push your ugly mug into this." The pilot's intervention with a proffered pint could not have been better timed. "You'll not get many more pints out of me in this Mess," he added.

"Of course ... of course," Texel was half whistling through pursed lips ending up as a prolonged hiss. "I'd forgotten you and

John were moving into the Officers' Mess. When's it to be? I'm not sure whether I ought to be standing to attention or not."

"Booze has constricted your bird brain," said Ace laconically as if it were the answer to any shortcoming.

"S'true as I'm standing here," quoth Texel wagging his number one finger at Pilot and Navigator. "They know in the Orderly room that your commissions have come through and while they're not very orderly the gen does seep through now and again." The Flight Engineer almost preened himself as a result of being first with the news. He smoothed back thinning hair and stood up straight with one hand on hip giving a loose impression of a cockerel about to crow at dawn.

"But what's the matter love?" Texel seemed suddenly contrite. "Have I put my big foot in it again?" Marion was staring at John in pained surprise.

"You didn't tell me you were up for commissioning," she accused.

"Oh Moses. Boobed again," moaned Texel and then, "Doesn't he tell you anything love. If you were my girl, we'd be like two peas in a pod."

John clutched pipe in one hand while the pint in the other sloshed over, but it was the pilot who came to the rescue.

"Couldn't be sure recommendations would be approved and in any case usually takes a hell of a time to come through channels." His reply was logical enough and could not be disputed.

"Immediate commissioning was the message I got," persisted Texel, "but have I got you in trouble Johnny boy or have I not." It was a statement rather than a question, and now Texel was positively gloating. "Never mind, I'll look after scrumptious in the long winter evenings. We'll cuddle up all nice and cosy won't we, Marion, my love."

"Belt up Tex." John was regaining composure. "If Texel is right," he said turning to the WAAF sergeant, "then I figured it wrong. I was sure we'd be through this tour of ops first, and then, going on to a training station as an instructor I need the commission." He stole another quick glance as she momentarily turned her face away but got her right in the eyes as her head turned again. The eyes were unwavering but there was moist anguish in them. What a fool he had been not to tell her of the recent interview with Wing Co. While all knew of Ace's gong, commissioning had not been mentioned by either Ace or John. All along he had confided in her his fears, his hopes and now, he supposed, she felt betrayed.

It was Sid's arrival that broke an uncomfortable silence and with a rare intervention he broke the ice simply because he had not known what had gone before.

"I'm in the mood for music. Perhaps John will favour us by tickling the ivories. Drink up chaps. You're slipping."

Ace fumbled with his tobacco tin.

"Good idea," he said. "Sid, as the proposer, it's your round. Better lay in a stock or Charlie will think we've all gone to our pits, and close the bar."

They barged through the ante-room door and John was comforted to find Marion's arm gently link with his. It looked as if she really did understand but there would still be some quiet explaining to do later. Scathing remarks came from several sergeants reclining in armchairs before windows open to the soft evening air.

"Boozing again Tex," someone said loudly. "You want to get some service in."

"Get knotted," Texel's reply was unusually brief, but there was a broad grin on his face, for he loved to be the centre of attention.

The second ante-room housed the piano, a battered, upright overstrung job, which owed its presence to a local benefactor who had assumed that its gift to the Mess would be a contribution to the war effort. The original shiny black gloss was dulled and severely scratched while all about the woodwork were the black scorch marks of fags ruthlessly stubbed out and on the top flap the marks from pint mugs. Notwithstanding its battered appearance, its tone and tunefulness was a substantial improvement on most Mess pianos, so often ill-used. John was not averse to playing it when in the mood but he was not sure of it now. There was too much on the mind, but as he ran fingers over the keys he felt the soft touch of a slender hand on shoulder which moved his interest up a peg or two. A quick glance over his shoulder was rewarded with a smile from Marion, whose eyes were still a bit sharpish, but her lips softer looking than red roses in the early morning dew. He played "Moonlight becomes you" first, because in looking at her he knew it was true, and then other popular melodies — "Tangerine," "My devotion," "A Nightingale sang in Berkeley Square," and "Deep Purple." It was all sweet stuff, nostalgic and popular, but entirely tuneful with words that made sense however sloppy they were. The company listened and sang untunefully for a while, but being broadly unmusical, and whose form could best been displayed on "Old Man Reilly's Daughter" with its lengthy exposition of crudity and out of bounds with a female present, left John to his music to lapse into subdued though inevitable shop.

"It's a rum do," Ace was saying as he straddled an upright chair, "I've got a bloody good crew, yet not one nor the other of us could call the other a friend. Socially we're misfits." He took a long gulp of his pint and waved the free hand around in the pose of most unusual expression. "Take a gander around. How many of my crew are here? John and Sid. Jock and Taffy have got regular birds in Lincoln. Frank's gone looking for a popsie without knowing what to do if he finds one, and who know's what Ken is up to." Here Ace paused for a comforting draw on his hand rolled fag for this sort of eloquence was not his style. "Mind you, I'm not complaining. I'm not a great one in others company, but it does prove that close friendship is not necessarily the essence of a good crew. It's discipline, self-discipline that matters."

Sid who perhaps had some small inborn musical appreciation or he would not have asked John to play, had one ear tuned to John's renderings and the other on the spoken word. Turning directly to Ace, he ventured his own opinion:

"I'm inclined to agree. At OTU the official line was chum up in a big way and get crewed. Possibly in some cases the idea was sound, because at that point we were all perfect strangers. But I make reservations. A crew of skilled chaps, not necessarily friends, will perform well but if one falls down badly on the job, out he can go without too much aggravation. But given the same circumstances with a crew of good friends, then you have a problem, for it's tricky to ditch a pal. So if you can't bring yourself to do the obvious, the crew is unbalanced and infinitely dangerous the outcome." Sid came to a stop feeling perhaps that he had not presented his views as lucidly as he would have liked. He was also aware that he had increased his audience for John had ceased to play and both he and Marion had picked up the thread of Sid's logic.

"We are living proof of your contention," said the navigator. "I remember at OTU we were the left overs after the others had crewed up. I remember too exactly how out of tune I was with the course pilots. I couldn't say why. I just knew. Quite frankly I knew the course was a pilot short and hoped for better luck next time, and also quite selfishly, I admit it, I thought if we did not have a driver we might get a spot of extra leave. Needless to say I was quite shocked to learn there was a driver left over from the previous course and we were expected to volunteer on the you, you, and you principle."

John turned to Ace. "Busted your collar bone playing Rugger, hadn't you Ace?"

"Sure, Johnny boy. You got me for better or worse."

Texel thought all this was hilarious. Ace turned on a faint smile.

"Look what you got Ace. A bunch of bloody scroungers."

"Don't seem to be doing too bad," replied Ace cautiously. "I'm told most of our original courses have met the grim reaper."

"Scroungers, Tex?" queried Sid. "Perhaps, but in those days the higher ideals of glory with glamour and death as the only reward weren't so poignant. To me, then, it was all adventure and the real feeling of fighting a war hadn't taken hold. I wanted the sensation of flying, not necessarily to fight." He added ruminantly, "S'funny how ideas quickly change. Over the first hurdle of our first op and the shock of it, I ceased to regard it as fun, realising that to get through a tour had to be a matter of dedication and bags of luck, all of the good variety."

"The complete answer to the what-did-you-do-in-the-War-Daddy, Eh Sid." Texel was strangely serious despite the flippant nature of his rejoinder.

"Bit premature." Sid still had his options open. "But there may come a time. They say there's no future in being one of Butch Harris' boys, but I hope to prove the statistics wrong."

Ace was nodding assent, but it did not come to more than that for thoughts were sometimes too deep for words. Instead he flicked ash off his battledress. Texel took up his pint again and found it distinctly refreshing. Sid was lost in thought or perhaps exhausted by his own verbal outpouring. John nudged Marion covertly, rolling his eyes in the direction of the door. She acquiesced and proceeded to action.

"I must go," she said and brushed her skirt down carefully.

"I'll send in a tray of pints." John hoped this bribery would cancel out the need for his continuing presence.

"They want to be alone," jeered Texel giving an extremely bad impression of Greta Garbo. "Can't you two leave each other alone for even one night. It's positively indecent."

"Jealous Tex?" John's question was practically an insinuation.

"I am, that I am." Tex was at least honest. "Send me in a double gin. I want to be miserable."

"Mother's ruin," warned the navigator.

"What of it?"

"You *are* an old woman, it'll ruin you. You will have beer and like it," said John.

"Mean sod." Texel was miserable already, with or without gin.

They said their goodbyes amicably for the repartee was hardly serious and having ordered the round, strode from the Mess into the twilight of a summer night. The air was still warm and only a variable breeze played around them as the shadowy outline of the village church loomed into the sky reflecting in the after glow of sunset. The village pub was active but not unduly so as Marion and John passed on their way to the WAAFery. They were at the entrance to the latter before John summoned up the courage to break a silence which normally would have been easily acceptable, but on this occasion was a shade uncomfortable.

"Are you still angry with me?" He really did not know how to break the silence and his question would have to suffice. Marion kept him waiting for what seemed like forever but finally she came on stream.

"No John. Not angry. A little hurt, but on reflection I realise you had reasons."

"Perhaps it was as well that Texel brought the matter up, although I really did not think that becoming an officer was imminent." Texel, the bastard, he thought. Always stirring up one pot or other.

"Didn't you think I would understand?" Marion was gently questioning. "Whatever is best for you I want. You must know that."

John took her hands and there was no resistance as he edged her closer.

"It's not as easy as it sounds. If what Texel says is true and I have not confirmed it yet, we'll not be able to eat together for we'll be in separate Messes and, we'll have to be more circumspect in our meetings — you know officers are not supposed to fraternise with non-coms. We could hardly stand on this spot and kiss goodnight without being seen by one of your officers. The next thing you would be hauled over the coals."

"You could have the same problem, John."

"Not me. Who's going to argue with aircrew? No you are the one to worry about. You could be posted. That's how it would be quietly arranged."

Marion was not a whit put out.

"Unlikely. There's a shortage of watchkeepers as you well know from all the hours I have to be on duty," she said. "Besides we'll just have to get away from the area in our spare time. That's not difficult for we have our bikes."

John knew she was right. It was not as if he was likely to make a valuable Sergeant pregnant. He just wanted to be with her. He enlarged the subject by way of providing a full explanation of his outlook.

"As I said in the Mess, the only reason I wanted to accept an offered commission, and that was what it was — I did not apply — was precautionary. If I finish this tour of ops I'll get whisked off to OTU as an instructor, and OTU's are not like Squadrons. Here we're the cat's whiskers spooned fed with real eggs and chocolate, with little military discipline in exchange for a tour of 30 ops. On a training establishment things are different. An NCO instructor is likely to be on the receiving end of the dirty jobs, whereas, as an officer I would be able to dig my toes in a bit."

"You make OTU sound dreadful." Marion could not really understand the basis of his pessimism. "It really cannot be as bad as that."

John began to warm to the task of explaining all to his girl particularly now that he was in good odour again.

"I've been to one, as a pupil of course, but it was not hard to see what a rotten job the instructors or screens as they are called had, taking up new crews — bloody dodgy, and I was not particularly impressed with the Group Capt who seemed to be from another age with an attitude to match — yes last war outlook. Besides, as more and more aircrew are fed into the system, the smaller fry we all become. No doubt about it, I would rather dice with the Squadron any day. Just think, we in Bomber Command are the only service hitting Hitler on his own ground, forcing him to move from production of his own bombers capable of taking it out on London, Bristol, Coventry and the Ports, into production of more fighters to protect Germany. We've come a long way from the cold war. We, in Bomber Command are hitting hard where it hurts."

John was a bit overcome by his own eloquence. He suggested that instead of standing outside the main gate to the WAAFery, they could sit on the seat a few yards beyond and under the hedge.

As they sat easily on the seat, donated by a local dignitary now deceased, Marion asked:

"What shall you do when the war ends?"

John's reply was more brusque than intended, for Marion had got him on the raw, simply because he had no idea.

"Don't see any sign of the war ending, and I think we should eschew trafficking in futures." He felt her hand slacken in his grasp so he continued quickly. "I'd like to say, that because we'll be married by then, it will be a joint decision, but I have little that is positive to offer you." Her hand tightened and he relaxed again. It was almost dark now. The fragrance of wild flowers hung heavily, but sweetly on the air, while the nocturnal wild life set up the summer chorus. Except for an occasional giggle from the WAAFery which was just behind the hedge, it was an evening that cried out for tranquility. John continued:

"I hope for the end of hostilities simply because I'd like to see the end of what is senseless killing, and also because, while I thrill to the sensation of flying, like Sid, I do hate the ties the service imposes. I'm no military man, just a civilian in uniform waiting to start a career. I have never known the elation of high ambition. I left college wholly undecided on a direction to follow."

"Surely there's something you specially want to do."

"I haven't decided yet. You see I was due to go up to University, to Oxford actually. Quite frankly, beyond expecting my academic ability to be stretched to the limit and gaining a good degree I had no other positive expectation. So it was that the War solved my problem temporarily. It allowed me to defer my decision."

Marion's face lit up with an idea.

"I know you don't care for the service, but what about the prospects in peacetime. You could have a permanent or short term commission at least. The thrill of flying in peacetime would surely override your dislike of a too disciplined existence."

"Perhaps, Marion my love." He laughed briefly and there was in it the bitterness of an old soldier. "You must know I'm the greatest pessimist of all time. Peace brings depletion of armed forces, stripped to minimum needs. It's happened before under the impetus of small but highly vocal groups of pacifists. Only limited short service engagements are likely to be available and that's no good for a married man, and his wife," he added pointedly.

Marion blushed in the dark and happily the flow of empathy recently dried up to a trickle had new substance.

"I'm prepared to face the future with you in whichever direction you choose to go," she averred.

"What do you suppose the RAF does in peacetime time?" John asked quietly.

"I really don't know. It was just an idea thrown out to assist your thought processes," Marion admitted.

"Well, I do." The navigator was positive. "If he's not consigned to some hot hell hole like Aden, then he's spending time playing squash and entering into petty social activities where the essence of advancement may lie in the ability to keep the interest of the CO's wife. I'm afraid that sort of pretentious conduct leaves me cold."

"There's always the flying." Marion was nothing if not persistent.

"Maybe. I can see flying to be secondary, conditioned by the finance available from a Government that may have what it considers more important priorities. I could go to University. Do you fancy being a Don's wife?"

"It's a new idea. As a farmer's daughter, it has never been remotely on my list of probabilities. What about an MP?"

"Absolutely no thanks. The last refuge of the devil. Have to be no good at anything else. Sorry love, if I'm to be recognised it has got to be for sincerity."

"You are beginning to think and that's all to the good," Marion said. "You might like to be a farmer, hey? Plenty of room for good men on my folk's farm. But I must go now. It's getting late and I'm on duty again tomorrow." She moved to rise but found herself locked in the navigator's steely grip.

"Don't go yet. I shan't sleep," he whispered.

"But I must," she whispered weakly.

"OK. OK, but don't be late for breakfast." He kissed her ardently on full moist lips and gently touched her face, so cool and soft. He could just about see the sudden stars in her eyes.

"Is that the best you can do?" she asked, her voice low and husky with emotion. For a moment John was startled at the sudden urgency in her tone. He crushed her hard against him, kissing her again and again, oblivious of various WAAF's filtering through the gate accompanied by the odd titter of either jealousy or approval. She clung to him as one clings to life itself. A tear or two rolled down her face to be lost in the miasma of a final kiss. Finally she tore herself from John's grasp. It had to be that way for he had little incentive to let go.

A week later, Ace and John were standing outside the HQ building centrally placed on the communal site, just having vacated the presence of the Group Captain, who with four thick rings had absolute authority at Holmdun. It was plain from their demeanour that something unexpected and unpopular had occurred, as indeed it had, for they had jointly been torn off a mighty strip. Ignominious dismissal had followed the brief but cryptic lesson and instruction handed out after having been given a lecture on what it meant to be commissioned officers in His Majesty's Royal Air Force:

"You have been in effect commissioned Officers for nearly a week, yet neither the one nor the other of you has seen fit to set foot in the Officers' Mess. I want no excuses. You'll take the day off — I'll see that you are not on the Battle Order. You'll go post haste into Lincoln, get kitted out. I expect to see you both in the Mess within 24 hours." It had been a command and no doubt about that, presented with a severity of countenance not under any circumstance to be ignored. The two young men had exited with salutes incapable of being bettered but with tails positively between legs.

"Oh Hell. I suppose we'd better beat it into Lincoln," said Ace. "What a bind."

In the late afternoon, they returned from the gracious cathedral city in a mood less than affable despite a minor binge at lunchtime, and repaired disconsolately to the billet. It had been a really trying day. The service tailor, or at least the civilian tailor who provided Officer uniforms had a largish supply of off the peg stuff, but was unable to fit either young man as a result of which emergency alterations had to be implemented. That had not been easy either, for the tailor had been loth to do other than work at his usual pace. He had to be persuaded that John and Ace would really be in the doghouse if he could not come up with some urgent action. In the end Ace won the day when the tailor noticed the New Zealand shoulder flash because he had a daughter recently emigrated to what Ace called God's own country. At all events it was the end of a chapter in their service careers. As Sergeants and more recently Flight Sergeants with the crown surmounting 3 stripes, they had enjoyed the easy going, no frills life in the appropriate mess. The bare little hut that had been their sleeping quarters for some months became suddenly home because they were on the point of leaving in favour of the Officers' sleeping quarters on the other side of the site, complete with batmen.

"Just look at this cheesecutter," moaned Ace as he took the brand new dress hat from his case and practically cut a digit on the peak. "It's so bloody new. We'll be seen coming from a mile off." John was not any happier either as he eyed the resplendent best blue uniform laid out on the bed. No doubt about it. These uniforms would stamp them from afar as sprog Pilot Officers. He could visualise the embarrassing barely concealed titters of amusement from all and sundry, not to mention the sure fire poignant remarks from closer acquaintances. Texel in particular would have a field day.

Tea time found Ace and John making progress towards the Sergeants Mess for the last time. Mutually, they had decided to have their final evening there before transferring their effects to the new quarters. They would attend the Officers' Mess in the morning for breakfast, inside Groupie's time limit. If they reckoned on a quiet last meal their hopes were misplaced. It was too much to hope that in so small a community that their absence had gone unnoticed. Moreover, news gets around even if the basis of it is inaccurate. As they made their way nonchalantly into the dining hall, Marion, Texel and the rest of Ace's crew were already chewing the fat. Ace and John took their chairs with studied normalcy and it was Texel who always demonstrated the curiosity of a woman.

"Where have you two been?" Texel's conversation at table was pretty well limited to questions or fragmentary gossip.

"On the booze in Lincoln," John replied a shade quickly since he had accurately anticipated the question, but taking care to give Marion an eye-ball message which he hoped she could decode.

"What, all day?" Even Sid was now jumping on the bandwagon. "Actually you both look as if you've been to a funeral."

Ace started in to say that they had and changed his mind.

"Not all day," he replied with a degree of accuracy. "Fact is we've just come from the billet. Been sorting out a parcel from God's own country."

"Where's that?" queried Texel as if he did not know.

"NZ, you bloody fool. Where else?"

Texel snorted indignantly.

"Didn't your parents ever teach you to share . . ."

"Jolly good shortbreads," interjected John. "Now if this country could only bake biscuits like those. . ."

"Now tell us where you skived off," pursued the flight engineer, wholly unimpressed with red herring. Ace sighed. He lifted his teacup with studied genteelness and then sharply replaced it in the saucer as if he had come to a snap decision, which action was calculated to gain full attention.

"We got a rocket from Groupie. Should have been in the next Mess a week ago. Net result an ultimatum. Get weaving or else. Been into Lincoln. Got pawed about by tailors. Scarcely had time for a pint." Ace issued this series of short statements to wide open stares for it was rare for him to exceed more than one at a time.

"You don't say," said Sid. He too was not so much surprised at the meat being purveyed as the way in which Ace had come out with it.

"Want to ask you jokers a favour." Ace went on before anyone else could horn in and his tone registered hope.

"Bloody sprog Officers still in the Sergeants Mess sponging off poor NCO's already," suggested Texel. "Conduct prejudicial to good order and discipline I call it." He managed to substitute mock disgust in lieu of his tombstone grimace.

"Belt up." Ace was beginning to get a bit irritated. "It's not money we want but co-operation."

"We really are all ears," said Sid.

"Well we've got to get into new uniforms and I don't need to tell you how bloody silly we'll feel," said Ace ruefully, almost sheepishly.

With the exception of Marion, the little group hooted in derision, but Ace persisted.

"That's where you roughs come in. We thought we could all go down to the Blue Tit and drown our sorrows. Perhaps mess up the new blue a bit."

"Am I included in the roughs?" Marion asked lightly.

"Course," said John but went on very quickly. "He doesn't include you in the roughs, but we do need your moral support." John's appeal was plaintive.

"Now you're talking." The others had paused for breath so Texel sneaked in. "We'll pour beer in your cheesecutters and mess up your best blue a bit, but I'm not going as far as the Blue Tit. Might run out of beer before we get there. It's the Old Cow or nothing and I don't mean you love," he finished, leering at Marion.

"OK. I'll wear that, to save you wittering on and on. It was only a suggestion. Forgotten your old age." Ace was prepared to concede a point.

"Are you sure you don't mind mixing with these bad characters, Marion?" John's genuine solicitude was obvious.

"As long as I take no responsibility for getting you back."

"Aw what a shame." Texel tried to look disconsolate.

Marion thought how strange it was that the human male who dared face death in the skies as a routine task was scared of looking even faintly foolish. If she could only get out of uniform and put on a swizz new dress she would jump at the chance, or even, if pressed, a WAAF OFFICER'S uniform.

"Count me out," intoned Jock mournfully. "I'm flat broke."

"Me too," said Taff with uncharacteristic agreement.

"Zat the only reason?" Ace looked in turn at both. "What happened to your popsies?"

"We're out of favour," replied Jock. With Ace's eagle eye on him he had to own up, and found some comfort in explaining. "I'm out of funds and she doesn't want to know me. She's had it in a big way from now on."

"Not surprised," said Sid caustically. "Can't imagine English girls wanting to date a couple of foreigners."

"Foreigners..." Welsh and Scots voices produced an exasperated but distinctly combined celtic soprano. Ace quickly smoothed ruffled feathers that were on the point of getting airborne.

"Reckon we can subsidise 'e, Eh John. 'Sides if it's wine or women, give me wine every time. Cheaper and with less permanent effect."

"Hark at the preacher. Do you know what Ace does if he meets a bird? No? Well I'll tell you. He always says 'is it worth my while to take you home?' If the bird prevaricates, he knows he's on to a good thing. If she slaps his face, he knows he's out and isn't going to throw good money after bad." Texel was really enjoying himself but if he expected an outburst from the pilot he was mistaken. All the pilot said was:

"Zero hour 2000."

"And Zero hour it will be," replied Tex, in such a way that put a perplexed frown on John's forehead. Texel exited with a fixed leer.

"What's he mean by that?" John asked Marion. "Sounds ominous." Marion nodded. She was inclined to agree, knowing the worthy flight engineer.

"Shall I meet you at the WAAFery?" he asked a little too eagerly.

"I don't like going into pubs unescorted, but you and Ace need each other. I'll see you inside."

"Well if you came with both of us, you wouldn't be embarrassed and no one would notice us with you there." John tried a little flattery, but it buttered no parsnips.

"It might be a lovely compliment," she said wistfully, "but in this instance it isn't, so fight your own battles."

"Deserted," moaned John, while Ace cupped his chin in the palm of one hand and stroked his hair mechanically. The latter seemed to be miles adrift. Marion was up and gone before the navigator could try other wiles, followed immediately by the rest of the crew and their fixed grins. John downed his cup of tea. It was cold comfort.

The evening was on the warm side of cold. Overcast cloud was building up solidly. Warm front, thought John. No wonder there was a standdown. But it was not raining yet as he and his pilot paused apprehensively before the public bar entrance to the Old Cow. They had walked into the village from their new quarters without attracting too much attention except that a pair of erks going the other way had pulled smartly into step as they perceived the two officers approaching, to put up stone bonker salutes that would have done credit to a couple of guardsmen, their faces the poker of all poker faces. Taken somewhat by surprise Ace and John had responded with salutes that were more in the nature of waves. Both knew the erks, crafty blighters, were demonstrating recognition of a couple of sprog officers without being remotely disrespectful.

The pause before the door was momentary. Texel had agreed 2000 hours and that it now was. They had supposed that the intention was to meet without, but it was transparently obvious that the others were within, for if there was one occasion when aircrew were really on time it was for the consumption of ales and spirits, and the minute hand on the church clock had already jerked past the hour. Summoning up a modicum of courage Ace thrust open the door smartly, and then paused. He half expected a deluge of water from a bucket perhaps placed precariously above the door frame until he reasoned in megaseconds that even the modern seer Texel could not foretell who would first cross the threshhold. John slipped in behind Ace's substantial square frame. They saw at once that the bar was tolerably well populated which state was in no way unusual when beer was in short supply and in variable terms of regularity of supply. But all seemed quiet enough. The two new officers breathed again. At the far end of the long bar Texel and Ace's crew had reserved their positions, already strategically placed to replenish supplies, and all grinning broadly. At a whispered warning from Texel they all moved into line abreast and as Ace and John walked towards them, in a loud voice Texel shouted, "Squad. Attention." The squad came very smartly to attention and saluted, their faces wooden, while the rest of the population grinned and whispered to each other, most realising the significance of what was a bit of a charade.

The two new officers walked the 20 miles to the end of the bar, their faces if not actually reddening, going into a pastel pink. Even the publican paused in the action of shining a glass tankard on a teacloth, frozen into immobility by the sudden quiet. Both officers and sergeants were aware that this was not really in the best traditions of the service, but who could fault management of the moment. It was all very precisely done.

"All right chaps, stand easy," said Ace while a slight twitch of his features signified ruefully that there was a modicum of humour to be accepted and replied to.

"Might have known you buggers would give us maximum publicity," grumbled John who was less amenable to the game than Ace had been. "And now comes the reckoning." He called to the landlord in a loud voice, "Bert, a whisky each for my colleague and myself and six orange squashes for the ragtag and bobtail." In a flash six grinning mugs registered sheer horror, while again the bar populace smiled their approval of so astute a move.

"And, you'll damn well drink it or I'll personally force feed you," finished Ace with evident satisfaction.

At what seemed a critical moment, the dark head and slim figure of Marion flowed through the doorway and all eyes turned towards her, the service able bodied storks eyeing her figure speculatively, while female eyes rapidly assessed her with becoming inscrutability to decide whether or not competition had arrived on their patch. Using the diversion John quietly beckoned Bert, the publican.

"Any Gin?" he asked.

"Might find a bit." The landlord was wary. Spirits were very limited.

"Stick a couple of gins in each orange squash, will you." John was speaking very quietly and Bert nodded. It was obviously an occasion. His co-operation would be appreciated. Aloud John said, "A Port and lemon please."

Marion's smile was becoming. She had the ability to turn winter into summer, and she was able to exude easy camaraderie in male company that was rare in women unless they were absolutely the centre piece. She did not have the female propensity for fluttering eyelids in such a way as to suggest "I'm all yours," but she did have an open attractive face that was capable of melting the hardest of men's hearts without even realising her power, or if she did, chose not to use it for improper purposes. She was the sort of woman men would like to trifle with but dare not.

"You both look very smart," she admitted quietly and John surreptitiously grasped her hand.

"Here you are Jokers." Ace being nearest to the bar acted as supply manager. "Port and lemon for a beautiful lady, double whisky for John and myself and orange squash for the roughs." Marion contrived to stifle a tinkling laugh.

"Not your usual tipple, Tex, surely."

"Getting their own medicine," burbled the navigator.

"Oh well," said Jock with total resignation. "I looks to you both."

"I catches your eye," chorused Ace and John.

Taffy sniffed his glass carefully. Although not "chapel" in the Welsh sense, he had the generally suspicious nature apparent in his race. Satisfied that it was not poison, he tossed the drink back, followed by Ken, Frank, Sid and Texel, not all together but consecutively according to their various degrees of scepticism. A wide enlightened beam shone on Texel's visage as the spirit warmed his throat.

"Wizard orange," he said. "Never realised it could taste so good. Cheers."

"You don't appear too happy, Jock," Marion probed as the company got into a general mood of gratification.

"Och, I prefer Scotch, but I was thinking."

"Almighty odd for an ass end gunner," put in Texel rudely.

"Noo, seriously, I was thinking how lucky are Ace and John." Jock ignored Texel preferring to reply to the lady.

"It's a matter of opinion." Ace was not convinced, but was uncaring anyway.

"Och it's noo joke, I'm serious. There was a gunner on this squadron, I'm told, before we arrived got grounded without reason, stripped of his stripes. They could hardly take away your royal commissions."

"I know about that." Texel did always, but for once he was serious. "Said to be medically unfit. Everyone took a dim view of it."

Marion was shocked and wholly unbelieving.

"Lost his stripes on account of ill-health. I can't wear that. There must have been other reasons, surely."

"Not so you'd notice it," replied Texel. But I suspect he got an LMF label pinned on him."

"What's LMF?" Frank had adjudged it time for him to make an intervention.

"Lack of moral fibre," intoned Texel. "Funked going on ops. Didn't want to get the chop. Can't blame him for that."

"This airforce is beginning to get too big," suggested John. "Currently the squadron strength is comparatively small, but when we get a couple of extra flights, we shall cease to be the cat's whiskers and become even more bits of Government property to be chivvied around and fed to the flames. I'm not surprised at Jock's story which Texel has confirmed."

By now the bar was full. A strong concentration of bodies in blue, of varied ranks, were in combat order striving to attain vantage points at the counter to gain the publican's attention, the latter now happily reinforced by Mrs Publican. These two gallantly plied the beer engines with the action of automatons heedless of who they were serving or order of so doing. So long as the till operated in continuous motion, they could properly be pleased with their endeavours. One particularly strong pincer movement threatened to break Ace's crew and additional company into two separate groups. Ace put his broad shoulders into defensive action, but superior force prevailed when finally Frank, Jock, Taffy and Ken got a divorce from the rest leaving Marion, Ace, John, Texel and Sid in a separate group. The latter were crushed hard against the solid oak counter and while this could be considered an ideal spot for the relatively easy procurement of repeat refreshment, it had the disadvantage of attack from three sides, pints of ale being passed over and all around spilling off the heads. Nevertheless in the true spirit of the service they stood firm like the bulwark of Land's End against the mighty assault of the ocean. John was not a whit put out. He was, to all intents and purposes embracing Marion, not from choice, but revelling in it never-the-less, wholly unaware of Texel's beady eye. In conformity with the jostle of the crowd so did the decibel rate rise until it was virtually impossible to hear or be heard. It was much like being on the train going on leave with compartments and corridors packed to suffocation. Tongues that were at other times silent or at best monosyllabic now wagged prodigiously under the impetus of alcohol input. The fact that very few words reached their intended destination was irrelevant. It was sufficient just to create a hubbub.

"Good show," bawled Ace as his navigator contrived against the odds to catch the publican's eye, and with success drinks were replenished.

"I like a bit of devotion to duty," said Texel, remarking on the navigator's success. Tex was loving every minute of it. The louder the noise, the more he was pleased just like any callow youth, unless of course he really was deaf as Sqn Ldr Denning claimed.

"Down the hatch," bawled Sid hoarsely.

"Not much hope of maintaining my promise to ensure soberness. I just can't move," said Marion. Only Ace heard her, and his reply was largely unsympathetic:

"I'm easy as long as I can raise my arm." It's doubtful whether this remark was heard either.

It was perhaps with a sense of relief that the bell tolled "Time Gentlemen please" and in a sudden quieting the Publican got the words out.

"And Ladies," roared Texel, beaming at Marion as he did so.

"Let's get mobile," advised Sid. Pausing only to drain glasses, they managed to link up with the divorced group to move as one body towards the door with Marion sheltered in the middle. She was like the rose in the ring of roses except that no one fell down. In truth to have effected progress on her own account would have been futile. It was some minutes before the enlarged group gained egress when both she and her manly escort practically fell out of the door in undignified fashion. But oh the joy of pure clean air after the smoke laden bar.

"There's something we've forgotten to do," Sid reminded as he got his breath back, while the rest looked askance. "We haven't mistreated the new gear."

"Soon remedy that," barked Ace. He flipped the navigator's hat on to the now wet ground and ground his heel on it.

Sid flipped off Ace's cheese-cutter and there was practically a competition to get a foot on it. The product of this lunacy was a sight to be seen. Brand new headgear was now muddied and creased. The crowd around them drifted away into what was now a drizzle of rain with the threat of heavier rain to come, and because of the overcast it was pretty dark. The immediate reaction of the group was to repair to the Sergeants Mess until it suddenly sank in that Ace and John could not go. They were Officers now — the Sergeants Mess was out of bounds. Ace said he would case his new joint. The majority would carry out their original intention and John was only in the mood to walk Marion to her billet.

"I've got quite fond of this village," he said as he led her away from the Old Cow. "It's a pretty little village and I feel a part of it, mainly I suppose because it's where we met. I'll be sad to leave. You know we've only a couple more trips to do."

"Perhaps you won't be posted far," Marion suggested hopefully.

"Well the service is not very co-operative when it comes to postings."

"But you'll still get leave. We can still come together," she persevered with a semblance of cheerfulness.

"Yes love, but only every 3 months. When I leave here I can kiss Goodbye to leave every six weeks, and three months away from you sounds like eternity.

"I was happy," Marion sighed. "But now you depress me. I was desperately trying not to think too far ahead."

"I'm sorry, but the thought of parting from you dominates me. I know it demonstrates a deplorable weakness of character, but there it is . . ."

"Let's forget it for the moment, John. Just walk and talk. It'll shorten the night."

"Not sure I want to shorten it." The navigator grinned and although she could not see the grin, she read the tone and gripped his arm more tightly. "But what of you. You're on duty tomorrow."

"Let the morrow take care of itself," she replied rashly.

"Whizzo. But I only hope Ace is in the land of nod when I get back. We have adjacent rooms and the walls are uncommonly thin. My creeping in at an unearthly hour, if discovered, would arouse speculative comment when news of our nocturnal ramblings got to Tex's ears. You know they are as thick as thieves. I'll be branded a philanderer, a dirty stop-out."

"Scared John?"

"Not me, but can you picture the story Texel's vivid imagination would contrive. Only a few nights ago he remarked that our disappearance in the evenings was highly suspicious and that the only venue he could expect us to be at was deep in a hayrick, out of sight of prying eyes."

"So? I've heard that from Texel before. It's his favourite dig. Who cares what he or anyone else thinks!"

"I've ceased to be remotely affected by his ravings," said John, "which I'm sure arise from sheer jealousy, but I don't want you to get a bad name."

Marion emitted a musical ripple of laughter that was just a shade naughty.

"You're a bad type John," she teased. "We'll have to collect a few bits of straw to put some value on his insinuations. Still . . ." She took on a more serious note. "I must have a word with him, a sharp word, for I've no desire to be regarded as an easy lay or any kind of a lay for that matter."

"You are already, at least in his mind."

It was still raining lightly but very dark and their progress was by the light of a torch, although for them it was a well trodden lane. It would soon be time to turn back, for there was only one way — the reverse of their current course.

"I think I have Texel weighed up." Marion said. "He's as steeped in the cast iron tradition of loyalty as we are, but for some reason he fears that by giving expression to it, he is adolescent, preferring instead to mask his feelings under a devil may care hard boiled exterior. He knows, for example that I'm no predatory female seeking to seduce you and yet he must publicly announce more or less that I am."

"You could be right, love," the navigator murmured. "He's totally loyal to Ace, yet you could not imagine a more opposite pair — on the one hand Ace who says little and on the other Texel who is garrulous. Trouble is he's got too much time on his hands, too much time to dwell on the precarious position of a bomber boy. I often feel that when a crew fails to return from ops, it twists a sharp knife in him. When I first arrived here, I thought he was the very end, horridly rude and a loud mouthed trouble maker, but I have since learned that he's really genuine, very kind and even pleasant at times, except to me," John finished ruefully.

"He saves it up for you, John. He thinks you've trodden on his corns as far as I'm concerned. Why I don't know. I've never ever given him any encouragement and in any case he's far from my type of guy."

"He'd bloody well better keep away from you, especially when I get posted." He half turned and stopped Marion in her tracks. "I love you so much I've begun to see a silver gleam of light for the future and I won't allow him to try to take you over while I'm eating my heart out in some bloody OTU."

"Now, now, darling." She was gently admonishing. "You're showing signs of jealousy and that's not a good omen for trust in each other. I happen to love you too, very much, but it is because of that love that I can endure temporary partings." John's arm tightened about her waist. Marion had said it all. He was happy. Momentarily as they reached the entrance to the WAAFery they automatically relinquished their holds, but then, oblivious of possible spectators he held her again while their lips met in a long breath-taking kiss. They were mere shadows in the deeper shade of night.

Chapter 9

IT HAPPENS TO THE BEST

The night was distinctly Novemberish and very dark. All day long stratus cloud had scudded across the sky with thick rain cloud banked up and over, giving a cloud base of about 500 feet and a possible ceiling of 18,000 feet. The heavy rain had now ceased but it was pretty chilly, so Ace lifted the heavy collar of his greatcoat to protect both neck and ears. Torch in hand he was on his way round the perimeter towards the caravan cited by the side of the runway in use. The problem was to retain in the narrow circle of hooded torch the tar macadam outline so that he was always on firm ground. As it was he was disconcerted to find that his feet seemed to pick out the biggest puddles, serving to chill those members more than somewhat. In fact, he thought irritably, he might just as well have blundered across the soggy turf to cut down the distance. But the caravan loomed in due course and he was just able to distinguish the black and white check-board pattern. As he steadily moved into the poor light from the runway flares he perceived the silhouettes of a small group of bystanders who, like him, had been brave enough to suffer the elements in order to give the battle order crews a hearty if unheard send-off.

For the umpteenth time the pilot glanced up with utter futility to try to pierce the blackness in order to estimate the cloudbase. In his opinion it was a thoroughly nasty night to take-off into. It would be pretty dodgy milling around with other Lancasters in nil visibility, all trying to gain maximum height before set course time. Not being on the battle order he had not the benefit of a Met briefing but experience was enough to convince him that tonight it was better to be anchored with both feet on the ground.

Tonight's target had to be an important one for the C-in-C to be taking calculated risks of this order. Take-off into thick cloud was a common enough circumstance and always dicey, but for some obscure reason the pilot was troubled by a vague sense of impending calamity, and it had substantial possession of his mind. He was unable to throw it off, try as he might.

From the distant dispersal the sound of Merlin engines coughing into life gradually extended into a steady murmur, increasing in intensity as more and more engines were started up. He then became aware of two vague but familiar figures standing close by. He moved up silently behind them.

"Hullo, children," he said. His subsequent hail and silent approach startled the two figures into an about turn.

"Oh H.Hello Ace," replied John. "Didn't expect you here. Still you are in better company than usual," he added meaningly. The pilot let the remark pass, for John was a dab hand at veiled insolence and his allusion to the missing Texel was not unexpected. It was not so much what the navigator said but the tone of voice. Anyway, now that he had reached his goal, Ace's irritability had largely subsided, despite the discomfort of his feet. He was impelled to see what footwear the other feet in the trio were using and was not surprised to note that his navigator had on a sensible pair of rubber gum boots. Just like John to be, like a boy scout, well prepared. Marion too had a pair of ankle high boots. Ace wondered whose idea it had been to be shod appropriately.

"Not on duty, Marion?" Ace was disposed to be sociable.

"Not today, thank goodness. My erstwhile counterpart in the watch office surprised me by getting pregnant and has been dismissed the service, which left me holding the fort absolutely, but she has been replaced now so life is a little easier."

"Yes, I heard you were having a rough time of it holding the baby — well metaphorically anyway." Ace could be considerate if he liked, but it was a remark so out of character that John gave him a quizzical look.

"What's the matter Ace?. Something troubling you?" The pilot was silent for a while and then perhaps feeling that a worry shared was a worry halved, he answered:

"Glad we're not dicing tonight. Don't like it. Can't explain. Just got a premonition of something grim about to happen."

"Imagination Ace?. Could be you know because we don't often stand here in this watching situation. If you stood here often enough, you could imagine all sorts of problems like engine cut on take-off, or a cookie working loose on the mounting."

"Maybe." Ace couldn't or wouldn't commit himself to that theory.

The first Lancaster from the far side loomed up, navigation lights dim and barely giving substance to its shape and size, seeming somehow smaller than in daylight, which was saying something when the wheel tyres alone stood as tall as an average man. With a final burst from the starboard outer engine it turned on to the runway, halting then with a hiss of brakes, lined up ready for take-off. Immediately the green aldis flashed out "clear for take-off" from the caravan and petered out as swiftly as it had appeared. From the cockpit only faint pencils of light could be seen by the watchers and the shadow of the pilot's movements as he and the flight engineer ran through final checks. Ace mentally went through the drill:

Flaps 30
Radiators closed
Lock throttles
Prepare for take-off.

It was taking a long time. He's making a meal of it thought Ace. The green light flashed out again impatiently, as if to say "get weaving", but still the Lancaster dallied, engines ticking over idly.

"Can't see whose kite it is," said John. The little group fidgeted in the cold. They had come for action, and action they expected.

"No I can't make it out." Ace's night eyes were equally inadequate. "But we may pick it up when she moves into the flarepath glow."

The motors took on an intensified note as the pilot advanced throttles evenly. The propellors previously turning over idly in a shall I, shant I jerky motion, began to windmill at speed. The delay had really only been a minute although to the spectators it had seemed much longer. The Lancaster began to quiver and vibrate while the tailplane rocked wildly on the tail wheel. Then as the brakes were released the plane lurched forward. The air to the rear was turbulent under the slipstream effect, and the motive power radiated shockwaves that smoke the eardrums. The Lancaster moved away faster now and the letter S was illuminated briefly. It was Denny's kite. Ace shot John a swift glance. His oppo Texel was aboard with the flight commander, both dicing with death. Acceleration was slow until the tail wheel came up, but finally S Sugar came off the deck, the four exhaust manifolds emitting sharp bursts of flame as the pilot strove for height. Then from each side of the runway, in turn, came the rest of the squadron, lining up, receiving the all clear and rumbling off in quick succession, finally disappearing into the low cloud. The air was alive with the roar of multiple engines like the sound of constant thunder. It was at least thirty minutes between first and last take-off, after which Marion, John and Ace turned away. The first scene in another act was over, the interval called. The last act would be hours later when the survivors rumbled back into the circuit and pancaked. In the caravan, the occupant relaxed and grabbed a cold cup of tea. He could rest awhile now unless there was sudden trouble like an emergency landing.

As the friends trod warily back towards the control tower, Ace voiced his concern in a question, that was really an appeal for reassurance.:

"How thick do you reckon that cloud is John?"

"Dunno for sure, Ace, but the main front has gone through and the ceiling coming down and breaking up. I should say, not more than 10,000 feet and that's generous. I was looking at the weather map and everything has occurred as expected."

"I don't share Met optimism," said Ace coldly. "They are at ground level."

"Must be a critical target," suggested John with a view to getting the pilot to unburden whatever was on his mind. It was unlike Ace to shy at weather conditions which were after all much better than on some occasions during their tour of ops. There was of course always the risk of collision when a large body of aircraft milled around indiscriminately in cloud, but looking at it objectively it was a big tall sky with immense capacity. Three hundred Lancasters massing over the whole county of Lincolnshire had a more than even chance of missing each other however dark the surroundings and however thick the cloud. By the time they had bypassed the control tower and got within a hundred yards of the community site, the monotonous roar of engines had lessened. Conversation had become conspicuous by it's absence and the three were looking for warmth. Then it was that quite startlingly Ace's premonition seemed to materialise, for out of the overcast sky, deep in the cloud came a tremendous flash like the fork of violent lightning followed by a yellow glow turning to red. Micro seconds later the sound of a violent explosion reached the ground and reverberated for seconds. Marion choked back an involuntary scream, pressing her knuckles to her mouth.

"What's that," she choked. "Is.. is it a plane?". She shuddered and John's arm stole firmly round her shaking shoulders.

"Sounds like a mid air prang," confirmed Ace grimly, but with a belated calm that arose from the realisation that his premonition had not been a figment of the imagination.

"Just listen to that," advised John as a new sound came upon the ear, increasing in volume all the while. The three stood transfixed listening to a high pitched whistling sound that culminated with the sudden appearance of the tail end of an aircraft shorn from the main fuselage, falling in flames seemingly very slowly. Remote the conflagration seemed at first but with every second it appeared to fall faster and in increasingly fearful aspect for it was bearing right down on them. Just visible in the mass of flame was the twin rudder section of a Lancaster.

They had an inclination to make a run for it, but Ace came up with the right reasoning:

"No point in moving," he cautioned. "It looks near but could hit the ground anywhere within a quarter of a mile." His own feet wanted him to run but logic signalled the brain to control the limbs.

Marion was in John's arms and what ever fear he had was overcome by this uncalled for moment of heaven which sent pulses racing, but her chillness sobered him up and he felt a chill run up his back like someone walking over his grave.

With a final spin and turn over, what remained of the tailplane crashed with a fearful rending sound some 60 yards away from where they were standing, just behind the Officers Mess, hurling blazing wreckage into the air. The conflagration burnt noisily, punctuated by the explosion of 303 cartridges from the rear turret, which presumably also accounted for the considerable fire.

"My God," said John, "Good job its not the forward fuselage complete with bombs or the Officers Mess would have gone up in smoke."

The pilot came to life. Previously held rigid by an inability to move limbs he went into action. He ran into the out-of-bounds Sergeants Mess simply because it was the nearest building to hand to phone the fire location to flying control from where the signal to activate the fire-tender would emanate and then dashed back to Marion and John who along with other bodies were moving towards the crash position. The fire itself was dying down but had spread into the hedge behind the Mess. The watchers were more composed now that the initial tension had eased. They watched the blazing pyre, for pyre it was — the rear gunner would have been cremated, possibly also the mid-upper gunner. The forward portion of the plane would have landed elsewhere, what was left of it and the crew would have perished, for the forward portion carried the fuel and the bombs. In fact they would have died instantly in the explosion that had rent the heavens.

"We'll probably never know whether it was one of ours or another squadron," said John. "There will be nothing identifiable left."

"Then there's the other kite," reminded Ace. Can't have a collision of one."

There were tears hanging on Marion's lower lashes threatening to roll down her face, but she had ceased to shake. Her tears were of sadness for the young men who had died over their own land, a misfortune without glamour. Involuntarily she turned to John again as she glimpsed the terrifying thought that he might have been one of them. It might have been you she almost whispered but choked back the words even as they were framed on dry lips. She had a sudden desire to seize his face in both hands and plaster him with kisses of pure possession. The navigator felt her mood and in any other place would have enjoyed the oneness, but the realities of wartime soon inched back into consciousness as he began to turn over Ace's remark. Yes there had to be another kite. If the first one was not from this squadron, this one could be, but he knew they would probably never know.

Ace was looking distraught and the look was wholly alien to him, but John sensed what it was all about. He had Denny and Texel on his mind and was unable to shake himself free.

"It couldn't have been Sugar anyway," soothed John. "Denny was in the first wave and would have gone long before it happened." The navigator's reasonable contention had something of the effect of a cold shower on the pilot.

"Yes — you're right John. I must be losing my grip."

Marion pulled herself together and linked one arm with Ace's and one with John's.

"Lets all walk," she suggested. "There's nothing we can do here." They trod a familiar route into the village without looking back and impelled by Marion, they entered the Old Cow. The Public bar was uncommonly depopulated, the atmosphere as sober as a vicarage tea party, a sure sign that the squadron was operating at pretty well maximum strength. In fact there was a complete absence of flying brevies and only a sprinkling of RAF administration bodies. In one corner two elderly gentleman stolidly moved dominoes in thoughtful fashion. Even Bert, the publican who one would have thought would have been glad of a rest, looked totally bored.

"I'll treat you both to a drink," Marion insisted. The offer produced immediate protests, but with only the insistence a women can bring to bear she brooked no argument and by way of conciliation requested Ace to order. Ace suppressed a smile and moved to the bar counter. Marion's ten bob note was burning an embarrassing scorch mark on his hand. It was pleasureable, though, to be in the company of a girl who even in wartime preserved sufficient feminity to eschew personally ordering drinks in a public house.

"Where did it fall,?" Bert the publican asked, with a worried look that reflected the concern of a man who existed almost entirely within the confines of his little empire. What news he got came to him and if it was a country mile from the communal site to the pub, then he had got the news pretty fast, though imcomplete. "Looked as it t'were comin' down on the green, I'm told." It was his business to find out all he could to relate later, for it was part of his trade, his living, to know exactly what happened in the small community.

"S'understandable," responded the pilot. "It's always difficult to judge where a falling object would fall, particularly at night." It could never be an official secret, so Ace added, "Fell behind the Officers Mess." The publican scratched his grizzled bit of hair located on the back of the neck.

"As far away as that." He came out of the effort of mental activity and applied himself to his responsibility. "Two pints of bitter and one port and lemon you said." He put effort into manipulation of the beer engines and asked: "Weren't one of ours, were it?" His mental appetite remained strong and the pilot did not fail to grasp the significance of that simple enquiry. One of ours, he repeated in soft soliloquy. One of ours might have meant any British aircraft, but the man had lodged his enquiry in the possessive sense — one of the village's squadron. It gave the pilot a peculiar feeling of warmth. It was indubitably clear that the stolid Englishman and his fellow villagers took the human affairs of the men in blue to heart in their undemonstrative manner.

"Difficult to say," replied Ace aloud. "Nothing much left to identify." He ended the brief converse by proffering Marion's ten bob note, grabbed the drinks and regained his friends who had taken up position before the open log fire drawing maximum warmth to unchill their bones.

The pilot sipped his drink with less pleasure than usual. Vaguely he perceived within himself the symptoms of that still nagging forboding, wholly unassuaged and made the painful experiment of going back over the course of the night, centreing finally on what he thought was the focal point of his concern. Why did Denny idle on the runway.? It was not as if he, Ace had imagined delay, for Denny had been reminded by caravan control to get weaving. He must then have got mechanical or electrical failure of a sort, but then decided it was insufficient reason to abort and certainly Denny would never abort unless he absolutely had to. His personal motto was like Bomber Command's. Press on regardless. Ace rubbed his eyes to bring himself back to the present aided by the sharp crack of a log bursting into flames on the hearth. It was foolish to indulge in futile conjecture.

"Cheers Marion," he said. "This tastes doubly pleasant since you were kind enough to buy the round."

"I was just beginning to wonder whether or not you were still with us," admonished the navigator.

"Sorry folks, but I'm always retiring and tonguetied in the presence of the opposite sex." Marion laughed, and replied:

"I was hoping to conserve a perfectly charming compliment from the beginning of your remark, but you ruined it by putting me in the general class of the other sex."

"No chance of that from Ace. He's much too blunt," murmured John.

"I've been meaning to ask you." Marion had got Ace going a bit and would not let go. "Have you a special girl in NZ?"

"Confessions?" queried Ace, lifting an eyebrow under which there was just a trace of a smile.

"Not if you don't wish to say. I'm not curious for curiosity's sake. I'm really interested."

"Well, there is a girl who writes to me regularly and sends parcels for which I'm grateful, mostly biscuits, not like the hard tack you get over here."

"That's lovely. What's her name?"

"Connie."

"I like the name. I hope you reply regularly." Marion was persistent and in the nature of women got to the sore point, while Ace lowered his eyes, a trifle shamefaced.

"I fear I don't." His reply was crisp. "It's difficult to say anything. I naturally can't talk about ops — I wouldn't want to — and then my literary ability is like my conversation, brief and usually to the point. That's not what a girl wants. I fancy that in the course of time letters will die a natural death."

"That would really be a pity." Marion had to take the woman's view and added: "She must be keen on you to send parcels and write, which is pretty wonderful for she must have other distractions far away in NZ." Ace's reaction to what amounted to a call for candour and to go to work on his part was devoid of any visible sign that might be construed as agreement. Certainly he did not give the impression of being madly in love when he replied:

"We grew up more or less together, but now it seems difficult to even visualise her despite the occasional prompting with a photograph."

"You are very hard hearted and unfeeling, unless of course you are putting on a face." Marion's sympathies were sundered, but she got a reply.

"Maybe, but it's not part of my wartime plan to have emotional ties. No future in it." Somewhat severely he looked in turn at Marion and John as if to say "not like you two."

"Oh my goodness." Marion slapped her forehead in disgust. "Not another one. You and John are two of a kind and I despair of your manhood. The trouble with you men is that in order to face up to what you perceive as reality, you forget entirely the human aspect. You presume, I venture to say, foolishly, that cutting yourself off from decent girls because of admittedly dicey occupation you are being wonderfully honourable. Have you ever stopped to think what we, the damsels might think? Have you ever asked?" She knew of course how John ticked but she did not want to pick on Ace as the sole sinner, or at least make it sound that way. She paused for breath and since she still had the floor, so to speak, continued. "It's not for me to advise. I'm not qualified to judge in your case what you could be to each other, but I really do think you could at least write more often. Let her feel she's important and wanted." The Pilot shook his head. He clearly did not want to be persuaded:

"No future in that," he persisted, but Marion could be equally pressing.

"Have you stopped to think that perhaps the most important thing in Connie's life is waiting to get your letter? Pretty hard on her when it does not come."

"Maybe." Ace's rejoinder was a cross between acceptance of Marion's advice and non acceptance, non committal. On the other hand Marion was aware that whatever was said to Ace would not go in one ear and out the other. He would chew it over and file for future reference, so she ceased to badger him. The navigator however was far from content to let the matter rest. He had not twigged that Marion was really only getting at Ace and preferred to imagine that he was also in the doghouse, but he could sort that one out later. In the meantime he was constrained to remember that Ace and Texel were jointly concerned in levelling accusations at him in respect of his relationship with Marion, even if Ace was the junior partner, so he decided to nibble at the bone a bit.

"No sense in talking to Ace like that, love," he advised. "Hasn't a drop of warm blood in his veins. Presumably he wasn't born like that so its got to be a case of all change and decay. Do you know I've never so much as seen him measure up a shapely pair of silken legs." But Ace was hard to provoke.

"There's a difference between cautious distant admiration and making a meal of it," he replied.

"Rubbish." John had no doubt about it. "Do you know that little blonde dental orderly, Marion, — attractive girl. Seemed to get a bit of a crush on Ace. She could not take her eyes off him and when they did get to talk, guess how he got rid of her.

He said and I quote "Is it worth my while to walk you home? God, I gather she made a run for it."

"Gotta have self protection, John boy." Ace was really grinning now, the first time this evening. "You could do with a touch of the same technique."

"I remember now." Marion remembered something Texel had said. "So it was true what Texel said. He was referring to the dental orderly."

"That's right." Ace was not out of countenance for his conscience was clear. "But Texel put quite the wrong construction on it. I was being pestered, more or less, so I put an end to it right smartly."

Closing time rushed up and by then the mood was pleasantly bantering, but as they moved out into the night Ace bid Marion and John an abrupt Goodnight and shambled off towards the Mess to await the Squadron's return. All his earlier fears were back again and he could share them with no one.

The night was cold, but the cloud had disappeared and the stars made a rare November appearance. It was no night to hang about.

It was 0100 hours. Ace sprawled across two lounge chairs in the Officers Mess, half awake, half asleep. By his side the radio was tuned in to short wave transmission, but only silence echoed from the receiver except for some static. He was alone as he waited to pick up the first ground to air, or vice versa communications between returning aircraft and flying control. The rest of the communal site was in total darkness and only a single lamp was on in the mess allowing restricted light. A mile and a half away on the airfield flying control personnel were, if not awake, on the brink of it for they could expect returning Lancasters during the next half hour and thereafter. There were too, in varying states of readiness the aircraft marshallers, motor transport drivers, ambulance and fire tender drivers, debriefing experts all ready to leap into action when the first call came, and the runway flares had to be lit.

Suddenly Ace was startled into complete wakefulness by sudden static from the receiver. In a flash he knew the incoming pilot had depressed the transmission button, and a vaguely familiar voice, somewhat distorted came on the air, "Manger Charlie to Bakewell. How do you read me?" and the silken voice of the WAAF R/T operator replied immediately.

"Charlie clear to land. Runway 30."

Ace's own prodigy was in Charlie. Plt Off Chatterforth had come with Ace on a trip to Hamburg as a second dickey and here he was, thought Ace, walking in the steps of his instructor, first back. Jolly good show. The recumbent pilot had a surge of elation in the knowledge that Bill Chatterforth, still relatively new to the Squadron had accomplished another op, presumably successfully.

"Hi Bakewell. Manger Freddie. Permission to pancake." Couldn't miss the rasping Canadian voice of 'A' flight's Ransom. The latter with his all Commonwealth crew were as flak happy as they come, dangerously so. Danger Ransom just did not bother about and that was usually a bad omen. Notwithstanding, he was a darned good pilot and second home tonight, a fact that would not please him overmuch since with Ace out of the running he had been expecting to make the first slot. The reply from the control was not quite so prompt.

"Bakewell to Freddie. Your turn to land number 2. Circle at 1000 feet. Standby."

"Ok Bakewell, but make it snappy," and then a moment or two later:

"Freddie from Bakewell. Clear to land. Call downwind."

And so it went on. Where the hell was Denny Ace asked himself for the Sqn Ldr liked to be home first and when he and Ace were on the battle order they vied for the status of home first. With a progressively sinking heart he listened to a string of calls, but no S Sugar. Then eventually there were no more. All were back except Sqn Ldr Denning and Flt Lt Hall the 'B' flight deputy commander. "A" flight had got away with it with all Lancasters returned safely. Fleetingly Ace Burnett recalled his flight commander's passing words much earlier in the day "You never know Ace you might be flight commander tomorrow." Ace hoped they would not be famous last words. But why did Denny have to make such a clottish remark? It was asking for trouble. Yet, Ace consoled himself, all was not absolutely lost. Denny might have had to lob down on another airfield for lack of fuel or even at the emergency airfield on the coast built for just such a purpose. Control might know. He sprang from his chair and reached for the blower.

"Flying Control", he asked for and got.

"Flying control here."

"Burnett. Any news of Sqn Ldr Denning and Flt Lt Hall. No?. Thank you.......Yes, I'll be in the Mess."

There was no news, but it was still possible that a landing had been effected elsewhere but not yet notified. Aimlessly he paced the ante room. What a cow of a day it had been. Miserably he recalled that his forebodings had had some substance, but there was nothing to do but wait. He paused in his shambling walk. It seemed that he would have to accept that Denny and crew had been consigned to a far distant grave or ended up as dust in the air, for it was now long past the time when even a crippled Lancaster would have made landfall. There was a chance they had bailed out provided that the aircraft was partially controllable and did not get into a spin, or explode of course, in which case together with escape packs they would first have to evade capture by the enemy to effect sanctuary in neutral territory and finally reach home later, much later. There was another possibility. They might have ditched in the drink, but that was cold comfort. Ditching in the sea was a hazardous circumstance in broad daylight when success depended upon the pilot's ability to lob down flatly at about 90 mph. If the sea was rough the chance of ditching successfully was considerably less and ultimate survival always depended upon being found by the RAF Air Sea Rescue Service. But ditching at night — Oh dear — a horrible thought. In pitch blackness, perhaps with the aid of the spotlight, but not necessarily so if the electrics were up the wall, it was all in a new dimension, for it would be terribly difficult to judge the height off the water and also to assess whether or not the sea was rough. Still it had been done and there was a slim chance that Denny, Texel and the rest of the crew were even now composing themselves in a dinghy that was at the mercy of the North Sea.

He was grasping at straws. He knew that, but suddenly he became coldly sensible and more controlled. What was the point of futile speculation? He had to be losing his grip. He slumped again into his chair, somewhat cold and chilled. Despite the cold, his head nodded onto chest as the will to remain awake lost strength. Sleep claimed him mercifully.

Midway across the English Channel, between the Dutch island of Walcheren on the one side and the English town of Southwold on the Suffolk coast, a lone Lancaster moved with some difficulty towards the homeland. If the aircraft's passage through the air was erratic and the tracking to the south of the planned route, she was heading in the right general direction. At the controls a tight lipped pilot struggled against pain that threatened to engulf him and a flying machine that had lost its natural flying equipoise. The slightest relaxation of firm manual control by the pilot allowed the Lancaster to turn itself into a missile, projected downwards under the influence of gravity towards the black chill sea, only 8000 feet below. Just the sheer physical strength of the pilot and matching will power stood between continued lame flight and a dive into the drink. It was a battle for survival cold and clear, for he was stricken with both arm and leg wounds. He only had to apply more than a little pressure to the rudder bars to feel searing pain that dulled the brain, sapped the will to go on. It was bloody cold too for there were gashes in the cockpit perspex and jagged holes in the fuselage.

"How long to the coast?" Sqn Ldr bit out the question with a hiss through clenched teeth as once again he relaxed pressure on the control column and had to correct painfully. But if there was agony in his voice the fact that he spoke at all was a tonic to his silent crew. The only question was — how long could he keep it up?

"No more than 15 minutes, Sir." The navigator's reply though coldly tense was controlled.

"Thank God for that," murmured Denny. It was an incentive to keep going. He screwed up watering eyes, peered through the damaged windscreen and prayed for some strange telescoping of time. For once he could tolerate a timing error in the navigator's calculations provided that it put his Lancaster nearer land than currently anticipated, but he knew there was little hope of that.

F.Sgt Tex Hanson was shaken but calm. He was unhurt but there was a large singed tear in his flying jacket signifying a very near miss and he had to consider himself lucky. For the hundredth time he glanced at the pilot's white face which seemed to stand out even more vividly against the dark surround of flying helmet with every passing minute. He, Texel, more than the rest of the crew, was fully aware of the pilot's extreme discomfiture and he, Texel, was leaving nothing to chance. He was poised to grab the control column should his skipper black out. At that point, he knew the Lancaster would go into a dive by reason of the hammering a number of it's mechanical functions had received. While he had schooled himself to accept the prospect of taking over he could not view the outlook with any less apprehension for he had no training as a pilot. It was true he knew all the settings and required engine revolutions. He could read the cockpit instrumentation as well as any pilot, but putting the theory to material use under the present extremely dodgy conditions was an altogether different kettle of fish and with that thought in mind he ruefully reflected that they might yet all provide food for the fishes. The biggest snag of all was that the Lancaster was without dual control. So, if the pilot flaked out he would have to lean over to grasp the column while the navigator removed the dead weight of a burly pilot from his seat. It would be no easy matter. Unless Denny could be got out quickly enough to allow Texel to gain rudder control the grim reaper would be holding out welcoming hands.

Texel had quietly arranged with the navigator to provide emergency assistance if required. Now he licked dry lips although the long drawn out struggle back from the target area had to some extent neutralised fear. All the way he had expected to have the riddle of death revealed to him, but hoped the event would be postponed. With each mile of progress his hopes grew, albeit cautiously. A glance through the perspex to starboard revealed the outboard engine still turning merrily beyond the inboard that was dead and feathered. On the port side the situation was identical. Thank God it was a four engined job and would fly on two. The bigger problem was the state of the rudders for the tail plane was clearly damaged and the tip of one wing had disappeared, which meant landing problems, to say the very least. Then again there had to be damage which at this stage it was impossible to assess.

While the navigator laboured on, checking and rechecking for a mere minute of time could be the margin between life and death, the wireless op was playing nurse to the mid Upper gunner who was lying on the bunk in the relatively hazy state induced by a morphine injection. The gunner's leg was pretty bad but the wireless op had stemmed the blood flow with a tourniquet.

It had all started at the termination of S Sugar's bombing run over the Big City (Berlin). Denny had just completed a masterly straight and level run and was holding steady for the photoflash when the Lancaster was hit by the blast of a heavy ack ack shell bursting close at hand, and it was at this point that the mid upper gunner had been hit. Two engines caught fire, were extinguished and feathered, but the resultant loss of speed left the Lancaster trailing to the rear of the bomber force and open to fighter attack, the lone bomber showing up as an identifiable blip on enemy radar. Within an hour to go to the sea boundary of enemy occupied territory, S Sugar became a target. The pursuing fighter homed in, but was spotted. With astute pilotage and integrated co-operation from the tail end gunner the first attack was rendered void, but the Nazi pilot sensed a lame duck or more likely he had noted only two exhaust emissions. Whatever the reason he came again out of the blackness squirting cannon shells which severely damaged the tail plane and at the same time wounded Sqn Ldr Denning. Then it was when the game seemed to have been played out, the enemy fighter came in again for the final kill with rather less caution to catch the full blast of the tail end gunners salvo and had to sheer of, flames spewing from it. Thus it was that having survived a close flak burst and three fighter attacks, the navigator had engineered an approach to the emergency landing drome at Woodbridge, and the height carefully nursed was down to 3000 feet.

Denny switched on to transmit.

"Mayday, Mayday, S Sugar requests emergency landing instructions."

Woodbridge was quick off the mark as befits an emergency landing drome.

"S Sugar, you are clear to land. State nature of your emergency."

"Request ambulance and fire tenders."

"OK Sugar. You are three miles from touchdown."

If Denny could hold out now, there was chance he could effect a landing of sorts. It was encouraging that there was greater clarity in his speech on RT, but it might be only a moment's uplift. He could pass out at any time.

Texel's worries were now really on line. The loss of two motors was not catastrophic, but the full extent of damage to the Lancaster was unknown. He had the distinct feeling of cold water trickling down the spine when it occurred to him that in all probability the wheels would not come down, or if they did, not lock down. Texel came out of reflection to the immediate present when the pilot's irate voice homed in on him accompanied by a smart slap on the back of the head, which was the pilot's normal method of attracting his flight engineer's attention, as the latter was supposed to be deaf in the air for no accountable reason. For once Texel enjoyed the slap, for it meant Denny was still conscious.

"Listen you clot. Can you see the coastline?"

"Yes Sir and Woodbridge landing lights slightly to starboard," replied Texel.

"Woodbridge? What the hell are we doing so far south?" asked Denny angrily.

"Emergency landing facilities", replied the navigator quickly for he did not want the pilot to burst a blood vessel in addition to his other problems. "Shortest route from enemy coast," he added.

"Sorry navigator." Even in pain the Sqn Ldr was apologetic. "Should have known you'd have your finger out."

The extensive emergency airfield was lit invitingly with its uncommonly wide 3 lane runways from East to West.

"Select centre lane," came the instruction from flying control, "Repeat centre lane."

"Sugar here. Confirm Centre lane." Denny was as brief as possible. "Turn out the bloodwagon."

"OK Sugar. Good luck."

No orthodox circuit was necessary. It was merely a question of losing height to touchdown, a judgement that at night was always dodgy calling for skill and experience. The approach had to be good this time for they could not afford to take the extra risks of an overshoot.

"Flaps 20 idiot." Denny spat it out.

"There ain't None," replied Texel. The pilot turned slightly to look at his flight engineer who half shrugged.

"Wheels down," Denny tried again.

"Wheels down," echoed Texel, whose eyes were on the dashboard where two green lights should come on to indicate wheels locked down. There were no green lights. Denny groaned. It was too much to ask for everything to be in working order. Hell, their life was one of taking risks. What was another one.

"Can you see if wheels are down," Texel asked the bomb aimer.

"Yep. They are down alright, but whether locked........." He broke off. The whole crew knew it was likely to be a crash landing for without flaps the Lancaster would have to come in fast.

"Skipper to crew. Safety belts. Bomb aimer come up fast." Denny was half way to being brisk.

They were over the leading glims. The navigator was reading the airspeed 125. 125. 120. 120. Texel's eyes were glued on his pilot. The port wing dropped. Denny painfully used two hands to regain stability.

We're coming in too fast, thought Texel, but then, what choice have we got.

"Get ready to cut throttles." The flight commander just about managed to get the words out.

"OK sir. Ready and waiting." Texel tried to sound confident.

"Cut." The command was brief. The flight engineer whipped the throttles back and braced himself as the Lancaster hit the deck with a sickening crump. With the speed not seeming to slacken the aeroplane began to slew starboard as the starboard leg of the undercart collapsed with a horrible grinding sound. Before Texel's eyes the landing lights began to gyrate clockwise like the window lights of a passing express train. He was jerked violently to one side taking a severe blow on the head. Senses swam and through the ensuing pain, oblivion reached out for him.

Ace slept uneasily, the prey of conflicting dreams. The telephone was ringing in the flight office. He picked up the receiver but it was as dead as a doornail. He walked the corridor to the other offices and the bell was ringing again. He picked up 'A' Flight office phone. It made no difference. The bell was still going it. Then it seemed that a host of bells were ringing, all insistently demanding attention. Louder and louder they shrilled out beating on Ace's eardrums like some vile Gestapo contrived torture. He had a feeling of total panic. Hands clasped over ears which made not the slightest difference, he ran out of the flights block, tripped and measured his length on the concrete path. He re-occupied the real world with a start to find himself unaccountably on the floor of the ante room in front of the chair in which he had dozed off, and in a posture rather less than comfortable. He fell to wondering how he could possibly have slipped from a reasonably capacious chair complete with armrests, until he began to recall vaguely his nightmare and those bloody telephones. God, he thought, the bloody telephone is still ringing and so it was. He recalled that he had remained in the ante room for the sole purpose of getting a good news call. He slipped through the open door and detached the receiver.

"Burnett here," he said. "Landed at Woodbridge?. Jolly good..... Hurt? Badly? Oh good. Any news of Flt Lt Hall.....Tough titty. Thanks for the call." The blood coursed freely in his veins again. Denny and the mid upper were in hospital, which wasn't exactly good news but it was better than expected. The wounds would heal and the shock wear off. Texel was in sick bay suffering from a concussion, as was the bombaimer. That would cut Texel's cackle for a few days.

Somewhat more brisk in movement, Ace returned to the ante room, turned out the single light bulb that had been his sole companion for hours, dragged on his greatcoat and plodded towards sleeping quarters.

Chapter 10

GET HIM OUT OF HERE

Two whole days had passed since the dreadful night when "B" flight lowered its pennant, so to speak, in memory of the deputy flight commander and his crew, missing believed killed, when it nearly lost the Flight Commander and crew, and when the tail section of a burning Lancaster had crashed just behind the Officers Mess. On this the third morning the flight office was crowded to capacity, mainly because the previous night had been non-operational.

Outside it was pretty murky with Lincolnshire's special brand of fog swirling across the airfield in thick banks, thinning only at times, just sufficient to be able to trace the outline of the maintenance hangar and the control tower. It was just as foggy in 'B' flight office, the atmosphere made up of a combination of infiltrated fog and cigarette smoke. Crowded around and on the few utility chairs or perched on the low window ledges, the pilots talked "shop." They talked about the last op, the numbers missing from the whole of the Command, the next target, aircraft faults or particular characteristics in the detached way of a group where fatalism and cynicism were easy habits of the mind.

There was however one difference. Where the Sqn Ldr normally parked his posterior, Ace was sitting leafing through serviceability reports, although his mind was not wholly in tune with the task. He had been told that Denny was fretting more than somewhat in an East Anglian hospital, causing no little distress to the little band of dedicated nursing staff in an effort to get himself discharged from what he regarded as nothing less than a prison, but the real bad news was that given him by the Wing Co, who had earlier summoned Ace to the presence.

"You're acting flight commander for the time being," Wing Co had said tersely.

"Yes Sir." One could not but agree with a Wing Co. "But I've only one trip to do. I don't want to be held back."

Wing Co sat up straight in his chair and looked for a moment as if he was grinding his teeth, but sternness gave way to the ghost of an understanding smile.

"Of course, Burnett. You've been so long with us by current standards, I had envisaged you and your crew as permanent features of the establishment. However, for the moment, I expect your sense of responsibility to override personal goals. I know you are not the most senior officer in the flight due to overdue commissioning, but circumstances require someone who knows the ropes." He paused for a second to see if there was a further reaction and receiving nothing more than a poker face of wintry aspect he continued quietly:

"Don't think I don't know how you feel Burnett. I've experienced the same emotion — you wonder just how high is the final fence."

Ace was not all that pleased to be regarded like a horse, but he understood the analogy. He had not worried unduly over previous operations, but now he was numerically one short of the final fence it was beginning to be a real barrier psychologically. The Wing Co was right. What was so important about number 30? Wing Co should know. After all he was on his third tour of operations and he was still around.

"Very good Sir, I'll do my best."

"I know you will." Wing Co could now afford to be charitable. "I assure you you'll not be held back a moment longer than necessary, the more so since chaps of your experience are badly needed as instructors. In the meantime, see that the crews get maximum bombing practice on the range."

Ace had saluted smartly and retired in good order. There was no point in doing otherwise. One could not argue with three rings. In any case he had got a bit of a glow from the interview, for the Wing Co's decision was a tribute to both his experience and standing. Thus it was that Ace occupied the chair without dissent.

The telephone buzzed, an event that usually produced absolute silence in the flight office, but for once no one paid it serious attention. It was accepted that with a fog forecast for day and more dense at night with a particular worsening in the early hours of morning, ops were unlikely, and Ace quickly confirmed the view.

"OK jokers. Pukka standdown. You can all scram, except for Plt Off Bushell. The flight office emptied so fast that the inside fog almost went with them, leaving Ace with a new Pilot Officer in the unsullied flush of youth and just 20 years of age.

"Better take a pew. I wouldn't offer you a fag as I roll my own. Found nobody likes them. Cheap way of smoking."

"Thanks, but I've got my own," replied Bushell taking a packet of Victory V's from his pocket.

"You don't smoke those things surely," said Ace. "I've heard they have already created more casualties than the war itself. I've heard say they're half camel dung, but I don't know what the other half is." Bushell grinned now wholly at ease.

"Don't usually smoke 'em but I've run through my supply of Sweet Caporals I brought back from training in Canada."

Ace leaned back in his chair and blew smoke-rings, aware all the time that the new pilot of equal rank had earlier eyed him with some puzzlement. He knew too, that the new man was wondering why a mere Pilot Officer was apparently in command and in his own time Ace took the mute enquiry to its logical conclusion by issuing a brief explanation.

"You're wondering about me," he said at last and the young man blushed like a young girl accosted by her first boy friend. "I've been delegated to act in the temporary absence of Sqn Ldr Denning, who is in hospital."

"Not seriously ill, I trust."

"Well he doesn't think so," replied Ace. "He's in hospital in East Anglia." Bushell appeared to be more puzzled than ever but repressed his inclination to enquire further in adult fashion, and then it dawned on Ace that the young fellow had not heard about Denny.

"Got chopped up a bit on a trip to the Big City."

"The Big City?"

"Berlin." Even Ace was surprised that the young pilot did not know the pseudonym for the German capital until he remembered that OTU did not really prepare young pilots adequately for the squadrons — it was merely an extension of flying practice. Ace went on, "and now he's taken the war into the hospital. Just doesn't like hospitality." He was quite pleased the way he'd put that, but pulled himself up a bit sharpish when he noted the slight palour on the new young fellow's face, with perhaps just a faint quiver about the lips which he was rapidly counteracting by sticking out a chin resolutely.

Bushell had not until this moment come up against a real battle hardened pilot, who it seemed, judging by his mode of expression, treated disfigurement and injury with such nonchalance. Ace, on the other hand was learning a lesson of his own and paused to wonder whether he had been so green when he'd first arrived on the squadron. On balance he felt that his responsibility as acting flight commander was to disabuse the new young pilot of the idea that going on ops was a tea party and bring home a sharp sense of realism when the apron strings must be severed unconditionally. He had to demonstrate here and now the brutal fact of life that flying bombers might well be a youthful adventure but that it was also a thoroughly dicey business. It was on the basis of this reasoning that he decided to rub it in a bit.

"Flt Lt Hall, the deputy flight commander also bought it the same night, which is why I welcome you to 'B' flight as a replacement for those gone before." To mellow the bald statement he continued: "We're not, I think, such a bad bunch, although a bit rough and boozy at times, but that's part of this life." He watched Bushell through half closed eyes, but there appeared to be nothing now but determination almost fiercely displayed. "So," he went on, "as far as ops are concerned you won't be pushed into the fray prematurely, so just mosey around and get the lay out, find where everything is sited. Weather permitting we'll have you in the air on bombing practice first. Then we'll send you as second dickey with an experienced crew just to see what it's all about and get the feel of it. Then you watch and start learning fast."

"But I thought Squadrons were short of crews and I'd be needed right away." Bushell was mildly remonstrative. He had obviously anticipated being thrust into the air from the word go.

"We are," replied Ace briskly, "but it so happens we're not exactly chokka with kites. You'll probably do your second dickey trip with me, since an extra bod in the kite is not popular with most crews as it crowds the accommodation, but I'm easy."

Ace forebore from explaining that some pilots regarded passengers as jinxes, since he did not think it necessary to overdo the heavy stuff. Thus he continued in informative vein, "In the daytime Lincoln Cathedral sticks up a mile in the sky and is therefore a decent landmark, so be careful not to knock off the spire. At night you can't see it so it's a dangerous obstruction. There was some talk about putting a red light on it, but I gather the Bishop doesn't want it viewed as a red light area." Bushell was now sufficiently relaxed to smile and Ace went on again. "There are so many bomber airfields around here you don't know whether you are on arse or elbow. At night it's a picture with all the ident beacons burping out morse identification and unless you can read morsecode you'll never find your own airfield."

"Have you ever landed on the wrong field?" queried Bushell.

"Sure thing. Twice due to bad weather and not because we could not read our own beacon. Main thing is to set your wheels down somewhere friendly on this side of the channel. But enough of all this for now. If the fog doesn't lift soon, we'll have forgotten how to fly." With that he rose languidly and unhitched greatcoat from a peg. "We're closing shop for today. If you're heading for the Mess, I'll introduce you to some of the shower."

"I'd like that. Would feel quite lost among new faces."

"You'll soon get to know them. As I said, they are a pretty good bunch — cream of Britain's youth, you know." Ace paused in the middle of buttoning his greatcoat. "There's just one other thing. When I first arrived on the squadron I was well advised. Don't be afraid to ask. Nobody will think it unusual. I suggest you get in touch with my crew. They're a curious lot, but have got a few clues. Came up the hard way. Let's go."

The two pilots reached the Mess a half hour later, but not without difficulty for although Ace knew the way like the back of his hand, a Lincoln fog was a force to be reckoned with. One moment it thinned to acceptable visibility and then visibility was nil, a dense bank blotting out the topography as effectively as an arctic blizzard. They missed the first entrance to the communal site that lead to the respective Messes until a sudden thinning of the fog threw the guard room at the main gate into proper perspective. Once the necessity for pathfinding was gone, they relaxed and Ace spoke again as they got to the Officers' Mess entrance.

"Is your navigator OK?" he asked innocently.

"Yes. He's classed as Above Average both at Air Observer School and at OTU," replied Bushell with just a modicum of possessive proudness that reflected sober confidence.

"That's useful." Ace acknowledged and meant it. "Good navigators are a rare breed and their unenviable task goes unrecognised in some quarters, although I wouldn't tell 'em so. Cocky enough at times. But a good nav has got to use his loaf as well as his training. It's like road sense — he's got to anticipate." Ace flung open the Mess entrance door. "I take it he was commissioned straight from training."

"Yes, like me." Bushell did not see anything unusual in that.

"Well so long as he's prepared to accept advice from more experienced NCOs, he'll get by. Some of the boys came through training before there was automatic commissioning and have been forgotten on the squadrons. Fact is, both my nav and myself are only recently commissioned and that only occurred by chance."

A long row of greatcoats surmounted by cheesecutters or the less dressy forage caps occupied pegs arrayed along one side of the hall. Normally at this hour in the middle morning the mess would have been practically empty, for either of two reasons. The first, they would have been sleeping it off if ops had been on the previous night, or if ops were scheduled for the current night they would have been down at the flights taking-off or preparing to take-off on night flying tests. Today the likelihood was that the Mess would remain pretty active, for not only was it just about the warmest place on the establishment, but also only fools would venture forth far from identifiable boundaries on such a day unless the fog lifted.

Ace made his way to the ante room.

"There's my navigator Plt Off John Howard talking to a new face," he said, and pointed towards a group of Officers who were warming posteriors before a roaring log fire. "Could be our respective navs have got together already."

"Looks like it. That's my nav there."

"Right, let's horn in. John can be sociable when it suits him and he's looking affable. We'll make the most of it."

John turned without surprise as Ace approached, to allow a little warmth to reach out to his pilot. He still had the ability to know precisely when his skipper was around without visual assistance.

"'Lo Ace," he greeted the pilot blandly. "Completed your onerous duties for the day?"

"Bad start. I was just telling Bushell here what a sociable fellow you are and all I get is sarcasm."

"Just plain curiosity Ace, coupled with a certain protective feeling. Don't want you to knock yourself up or I might have to do the driving as well as the navigating."

"Well, effect a landing," suggested Ace, "and cut the cackle. This is Plt Off Bushell, new to 'B' flight. This is John Howard, a better lover than navigator."

"How d'ye do." John shook hands with the new pilot. "Just been talking to Johnny Fairfield here — your nav I believe. Johnny, this is Ace Burnett, prune pilot and acting unpaid flight commander."

"Hi." Ace shook hands. He could expect his navigator to continue and he was right.

"It's an education flying with Ace, or rather landing with him. After the first touchdown bump, we add a few minutes airborne time before the wheels stay down." The remark produced a couple of laughs which had the merit of breaking the ice.

"What are you planning to do, today, Ace?" asked John. "Marion and I thought you might come into Lincoln with us later if the fog lifts." Ace scratched his head before replying.

"If the fog clears this afternoon as Met say it will, I'm figuring on making a flying visit to Denny and Tex."

"That means it'll persist all day," muttered the navigator with unfounded pessimism.

"Met are confident enough, but it'll close in again after dark. Want to get airborne with me?"

"I see. You need me to show you the way." John grinned at the two new officers who were a bit bemused for they were not certain if the navigator was being serious and their own relationship was so very different. "Never did meet a driver who could find his nose before his face."

"Only wanted you to carry the maps," Ace replied. "Are you coming or not, or do you need to get your girl friends permission first?"

"She's not off duty until this evening, but we had better be back by nightfall, fog or no fog." It was Ace's turn to do a bit of stirring and he did wink at Bushell.

"You won't be so keen when you know which kite I'm taking," he said.

"You — not the Oxford. You've never flown one before."

"Piece of cake, Joker. Only two engines. Much simpler altogether."

"Count me out," moaned John. "I'm no longer keen — in fact I'm dead scared. Don't mind so much buying it on ops — seems pretty respectable way to go, but in a two engined Oxford with the pilot going solo, so to speak — any of you chaps like to volunteer?" All his entreaty got was restrained mirth.

"When you've finished burbling, I'll have your decision," said Ace.

"Oh Lord. Can't let the side down I suppose. Can't let you get lost, but take note everyone — this is my Last Will and Testament. I want a wreath of red roses."

"Hark at him drivelling," scoffed Ace. "All he has to do is sit tight and pray." He turned to Bushell and Fairfield. "With a bit of luck we'll be back for dinner. What about wading down to the Old Cow in the village after dinner. Not a bad pub. Can't speak for the company of course." The two new boys nodded eager acceptance, pleased to feel not so alone.

"It's a date then. 2030 hours. Coming John?"

"Sure. Anything you say Flight Commander. I'm in your hands."

As they stepped out of the Mess, the sun was shaking itself free of the fog.

The Hospital was administered by the RAF, although it sometimes accommodated patients from the lesser services like the Navy and Army. Its reputation as an establishment for specialized treatment was of the highest order, particularly in the matter of repairing war wounds, not too serious burns and crushed bones One would hardly have reasoned that it was indeed a hospital from the exterior view, for it looked more a mellowed mansion with Georgian windows over which a mass of ivy strove for absolute control. Standing in five acres and a quarter of fine, well tended grounds on which a fair measure of Jankers must have been lavished, it looked secretively out of a cluster of tall beeches on to the generally flat countryside. At some time in the distant past it must have been owned or at least tenanted by a noble Lord or at the very least the local moneyed Squire. The only thing that really spoiled it all was a pungent aroma of ether or other allied medications that easily escaped through the massive front door like a sort of welcoming scowl.

Ace and John entered the main entrance with some trepidation that was not altogether unjustified since they were immediately accosted by a superior looking woman of indeterminate age, who demanded to know the reason for their attendance in a peremptory manner and in a voice like a cannon in a subterranean cavern. Her piercing look held all the menace of a rattlesnake about to strike, which, to say the least, was highly disconcerting.

"I'm visiting Sqn Ldr Denning," said Ace doing his best to emulate the dragon, while John took shelter in the lee of Ace.

"Oh. Him." She said it with a capital H after drawing in her breath in one enormous swoop before exhaling loudly. "Have you made an appointment?"

"Our visit was arranged by phone, Madam," replied Ace, courtesy itself, putting on a pronounced colonial twang as if to suggest that he'd travelled from the antipodes to effect the visit. It worked — more or less. A touch of humanity seemed to be radiated as she said with much less of a bark:

"Have the goodness to wait in the Waiting Room," whereupon she departed to duties unspecified in a truly matronly manner.

John and Ace backed into the waiting room a shade sheepishly, but almost immediately a nursing Sister of more pleasant aspect appeared, white cap jauntily mounted on a superb head of hair.

"Sqn Ldr Denning's visitors?" she asked.

"That's us," said John.

"Then come this way please." She preceded them in stately gait with brisk steps beneath a most shapely pair of legs not overenhanced by rather thick stockings. At the end of the hall she halted before double swing doors from behind which subdued murmurs of conversation were easily audible. "Your patient is in the room on the left just inside this ward," she volunteered. "Quite a boy. You can have him." Despite her tone of deprecation she managed a smile, which Ace and John returned more openly.

A long ward was revealed with beds aligning the long walls, all of which were occupied by patients mostly in a state of some disability and who seemed pretty cheerful, despite the dragon in the wings. On the left was a smaller room, enclosed and remote from the rest of the ward. It was not long before it could be seen that the state of cheer in the main ward arose from the goings on in Denny's room and then Denny's voice boomed out:

"Get out of here. I don't want you bloody females around me."

"We're in the right place," murmured Ace.

They pushed open the door and flattened themselves to the wall as a distinctly attractive wench of a nurse with angry inflamed countenance and set lips flounced past carrying all before her, mincing away rapidly.

"Sqn Ldr Denning, Sir," said Ace. "We heard you were in residence."

"Get OUT. Oh, it's you Ace, come in my dear fellow. Thought you were the quack. Come in Howard, don't be shy. I won't bite and put the bit of wood in the hole. It's a change to have human beings around me again. Pull up a couple of pews. I'm honoured to have a member of the navigators' union visiting a poor bloody driver."

"How's tricks? Feeding you well?" asked Ace.

"Where do you think we are — at the Zoo? Oh hell. Yes food's not bad. I keep telling them I'm OK, but they won't let me out of prison. All I get is honeyed phrases and what do you think? They pinched my clothes."

"How do you know?" Ace cocked an enquiring eye.

"Because I got out of bed and bloody well looked."

"Take it you're not considered well enough to blow," John said helpfully.

"So they tell me." Denny was simmering down and spoke wearily. "I've got a chunk out of my leg which is no problem. Same with the arm." He half waved a bulky sling. "Only a matter of time."

"You do look a bit seedy though." Ace was trying hard to help the nursing staff by piling on the agony and getting Denny to view his temporary incapacity with more forebearance.

Denny glowered, pale as he was:

"Look here Ace, If you are going to align yourself with the enemy you can sling your hook. It's like a prison camp." Ace and John were unable to restrain mirth at Denny's dejected look. Denny had to relax.

"Can it you two. Tell me the news."

"Well I've been detailed to keep an eye on things by Wing Co, till you return. Piece of cake so far. Nothing doing with widespread fog around."

"Where's Hall?" asked Denny quietly.

"Got the chop, same night as you had a minor problem." There was a short silence, a sort of remembrance.

"Hell's bells," said Denny at last. "At this rate, I won't have a flight to come back to. You must only have one to do, Ace."

"Too right."

"No idea what happened to Hall of course." Denny was still shocked at Ace's news.

"Usual — just didn't return. Got a new crew, pilot Plt Off Bushell."

"Trust you had a little heart to heart talk in the Denning mode."

"Sure, Sir, shot him all the big lines. Not a bad chap."

"Cheeky sod." Denny managed to get in a short laugh. "By the way Texel left here this morning. Should be back on station by now. Over his concussion but got to take it easy for a while. Nasty knock. My bombaimer is also discharged, but mid gunner will be non-operational for some months."

"You were not concussed then." John thought he ought to justify his attendance by getting in a word.

"Too hard a head, my boy."

"Texel should have waited. We would have given him a lift in the Oxford," Ace said, and John groaned.

"He wouldn't be such a bloody fool." John was quite sure of that and said so.

"You want to watch that, Ace. Oxford's not built for your rough handling."

"How right you are Sir," said John. "When we took off we practically went straight up. Ace must have thought we had a bomb load to get off the deck."

The three men nattered consequentially and inconsequentially until a timid knock preceded a pretty brunette nurse complete with tea tray, which rather looked as if Ace really had impressed the Matron.

"Bring on the dancing girls," suggested Ace and the nurse coloured up most attractively. Denny was surprised. He remarked that the first sign of hospitality seemed to have arrived with visitors. The way he said it gave one the impression that he had been in solitary confinement on bread and water merely. The very trim armful of femininity allowed a ghost of a smile to dimple oval face. She had not before had the dubious privilege of attending on the erratic Sqn Ldr. She carefully removed some clobber from the bedside table to make room for the tea tray and Denny smiled at her. Bearing in mind his reputation she averted her eyes shyly, but then she felt drawn by some hypnotic influence and ventured a timid glance. She was quite shocked this time to be on the receiving end of a broad wink together with a distinct look of appraisal, although clearly with nothing remotely indecent to it. A slow flush measured the distance between her dinky pair of ears. It was not that she had not been winked at before, oh no, she was used to such goings on mainly from young men scarcely dry behind the ears. It was just that the wink was totally unexpected after all the chat about the liverish Officer. Nevertheless all the skill of budding womanhood came to her aid as she allowed long eyelashes to drop demurely over twin pools of brightness in a most becoming manner before turning calmly towards the door, contriving to appear wholly controlled, while the now fading flush of the cheeks starkly contrasted against the pure white collar of her uniform.

As the door closed, Denny laughed. With the devil flashing in his eyes he said: "That'll set 'em talking when that dainty piece of frippet sets the telegraph going in the nurses' quarters. Like as not they'll be queueing outside my door after you boys have departed. I'll be able to take my pick. There's nothing like an old one you know."

"Casanova born again," suggested Ace. "New style of course. But I suspect she'd rather be a young man's fancy than have a sugar daddy. Does it mean though you're turning over a new leaf?"

"Could be my boy," murmured Denny, adding a cackle that could bode either good or ill. "Depends on what the quack says when he slithers through the door on his morning round tomorrow. I'll be wading in with a warning that unless I'm discharged from here at the double, I'm going into battle that'll rock the foundations of this mausoleum."

"In that case we won't expect you back for some time," cautioned Ace. "It's a cert they'll keep you here to ensure no complications in your condition and to avoid the possibility of your having to return to this honourable establishment."

"Wild horses won't get me in here again," quoth Denny grimly. "I'd rather expire by the wayside."

Ace gulped down the last dregs of tea and feeling that he had perhaps been unusually loquacious which was very wearing, he consulted his airforce issue watch. "We'd better be on our way. Fog's expected to close in again tonight and John's got a date."

Denny groaned. "You would have to leave just when I was beginning to feel sane, and, I'm worried about my Flight."

"No problem — all in good hands — never been better. Just got to find our way home. You know what these navigators are."

"P'shaw." John had been pretty quiet up until now. "Never did come across the driver who could map read let alone navigate," he said deprecatingly.

"Get him out of here Ace before I burst a blood vessel."

They shook hands and vamoosed. The corridor was deserted as both set course for the main entrance. It had to be supposed that practically everything stopped for tea.

Chapter 11

FINALS

The intercom crackled as one of seven microphones was switched to the "on" position and a momentary harsh breathing was audible. Each other crew member experienced tension of muscle and mind, for at this stage well into enemy airspace, a quick verbal communication might easily be of most urgent import. Each man expected the worst and hoped for the best. But when the voice identified itself it was an anticlimax for the voice of the navigator was quiet and devoid of any sense of particular anxiety.

"ETA target 2050 hours," he advised the pilot. "30 minutes hence."

"OK John. 2050 hours." Ace's voice was lacking in anything other than the commonplace. It was all a part of the recognised patter, brief but clear in meaning. He might just as easily have been agreeing the schedule for a booze-up in the local pub. In 30 minutes then they would be on target for the last time, at least for a year or so, and on target would mean halfway on the last trip. The crew had during the last nine months been to Duisburg, Dortmund, Dusseldorf, Essen, Wuppertal made up of the twin towns of Elberfeld and Barmen, Bochum, Oberhausen, Cologne, Krefeld, Gelsenkirchen, Turin, Reggio, Leghorn, Hamburg, Leverkusen, Nuremburg, Munich, Hannover. They had in fact been twice to Duisburg, twice Dusseldorf, 3 times to Cologne, twice to Hamburg, twice to Essen, once laying mines in Kiel Harbour, and now this was the fourth time to the Big City of Berlin, the very heart of the enemy. It was the third attack on consecutive nights. The fact that the target was Berlin again despite substantial losses on the preceding two nights indicated that Butch Harris and his Bomber Command were getting a real grip on the defenses by sheer weight of numbers.

If it was a milestone, so to speak for Ace Burnett and his crew, it was no less so for Plt Off Bushell, the second dickey, who was on his first op. He sat next to Ace, in the flight engineer's seat watching and learning. Already he felt that Ace was an example of a Bomber pilot to be emulated, seemingly as cool as a cucumber but as wide-oh as a cat watching a mouse.

They had already come through some pretty dodgy weather. At one stage, for many miles cumulo-nimbus cloud formation had towered above the operational height and passage through had been anything but a doddle. The massive cloud had produced its orthodox characteristics of violent turbulence which hurled the massive Lancaster up and down in the ebb and flow of powerful up-currents. The pitot head had iced up causing the Air speed indicator to fail to record properly, which meant there was no certain way of knowing whether the Lancaster was travelling at the right speed to achieve ETA at the turning points, let alone the target. They had ploughed through frightening thunderstorms, when lightning flashed, the brilliant St. Elmos Fire played statically along the windscreen, the leading edges of the wings, the tailplane and the gun barrels. It was a spectacle the crew had witnessed many times but it remained as awesome as ever. Now however the storms were to the rear and the thin upper stratus cloud dissolved permitting a full view of the celestial ceiling with the stars winking remotely but ever-enduring.

Sitting without perceptible movement except for very limited correction of the control column, Ace's eyes moved from Air speed indicator, to artificial horizon as rapidly as the green illuminated needles flickered and then out through the perspex canopy, forward and to each side. As he went through the pattern he considered the possibility that fate was perhaps dealing him a hand essentially favourable to the completion of his first tour of operations, for earlier in the day the long suffering flight Commander, although unfit for flying duties, had appeared to re-establish control of his flight, thus releasing Ace for the battle order.

About three yards to the rear of the pilot's seat, the distance bisected by a blackout curtain, John sat in his office illuminated dimly by the angled lamp, thankful for a few moments respite from the continuous pattern of changing calculations that gave substance to his chart plotting. As far as he could ascertain they were pretty well on track and on time. He was using new radar equipment which within a limited range showed up towns as blips on the green screen. But which towns? There were obviously no names on the blips. It followed that radar indications had to be used in conjunction with dead reckoning navigation. He was confident that he had married up the two sources. Like Ace, he was not unduly worried about completing his tour and it would be very bad luck if he did not. After all, Texel Hanson had said that Ace and his crew would never have the evil finger on them and Texel was the Oracle. The main thing was to get on to the target, get out right smartly and back into the weather frontal conditions that would frustrate enemy defences. Then all they would have to do was to hit the British Isles and on this occasion anywhere would do. Thus it was that John's confidence was on the plus side of neutral. The Target? Well that was a different story which he was used to by now. He had found that the best way to resolve anxiety was quite simply to keep busy.

Ace switched on his intercom. "Hey gunners. Cloud's broken up. Keep your fingers out."

"OK ACE." It was very nearly a chorus from Jock and Frank who had not really needed the reminder, but it did positively sharpen their vigil. Ace turned to Plt Off Bushell and spoke into his oxygen mask. "It's bloody quiet, but don't let that fool you. It's the bugger you don't see that's the killer." Bushell stuck up a thumb in front of Ace's mask to signify he'd got the message loud and clear. He had no false illusions about the latent danger lurking in the fathomless night. If one had any sensitivity at all one could feel the threat like a tight band round the chest. Above the throbbing pulsating Lancaster the universal parabola of heavenly bodies identified the ceiling to infinity. Down below there was a stygian blackness, a floor without substance.

"Looks like it'll be a ground marking attack after all," suggested Sid, the bombaimer.

"Ought to be," replied Ace. "We're out of cloud, but I don't know about below." The probability pleased him. He never liked sky marking attacks, for while this technique could be very effective and accurate, it required aircraft to bomb on a set heading and it does not require much intelligence to see that enemy fighters, knowing what sky markers portended, would home in. He banked over to Starboard after warning the mid upper gunner of his intention and rolled back over to Port.

"All clear," called Frank confidently as the course was resumed.

"15 minutes to ETA," the navigator advised. "We should see markers at Zero hour minus 5."

"We've got activity," said the flight engineer. "Unidentified aircraft, two of them on reciprocal course with navigation lights on."

"Lights on hey." Ace was thinking. "If we see any more like that, especially coming away from the target, we'll put ours on. Probably fighters identifying each other. All eyes out now. John, come up and add your peepers."

"Not a bad idea," murmured Ken. "You could be right."

Ace was silent now, increasingly watchful and wholly alert, flying by the seat of his pants.

"Target slightly to Port ahead." Sid was wide awake and peering out. "Must be some cloud below. There's a glow."

"Likely a dummy Sid," suggested John. "Too early for markers. 2 minutes to go."

"Could be searchlights." Sid was having second thoughts.

"We'll see." Ace was ever non-committal.

Target or not, they were approaching the vicinity for flak bursts began to puncture the darkness with winks that appeared to be innocuous but were in fact pretty nasty if too close. It was a sure sign that pathfinders force was sniffing around in the darkness in an attempt to locate the exact aiming point for main force to bomb.

"There she blows. Sky Marker," yelled Sid. "Must be some cloud after all." A single Target Indicator hung in the sky at around 16000 feet, positively identifiable, seemingly constant but actually subject to gravitational pull together with wind effect. Immediately a series of heavy flak bursts broke around the marker which suggested that even if there was cloud below, it must be pretty thin or the Ack Ack gunners would have not seen the marker. Cloud or not, pathfinders were under fire and substantially so.

"That marker will be gone by the time we get there," suggested Sid.

A few moments later, but hours it seemed, down went the first ground markers, red waterfalls of coloured brilliance. Clearly pathfinders were covering all the options, sky and ground markers. Sid preferred bombing the ground markers. It seemed to him much more positive to bomb identifying flares that burst, say 2000 feet above the deck, than sky markers that moved with the substantially stronger winds at 16000 feet, even though, if the right bombing technique was followed, sky marking was reputed to be just as accurate.

"There go the greens," Sid called. "Almost right on top of the reds." It was a wonderful sight. Then the Master bomber came on stream, a controlled voice out of the darkness on VHF:

"Bunker aircraft, bomb the greens." There it was, the positive instruction.

"Right, right, Steady . . . Right . . ." Sid had the reins now, so to speak and was directing Ace.

"OK Sid." The pilot pushed the rudder bars gently slewing Robert to starboard before steadying on Sid's direction.

"That's bang on. Keep it there Ace." Sid was awake and dead keen.

Now the flak bursts were fast and furious, but rather less so than Ace expected. The defence, so far at least, was nothing like as intense as it had been on some trips to the Ruhr and with all Lancasters in the force windowing there was an absence of predicted flak. It was as light as day now with hundreds of searchlights flickering around. Together with the brilliance of the flares, the flash of bursting bombs and the photoflashes, the sun could not have done better.

"Keep her steady, Ace," warned the bomb aimer as a near flak burst rocked the Lancaster. There was a metallic clang as a piece of shrapnel struck Robert somewhere, but Sid was oblivious to extraneous matters. All he wanted was a controlled approach and it was up to the pilot to keep it that way, by hook or by crook.

The seconds ticked by: hours it seemed until the bombaimer came again on to intercom just as the Lancaster, relieved of its load leapt upwards.

"Bombs gone," he confirmed. "Steady for the photo flash." Then there was a gi-normous flash nearby causing the pilot to duck as his side window shivered into a thousand flaws. The big aeroplane was lifted sharply, falling then into a sickening side stall. Ace swore loud and long as he fought to get the Lancaster under control again.

"Turn on to 359 degrees true," John yelled above the profusion of indelicate language. 'Ware of aircraft turning." There was always a danger of collision from a 90 degree turn.

"359 true. 3000 revs Ken. On course," Ace called. It was a bit hectic for a few moments, altering course, getting up to maximum speed to exit the target area and watching out for other Lancasters as he turned onto the new course while at the same time wondering whether the damage was hopefully superficial or more worrying.

Eight flyers had the sudden joy of feeling their reflexes re-establish normality when it seemed whatever damage had been sustained was not immediately crippling. The navigator breathed an audible sigh of relief which was on stream since he had forgotten to turn his mike off in the confusion. Not for the first time on this tour was he relieved to know the cookie had gone and with it the fear of sitting for most of the outward trip on a live volcano. It occurred to him that he had never heard of a 4000 pound bomb exploding in the air, but of course, dead men tell no tales. Midst these rambling cogitations he awoke to the fact that the 5 minutes flying time on this short leg was expiring.

"Prepare to turn on course 275 true, Ace. I'll tell you when."

"OK Navigator, 275 Standing By Everyone alright," There was a chorus of assent and the pilot breathed again. The leg out of the target area was a frustrating one since instead of directly heading for home it was practically due north, heading for the Baltic Sea. Yet, the strategy was clear. A large force of bombers could not at night turn straight onto a reciprocal heading without considerable danger of collision with other Lancasters coming in on the final wave of the bombing run.

"Course 275 true, Now," requested the navigator.

Heading west now and very roughly towards home base, they were at least past the halfway mark, but it was a sobering thought that it was a long way home, in the order of 3 hours of flying time. The needle of the distant reading Compass hunted a degree or two either side of the correct course, but it was not possible to steer with greater accuracy by reason of wind effect. But for the rumble of the four engines fully synchronised on cruising speed of 165 indicated, the night now seemed unusually quiet, and Ace had put on his navigation lights. It was a calculated risk. He hoped that to a possible attacker this action would signify "friend", but he just could have made a wrong assumption. The lights would only remain on while they were still within sight of the target now blazing to the rear.

"What can you see, Jock?" Ace wanted a preliminary briefing.

"Och. Can't really tell because of the cloud, but there's certainly a concentrated glow." It would not really matter a great deal. Berlin was a big city. Most bombs would have fallen within city limits creating significant damage and chaos. Hitler was getting back what he started. Goering's proud boast that no British bomber would be able to bomb the Fatherland was a dead, dead duck.

The pilot banked R Robert over, both port and starboard in turn to allow the mid upper gunner to have a comprehensive gander underneath with eyes straining to pick up fast moving phantoms of death, but for the moment it was all coming up roses.

Down in the bomb compartment Sid resisted the tendency to doze off and swallowed a couple of wakey-wakey pills, for this was the last trip. There must be no neglect for such would be tempting fate.

A little out to starboard the night exploded with a gigantic flash and Ace rapidly switched off the navigation lights. Momentarily the crumpled shape of a bomber stood out starkly just prior to disintegration. A ball of flame hung in the sky and then sank apparently slowly into cloud.

"Bomber shot down," said Ace warningly. "Fighter attack. Peepers wide open, jokers. John, log details."

The crew tensed to the nth degree. It was a feeling both exhilarating and frightening. Every expectation was now tuned to the possible silhouette of a marauding enemy fighter.

No such danger presented itself, and every minute ticked off 3 miles nearer home.

The towering cumulo-nimbus tops experienced on the way out seemed now to have lowered their tops, but they were still in evidence and a possible refuge.

At estimated time of arrival at Dutch coast, Ace stuck R Robert's nose down gently, losing height gradually from 21,000 feet, but increasing speed and informing the navigator accordingly. There was in his mind, a gut feeling, a hunch, a doubt about the Met men's confidence that fog would not close in until after midnight. It was a constant fear that Met would get the timing wrong.

It was not long before Ace's notion that fog could be a hazard back at Base was advanced to fact, for Taffy, tuned in to the half hourly broadcast came up with a warning of reduced visibility. And that could mean a little or a lot, especially in Lincolnshire. Since however a warning had been positively transmitted it had to be assumed that the outlook was poor. The old enemy was rearing its ugly head. No doubt diversions were planned but Ace had no particular desire to doss in a strange bed.

"Pushing up the speed to 200 IAS, John, while descending," he advised. "Possible fog at base. Revised ETA when you can please." Press on very smartly was his pattern from now on.

They crossed the Lincolnshire coast without seeing it. Only radar told them it was there. At 2000 feet now the occasional wink of airfield ident beacons flashed out the two letter morse characteristic, but there were not as many as there should be and the conclusion to be drawn was that fog was undeniably around masking some of the beacons.

"Watch for our beacon, Sid," instructed Ace. "DP in case you have forgotten."

"OK." Sid did not mind a bit nor had he forgotten. He had the best view out through the blister, but he had not picked it up yet. Ace heaved himself into a new position and breasting the control column peered forward hopefully.

"How are we tracking navigator?". There was just a touch of concern in his enquiry. He was past visualising a strange bed — he was even considering the ultimate — having to bale out.

"Spot on. Two minutes to ETA." The navigator was supremely confident. He had to be for nobody else was.

"There it is." Sid had picked it out despite the poor visibility and was happy to have done so. "Slightly to port."

"OK Sid. I'll have to run over it on the QDM. (Magnetic course from beacon to Base) Keep your eyes on it. I can't see it."

"Left left steady." Sid was smiling grimly to himself. It sounded like a bombing run.

"Manger Robert to Bakewell. Permission to pancake." Ace was not going to mess about. He pressed the transmission button and got the immediate if sleepy voice of the WAAF R/T operator.

"Bakewell to Robert. Pancake immediately. Clear to land."

"Rodger Bakewell, downwind I think. Can't see a bloody thing."

"Airfield on the port side, a mile or so." Plt Off Bushell was doing his bit.

"I've got it." But he lost the flare path almost immediately. It would be sheer guesswork in deciding when to turn on to the penultimate leg and be near enough to see the runway flares and yet far enough to have a decent approach. Cursing softly he ordered Bushell out of the flight engineer's seat so that Ken could take over. Tonight they needed the co-ordination which flowed naturally between them. He turned on to the penultimate leg, but he could see nothing. God, he hoped he would not have to overshoot in this shit. The navigator was already watching the ASI ready to call the airspeed on the final approach. Ace turned upwind. It was just a guess. There was no sign of runway flares.

"20 Flap, Ken." Ace had to assume that the runway was ahead. Ken selected and confirmed. The nose came up. The air speed indicator dropped to 140.

"Revs up." The constant speed propeller controls were pushed forward drawing from the engines a pronounced whine.

"Wheels down." The pilot needed instant action and got it from Ken, who again confirmed.

"Radiators closed."

"Radiators closed," echoed Ken.

Two green lights came up in front of the pilot, indicating wheels locked down.

"Full flap." Ace could not see the flarepath, but he had to assume it was there.

"There's the funnel," called Sid quickly. "Slightly starboard." The pilot slewed the Lancaster to the right just in time to see a green aldis light flicker out from the caravan. Control obviously understood the problem created by fog.

"Speed 130 ... 125 ... 120 ... " It was the navigator allowing the pilot to fully concentrate on his height, the angle of approach and the point of landing.

The pilot got the throttles forward. It looked as if he was undershooting.

"130 ... 125 ... 120 ... 115 ... 110 ... 100." The navigator raised the tenor of his voice to make sure the pilot knew that speed was down to 100. How he hated these night time approaches on to an ill lit flarepath. It only needed an engine cut now to tangle them in the trees on the eastern boundary.

"Can't see the flares. There they are. Cut." Ace bellowed the last word. Ken snapped back the throttles. The exhausts popped and spluttered. The pilot was literally feeling his way to touchdown. The Lancaster jarred suddenly and continued to float before finally settling to a bumpy landing, which was a triffle unusual. The concrete should have been relatively smooth. On one side of the Lancaster was a line of flares. Where was the other?

"We're not on the runway. We're on the grass." Ken was quite certain of that. "Think you flicked the caravan with the starboard wheel," he added.

"You don't say. Wondered why I could only see one line of flares. In any case I've always said the caravan is parked too close to the runway, specially on a night like this." Ace was not inclined to be sympathetic, but he *was* wondering about the bod who occupied the caravan and who indeed had given him a helpful green for the approach. He pressed the transmit button to call flying control.

"Robert to Bakewell. Clear of runway. Think I have bent the caravan."

"Bakewell to Robert." It was a male controller's voice. "You did. Report immediately to flying control, repeat immediately."

"That's it," Ace mused aloud over the intercom. "We just made it. Pound to a penny kites here on will be diverted." He ran Robert uncertainly round the perimeter track while Ken, head out of window called the directions. Once it was necessary to come to dead stop as visibility dropped down to nil. Then the fog bank rolled on allowing Ace to continue, albeit very slowly indeed. He was not at all sure where he was and would have to rely on the marshaller to guide him into dispersal.

"There he is." Ken had seen the flash of a torch. There was dispersal and a waving torch to steer by. Home at last. The engines coughed and died. The silence on intercom expressed the weariness of the crew after 6 hours of tense vigil. Even Bushell, the second dickey, who still had questions to ask the experienced pilot, had not the strength to pursue his intentions.

It was Jock the rear gunner who made the first move to evacuate and the urge to do so was impelled entirely by the need to ease cramped legs. "And that's that." His tone was at once both jubilant with the laurels of a completed tour of ops and regretful like a man who has tasted blood and liked it.

"Tour expired. Whooppee." The mood was catching and Sid gave expression to it. "Pints all round in the Old Cow," he promised.

"So long as you pay, tonight or any other night," replied Jock.

"Bloody mean Scottish bugger," taunted Taffy.

"Save it you two bloody foreigners. After the party you can disembowel each other for all I care, but don't spoil it all beforehand." Sid was not a man of many words, but he could put his view succinctly.

"Bloody cockney, belt up," advised Taffy.

"Och aye. Wrap up." For once Wales and Scotland were united.

"Pipe down all of you and get weaving. Transports here." It was the captain's last command of the tour.

Unusually, as the crew transport shuddered round the perimeter towards the distant briefing room at a lick that paid scant respect to the fog, its occupants were prepared to tolerate the prospect of a long winded briefing with equinamity. Even the WAAF driver, grating the gears, caused no adverse comment, nor were voices raised when the transport came to a stop with an almighty jerk to let Ace disembark at Flying Control, where he, still clad in his tough fur lined leather flying jacket stamped up the concrete steps and barged in to the holy of holies. There he found the Station Commander, Wing Commander and principal control officer in muted but earnest conversation and as Ace came in Groupie acknowledged his presence.

"Ah. There you are Burnett. Sorry to bring you here. Wanted an opinion on the all round approach visibility, but we have already taken the decision to divert. So you are the only aircraft to get in. Good trip?"

"So so, Sir. Cloudy over aiming point. Dual marking attack. Seemed concentrated."

"Good show. I believe this was your last trip. Congratulations."

"Thank you Sir." A few words of praise from Groupie had to be absorbed. "But I'm more worried about the bod in the caravan."

Groupie grinned. "No injuries. You must have just glanced the box with a wheel. Pretty bad vis, what?" It was a statement as well as a question so Ace felt obliged to answer.

"Very bad Sir. Never saw the caravan. Didn't see the runway until the last minute and then I could see only one line of flares."

"Pretty good show getting down at all," Groupie was full of praise. Ace wondered if the reaction would have been the same if he had bent the Lancaster. "Well skate along now for briefing, Burnett. You'll be popular with the specialist officers today, all wanting your attention."

Ace saluted and skated. Not long now before consciousness would slip away in the warmth of his bed.

The well worn sign depicting the Old Cow swung gently with a protesting squeal while the gnarled boughs of the old oak tree nearby seemed to creak in like protest at the cut of the wind, or perhaps the protests were in respect of a crescendo of voices thundering to a new high point from within the pub and easily heard without. It was but a few moments from closing time when the mutilated strains of "Nellie Dean" reached an absolute climax before dying suddenly, followed then by a thunderous roar of cheering from the assembled company that literally shook the timbers of the old pub like the shock wave of an exploding "cookie" (4000 lb bomb). Even the waxing moon peeped out scared-like from behind fast moving cloud and retreated.

It had been a party above all others and had had to be held in the pub rather than the Mess because the gathering was a mix of Officers, NCO's and ground crew erks, all celebrating end of tour for Ace and his crew.

Ace, more animated than was his habit had dominated the company, Marion had smiled and laughed freely, starry-eyed in the knowledge that her man was reasonably safe now for at least a year while John, who had performed on the piano to everyone's satisfaction with the abandonment of a virtuoso, was pleased to see Marion so happy.

Then there was Texel who had raised his less than tuneful voice in song along with the others but who, in between times, was strangely silent, choosing instead to concentrate largely on dirty great pints of wallop. It was not that he had been in any way unsociable. He had listened to the conversation. He had interjected at times but was mostly monosyllabic allowing for once the ops expired crew to get a word in edgeways. Just once he had branched out to propound the sequel to the "brooms for sweeping out 'B' flight Sergeants' sleeping quarters problem" following Denny's complaint about the filthy state of the huts some months before.

"You remember I got torn off a horrible strip and I told Denny we didn't have any brooms," he said. "Well I never did tell you what happened. One night we diced to the Happy Valley, Essen I believe it was. We'd just dropped our load when one of those dirty blue radar searchlights fastened on to us and within seconds we had a dozen more searchlights dead centre on us. It was like bright sunshine in the cockpit. We were well and truly coned. Well, to cut a long story short, Denny got his head down like he always does to get out of the dazzle and what do you think? Just before we went into an almost vertical dive he slapped me round the back of the head 'cause I've always been deaf in the air, and yelled, 'By the way Tex, I've got some brooms for you to sweep out your quarters.'"

The wide-eyed company had looked askance at Texel and then produced a roar of derision followed by a combined rendering of a nifty ditty:—

"That was a cute little line, tell us another one do." Texel was not at all amused. His customary grin was not in evidence.

"You can laugh," he had said, "but its as true as I'm standing here. We got the brooms didn't we. Blimey, you ought to remember. You were all binding about being housemaids, yapping about reporting sick with housemaid's knee." His remarks had certainly silenced the company. It just could have been true. Yes. It was all within the realms of possibility for the Flight Commander was capable of it.

Rooty Arrows, the "chiefy" in charge of "B" flight Lancasters together with his little band of technicians had downed the pints, fully keeping pace with the aircrew, and enjoying the bonus of free drinks.

Finally there were assorted airmen and WAAFs and locals who, upon Ace's promise of free drinks, had found themselves drawn not unwillingly into the impromptu farewell party, for farewell party it was since Ace and crew were all posted on the morrow, each to separate units around the country. The postings had come through so quickly that Ace had ventured an opinion that he and his specialist crew were badly needed back up the line. He was right of course, although authority would not have expressed it in those terms, since a massive increase in Lancaster bomber production called for more available aircrew, which, in turn begged the need for more experienced instructors.

Now it was all over. The pub slowly emptied, the beer engines covered with cloths and the lights turned down. The clientele filtered away into the darkness on their several ways.

Together again and alone with each other Marion and John trod the route to the WAAFery. The moon was in evidence but partially hidden behind cloud. There was enough light to proceeed without the aid of a torch. A cold wind gusted about their ears and it was a good excuse for John to encompass Marion's delightfully slim waist with one arm to establish proprietorship and generate warmth. Marion was not complaining about that.

"You'll write me often," Marion said. It was a statement made less dictatorial by the impassioned tone that only a woman in love could produce.

"I will my love," he replied fervently. "As far as possible every other night."

"How long shall you be at OTU?" she asked.

"No way of telling. It's supposed to be a rest from ops. Perhaps a year..."

"Unless what?" Marion was sharply interrogative and John drew in a long breath. He had hoped this particular question would never arise, but he had to be honest and confide, especially since he had once given Marion the impression that he could not trust her judgement or reactions and had been sharply criticised for it.

"Unless Ace decides to pull a few strings to get back on ops. I can't see him enjoying screening new pilots on circuits and bumps." The wind grew colder and so did the atmosphere. Marion disentangled herself from the nav's embrace.

"But you can't, he can't." It was almost a sob. "You have earned a respite and you're lucky to be alive. One should not tempt fate."

"Haven't got any twitches yet." John made the remark in wry humour. It deserved to and did fall flat for Marion did not reply straightaway.

"Not yet you haven't." Her remark sobered him up a bit and the more so as she continued; "It takes an outsider to see the signs and Ace has them. It's just as well you've completed your tour."

"Oh I don't know about that." He was not at all convinced that she was right, but in any case he could not allow her to entirely dictate the course of his actions on personal grounds for the war was not yet over and a chap had to do his bit. "We had a dodgy moment or two on our last op, but Ace was, I thought anyway, even more cool than usual. I'm not at all sure your analysis is correct."

"That's just it. He may have been getting a bit flak happy, over confident, a state of mind, I'm told, which is most dangerous." John thought about it as they walked on. Marion could be pretty acute at times.

"Maybe you are partly right," he admitted at last. "As I said he was ice cold in danger, but he has been more easily irritated by small things. I put it down to sheer frustration at not being able to complete the tour earlier. Never-the-less I can't see him being satisfied at conversion unit."

"Perhaps so, but he will be away from ops," and from Marion's point of view that was the clincher.

"True and so will I, but that does not mean I'm going to enjoy my time at OTU, stooging around the country, looking over the shoulders of navigators under training, and in Wimpeys too. And if there is one kite I've never been comfortable in, its the

Wellington. Continuous smell of oil. Everything you touch leaves a fine film of oil on the hands and clothes. Probably smell of vomit too."

"Vomit? Don't be disgusting." She was going off him.

"I'm not joking," John went on unperturbed. "Many an aircrew bod gets air sickness and Wimpeys do seem to wallow about more than most. It's even worrying to watch the wings. They actually flap, just like a bird's wings, not at all like the Lanc which is not only smooth as silk, but promotes confidence. It's unlikely I'll see a Lanc at OTU, but if one lobbed down for any reason, well, I don't know how I'd feel. Pretty sick I guess."

"Surely though, there is a minimum period of rest," Marion ventured with little confidence.

"As I said earlier, it's reckoned to be about a year, although it's always possible to jump the gun if one knows the right people. But most chaps posted to OTU seem to get stuck there, or so I'm told. The net result is soul and drive remorselessly destroyed. The only way to get out of that sort of deadbeat situation is to put up such a shocking black that it cannot be ignored. Then you have a situation, when Groupie, probably a dead beat as well, looks down his long nose, gives you a pep talk on the need for devotion to duty, asks you to sign an adverse report to incriminate yourself and then has you posted back on to ops as a penance, or so he thinks. That is one of the ways that chaps have got back on ops." Marion emitted a strangled sound expressing total disbelief.

"I just can't believe it," she said. "I have had reason to see how efficient Bomber Command is operationally, and yet you are saying or suggesting that in the background there is a less than efficient group."

"Yes, I am." John was categorical. "But don't forget when I leave here I shall no longer be in Bomber Command. Effectively it will be Training Command and that's a different bag of tricks."

"I see. I'll have to take your word for it, but don't do anything foolish John," she pleaded.

"I'll not ask for trouble unless it comes to me, I promise you," he replied. Marion knew she would have to be satisfied with that. She had rather foolishly supposed that being tour expired John was relatively safe from the perils of war and she had never once considered that he might not want to vegetate. The tears ran freely again in the darkness as fears took imaginative hold. She saw again the terrible night when half a Lancaster fell blazing out of the overcast, behind the Officers' Mess. She struggled valiantly and secretly to quench the emotion that threatened to engulf her, until finally, momentarily out of control she stopped walking, turned and threw herself into the navigator's arms, her whole body shuddering in a passionate aura.

John was surprised at her reaction to what after all was a discussion on the immediate future. It had not occurred to him that Marion had been looking much further ahead, and in any case there was no accounting for a woman's reaction, but he was on to a good thing just at the moment and took advantage by wrapping her in a manly embrace. That didn't seem to do any good for her tears were now accompanied by outright sobbing, which was a bit tricky right outside the WAAFery gate.

"I'm sorry," she sobbed brokenly. "It's just that I had thought you were finally safe and that I would not have to face up again to your not coming back. You don't know the sleepless nights I have spent in agonised suspense, fearing the worst, hoping for the best, and now you are hinting at a second tour. I don't know that I can bear it."

"Tush, don't cry love," he murmured with really touching solicitude. "It is only a possibility if the war goes on long enough and I'm only doing what you yourself said we should do, live with the present and let the future look after itself. Do you remember saying that, or words to that effect?"

"I remember," she admitted ruefully. "It's not easy advice to follow."

John kissed her dewy eyelids lightly and caressed her neck and hair, oblivious of the transit of WAAFs going through the gate. She had been a great comforter to him through this last nine months and more than usually supportive in so many ways, but it was really only just getting through to him how much it had cost her in anguish. He knew now why so many WAAFs kept clear of flyers, and understood.

"I have not been very tactful." His admission came suddenly. "I'm something of a fool. I have been lacking in human understanding. You'll have to put it down to lack of experience in these things, but I hope I am learning and will be the better for it. But you must know that I would never hurt you willingly for I love you too much."

Marion wiped her tears on a wisp of lace handkerchief and tried to smile through misty eyes. "I'm afraid my heart doesn't allow for your sense of duty," she said.

John tried to be consoling. "The war will probably be over before I need to think of going back on ops," he said, hoping that she would grasp that particular straw. It seemed she did grasp it, for she lifted her head, breathed in strongly and relaxed.

"I'm tempted to cross forbidden territory," said John. "So avert your lovely eyes or I won't be able to leave you tonight."

She perceived his changed mood, at once light hearted yet serious. She replied with a touch of wickedness.

"Don't leave me then. I dare you."

"You alluring witch. If you are not careful I'll take you into the first hut."

"It is empty," she replied. "Wholly unoccupied."

John's heart beat faster, but after a moment she whispered, "You had better go. Too many people have seen us already and I've no doubt others are watching." His only reply was to kiss her again, long and ardently with new persuasion.

"Please let me go, John," she pleaded, "or I shall make a complete fool of myself by ditching all my principles which are very soundly based. I'm only just under control, and it must remain so until we are married." He released her slowly seeing the wisdom of her appeal. If she would have agreed he would have risked discovery in a compromising situation, but she was not an easy touch and both might regret precipative action.

Marion put an end to further temptation.

"It must be Au Revoir for now," she said. "I'll see you tomorrow before you leave. Kiss me quickly and go quickly, please."

Watching her slim form merge into the shadows John had a mad impulse to go after her and claim her wholly, body and soul, but it would inevitably get her into trouble. He was unashamedly aware that his eyes were on the misty side of dry, an experience never before visited upon him. She was wonderful. Well worth waiting for. He hoped she would eventually become his wife, although he must not think of that now. If she had given ground he would have married her as soon as it could be arranged and in wedded bliss they would have achieved short spells of heaven on earth during periods of leave, but the shadow of the future remained in the back of his mind.

He turned up the collar of his greatcoat against the wind that seemed to have turned positively arctic and trod the lonely path to his own cold and lonely room.

Tomorrow, Ace would be off to Heavy Bomber Conversion Unit near Newark. Sid, Taffy, Jock and Frank were off to Operational Training Units, as was John. The crew had overnight changed from one integrated unit into seven separate parts.

Chapter 12

THE AFTERMATH

The bus pulled up outside the Old Cow to disgorge several passengers. All but one slipped away with the urgency of purpose to respective homes; two middle aged women with hard won groceries from Lincoln City; a man with a pork pie hat dressed in a drab worsted suit who looked like a salesman, although what he would have been trying to sell in the post war years of austerity was anyone's guess; a middle aged man in grimy overalls perhaps off a factory shift; a young girl neat and tidy in a not entirely new two-piece suit which must have set her mother back a bit in clothing coupons. She could be a typist perhaps returning from a job interview, seemingly successful judging from the perkiness of her gait.

The last person stepped down from the bus in unhurried fashion, pausing momentarily as if at the last moment he doubted the wisdom of this journey. He was altogether hesitant, like a traveller in an alien land. Dressed in a dark suit with a faint blue stripe running through the pattern, he lingered for a further few seconds taking in what was essentially a familiar scene. The colour of his hair was ginger, streaked prematurely with white. He was thinning fast on top. Altogether he looked like a city man who had never really cottoned on to wearing a black suit with Homburg hat, complete with walking stick or umbrella. He was in his late twenties but looked considerably older.

The mellow stone church, not far divorced from the Old Cow pub, the cottages with clematis and wistaria climbing against the walls were unchanged in the stranger's eyes, but what was different was the total absence of blue RAF uniforms.

The scene contrived to usher back memories of eight years ago, memories that were pleasantly nostalgic, those of excitement and those that were as bitter as aloes in the mouth, none of which would ever be erased in his lifetime. Involuntarily the man glanced down at his civilian clothes as if he expected to find himself still in RAF Officer's uniform, but a sudden tightening of the lips and facial muscles indicated a sharp reality of the moment. Why he had come to suffer the painful experience of going back over the years he did not know. All he knew was that he had been impelled by some irresistable inner driving force to return to the venue of the happiest time of his life and the crunching tragedy that followed.

He crossed the road slowly to enter the public bar of the Old Cow where the landlord, lethargically polishing the brass beer engines sticking up like sentinels along the counter, looked up with a spark of interest, for business was not as good as it used to be.

"Morning, Sir. Lovely day," was his friendly greeting. The young man slapped a ten shilling note on the counter.

"Pint of black and tan, please, Bert."

"Roight Sir. Pint of black and tan coming up." He laboured the beer engine handle whilst covertly eyeing his customer. "I ought to know you Sir, since you know my name, but I can't put a handle to you. Musta bin during the war cause I ain't seen you recent like."

"I'm John Howard," the young man said. "There was a crowd of us, Ace, Texel and Sid."

"That I remember. I know'd your face was familiar like, a bit older, of course. Ain't we all," and he polished his scalp with one hand where there was nothing but a skating rink with a brush of hair on the neck. "You used to be friendly with that nice WAAF Sergeant..." Bert stopped. "You'll forgive me, Sir, tongue runnin' away with me. I forgot she ..." John's tone in reply was grimly measured.

"S'alright, Bert. Long time ago now."

"You'm roight there. Time flies and more as you get older, I find. How long now since you bin in here?"

Nearly ten years ago I first walked into your bar and the last time was eight years ago. Trade not so good today?" John asked.

"You could say that," the Landlord gulped as he thought about it. "In them days I sold all I could get and often ran short. Today I've got the stock, but only a trickle of customers. When the RAF left, so did my main trade. But what brings you here today, if I may be so bold as to ask?" John lunged at his beer.

"Don't really know. Irresistable force I couldn't control, trying to recapture a chunk of my life and wondering what life is all about anyway."

"I wonder too, sometimes. You were a bright bunch of buckoes and too few lived to see the end of the war, and what do we see now? A country bankrupt and in the grip of austerity. Not much money, not much fun either. What happened to your lot then? You chaps went off and a new lot came, but the last lot didn't have the gumption you did. Your lot was full of fun."

"Scraping the barrel, I suppose," replied John. "You know, don't you, there were 75,000 aircrew in Bomber Command and 55,000 were killed or just missing and never came back. Ace, the pilot was repatriated to New Zealand. Texel finally got married and moved up north somewhere. Sid was killed in a motor accident and I've lost touch with the others."

"Pity about that Sid," said Bert. "Fancy going through all that and then got killed on the road. Terrible, I say." Bert was genuinely sympathetic as he remembered how he used to talk to Sid perhaps more than the rest.

"Yes, he was married. Got two kids. The family are reasonably happy now, though. I call in when I'm in the area."

"And you, Sir, you set up alright?"

"Work in the City of London," said John.

"Married?" Bert was not sure that he should have asked the question, but it just came out. John bit his lip.

"Not married," he replied. "Couldn't after . . ."

"Sorry, Sir. Didn't think it would do any harm to talk."

"It's OK, Bert. Not to worry. As I said it happened a long time ago, but it still hurts like hell. Can't settle at all."

"That's bad. Aiming to stay around?"

"I don't think so. I just want to look around and . . . Have a pint on me."

"No thanks, Sir. Very kind of you. Can't take it on an empty stomach. Draw you one on the house though when you've finished that one."

"Must be going." John drained his mug. He had to get out into the air. "I'll call again if I'm this way. Nice to see you again, Bert."

The landlord's eyes followed John until the door swung closed. Rotten luck for that young fellow, he mused.

John walked slowly down the road, past the lane that used to lead to the sleeping quarters, and reached what used to be the communal site. Only the shell of the site remained. Delapidated, half torn down, prefabricated buildings were as empty of life as death itself. Across the main entrance an attempt had been made to keep out vandals by positioning rolled barbed wire in front. Along the grass verges weeds grew uncontrolled.

His thoughts ranged wildly into the old Sergeants' Mess, a ruin now, where he had spent most of his time, seeking ghosts that responded only in painful memory.

He recalled as easily as if it were yesterday when he had first met Marion, pretty well crashing into her just inside the entrance. The ghosts were still there.

His feet took him down the long road to the airfield and flight offices. The latter were still there though vandalised or at least cannibalised, for building supplies of any quality were hard to come by. The control tower remained as did the navigation centre, both tarnished by the elements. The concrete runways were still there but cultivation between them was evident. Whether or not the farmer had the Air Ministry's permission to use the land was irrelevant. Good fertile land could not be wasted. The hangar was gone but the bomb dump mound still survived, its original camouflage superseded by nature's hand.

John retraced his steps to the village. One or two people stared at him as villagers do when a stranger is about. If he was the object of some suspicion he was unaware of it. Then he came to the WAAFery. There was no longer a gate. The site was just a clutch of broken down huts. He stood there motionless with thoughts running wild. Rumination took him back over the years from the time he left the Squadron to go to an OTU, near Banbury in Oxfordshire, as an instructor . . .

OTU was typical of its kind.

John had been to Operational Training Unit before, as a trainee of course. It was at one such establishment that he, Taffy, Jock and Sid had crewed up with Ace to learn to work as a team, to bring their individual skills together into a smooth pattern before being passed on to Heavy Bomber Conversion Unit and ultimately an Operational Squadron.

Pilots probably had the most to gain from the course for it was then they graduated to a bigger aeroplane than heretofore in the shape and substance of the Wellington twin-engined ex-bomber, sometimes known affectionately as the Wimpey. For them it was circuits and bumps in daylight followed by the same pattern at night. Once proficient in the art of take-off and landing the pilots then took on board their crews when they proceeded on cross-country exercises both by day and night.

John's return to OTU was not exactly a new experience except that this time he was one of the instructors or screens, an experienced operational navigator with a good deal of knowledge to impart to sprog navigators on their way through the long training programme.

It looked good. The airfield was set in more attractive countryside than the County of Lincoln could muster. It was a well-planned permanent station built solidly of bricks and mortar that had mellowed over the years. Along the roads between the functional buildings were trees and shrubs that in Spring and Summer would be a sight for sore eyes. It was like a large self-contained village.

The Officers' Mess was a two-floored building, accommodating on the ground floor the dining room, kitchens, billiard room, reading room, lounges, and bar together with sleeping quarters in the wings. The upper floor was given over entirely to sleeping quarters, individual bedrooms with plenty of hot and cold water. It was all pretty cosy and a batman was always around to ensure that uniforms were properly valeted and shoes cleaned. And it was a far cry from the discomfort of the temporary airfield that had been John's home on the Squadron.

If it was warm and civilised in the Mess, an interview with the Senior Navigation Officer chilled John more than somewhat.

"Where do you hail from?" The question was abruptly delivered and in a distinctly unfriendly tone.

"Five Group – Bomber Command." John was proud of it and it showed, but the Squadron Leader was unimpressed. Clearly the latter's experience was not in the orbit of Bomber Command.

"Huh." It was practically a sniff. "One of the C-in-C's glamour group." He spat it out as if John had been part of a criminal organisation, and John, although beginning to seethe, decided to play it cool, or partly so.

"You could put it like that," he agreed, but rubbed it in a bit by adding, "Damned good squadron. Fine results."

The navigation leader affected a hard-of-hearing pose and proceeded with the interview or pep talk or whatever.

"Well, now you are a screen you will be responsible for ground lectures including Astro navigation. You are required to watch the time table and provide instruction at the required times."

"Bloody Headmaster," John said to himself and with admirable forthrightness decided to project a view. "I have not touched Astro since I was at Air Observer School. Skipper on the squadron would not allow it. Too dangerous to fly straight and level for a two-minute shot."

The Sqn Ldr leaned back in his comfortable looking chair and drummed fingers on the desk with marked impatience.

"I find it disquieting when a navigator posted to my staff admits to not practising Astro navigation," he said, "when Astro and DR are the fundamentals for getting from A to B in the air. Whatever are the squadrons coming to?" he said.

For crying out loud. John was exasperated. Where had the mush been all these years. Must have been on the Ark with Noah, for certainly he did not seem to understand present day needs in the bombing force. But it was much too early in his stay to create too much aggravation so he said simply, "In Bomber Command decisions are made by the Skipper and I was subject to them."

"Then you had better draw AP1234 Mannual of Air Navigation and relearn it. That's all." It was curt dismissal, so John got up, saluted vaguely and retired, aware that he had made an inauspicious start. He had expected to be allocated to one of the flights for the purpose of overseeing trainees on cross-country flights, and as much as he disliked the Wimpey it would be far better that lecturing on Astro, for crying out loud, with an old fogey of a navigation officer sniffing around trying to find fault. How the hell does he hold down his job, John wondered. Someone had to know that his ideas were out of the ark. Another thing, John did not care much for the Sqn Ldr's thin lips propping up a pencil line moustache.

That night in the Mess after dinner, John got a marked snub from the Sqn Ldr What's-his-name (for the life of him John could not remember his proper handle). The Sqn Ldr with conduct unbecoming an Officer and Gentleman had turned his back with the result that John's hair positively bristled and conceiveably went a shade redder. When the steward attended on John's needs, the latter in a loud voice requested, "One dirty great pint to take the bad taste out of my mouth." The steward looked askance but soft-footed it away to meet the request. Nodding heads perked up, a few whispers floated on the air accompanied by scowls and happily for John some admiring humourous grins, which partially restored his faith in human nature. John downed his pint in an ungentlemanly gulp and stalked into the writing room where he wrote a long letter to Marion describing comprehensively the demerits of OTUs generally and one in particular, finally signing off with a declaration of everlasting love.

NINETEEN FORTY FOUR dawned. John had made some friends in the Mess who together maintained a barrier against some of the unpleasantness and life proceeded without too many difficulties until the D Day flap occurred. Then trouble loomed.

Instructors were called together and told that they were to hold themselves available for operational duties if the need should arise. John was pleased to crew up with Ft Lt Dawson DFM., a former Stirling pilot, the crew then carrying out a successful cross country exercise spot on time at the turning points and spot on track all the way, much to the chagrin of the navigation leader who interfered to find fault and was disappointed.

It turned out to be a waste of time really for the instructors' services were not needed operationally, but from John's point of view his stay at OTU hinged on a technical matter which had come to a head at practice briefing. The Sqn Ldr had suggested that crews should carry out a time and distance run from an M/

F (Medium Frequency) fix which brought John straight to his feet.

"I can't see that an M/F fix is anything like accurate enough on which to base a time and distance run," he projected. The atmosphere chilled. The Sqn Ldr turned pale, to puce and finally to blood red, at having his suggestion pooh poohed by a junior officer. Half an hour later John was in his office.

"Fg Off Howard," The Sqn Ldr had gone back to pale. "I consider your conduct to be reprehensible and too critical on a subject on which you are insufficiently knowledgeable. I've had enough of you. You can pack your kit and join the section on the satellite aerodrome. Now get out."

"Bloody old deadbeat," murmured John as he got outside, but he was not displeased.

The satellite functioned mainly for circuits and bumps and the navigational requirements were minimal. He had to give up comfortable quarters for those of a war time built unit where daily shaving in cold rusty water was an occupational hazard with impetigo the frequent outcome.

It was however a pleasant exile. The only significant duty he was called upon to perform was to lecture a local Air Training Corps on the mysteries of aerial navigation, and it was fun. You could not blind the youngsters with science. They wanted to know the whys and wherefores. They were as sharp as needles as prospective pilots and navigators should be. He managed to inject a good deal of humour into his lectures and was popular, so much so that he was invited to their annual dance. Even that did not turn out as expected for the dance band either ran out of petrol or broke down on the way to the hall, so John felt obliged to offer his services as pianist, which turned him in the eyes of the ATC into a saviour, or at least a tin god.

The overall damage was done however. You cannot buck authority and get away with it. Just a year to the day, he was called over to base and briskly informed that he was posted back to operations. The Sqn Ldr had clearly had a vindictive hand in the arrangements for he was almost smiling, but what the Sqn Ldr did not know was that John, aware of what would transpire, had been in touch with Ace who had pulled strings successfully. He was posted with Ace and original crew back to his old squadron. The OTU navigation section thought he had gone mad when with joy in his heart he announced that he was getting East of the Wash again. I can't wait to get out of here, he told them. That night he bought drinks all round in the Officers' Mess, with one exception.

It was an even greater surprise to the staff of the OTU, when Lancaster O Oboe lobbed down to a perfect landing on three points, the next morning. It was John's taxi arrived to speed him from the Oxfordshire OTU to Lincoln, and the Senior Navigation Officer looked as if he was about to be sick as John waved an airy goodbye. A Lancaster was a fairly rare bird in the Oxfordshire area. As a consequence its arrival caused a bit of a stir and not inconsiderable interest, particularly from those trainees who aspired to fly the aeroplane at a later date. With John safely aboard, Ace treated the spectators to a steep breath stopping climbing turn and a measured ear splitting run across the airfield, while John metaphorically lifted two fingers. It was not necessarily a victory sign.

"Here we are again John boy," said Ace unnecessarily as he cut the engines in the dispersal at Holmdun.

"Grand, Ace." That was all John could find to say. He was happy. As they awaited transport, Ace said quietly, " I must tell you now that Marion was posted yesterday. I didn't know myself until this morning."

"Posted?" John could not believe it. After a year away, apart from brief meetings while on leave arranged simultaneously, he'd been looking forward to having more time with her. "Where's she been posted to?"

"Malpen, on the Anglian coast, urgently needed apparently. Got only 48 hours notice. She left a letter for you."

John looked out across the airfield towards the familiar flight offices. Quite suddenly the prospect of another tour, albeit only twenty trips this time, had diminished. "Reckon she was posted on account of my return?" he asked Ace, who was positive.

"No chance. All the cobbers we knew and would know of you two have gone, except for ground crews of course. Denny's got his own squadron now at base and the flight commanders are new. Just about the only one who's left is Bert Apsley, and gumming up the works is not his style. Even got a new Wing Co."

The Mess looked to be less tidy, the furniture inevitably more battered. The faces were different, mostly of young bloods recently from Operational Training Unit and even more recently from Heavy Bomber Conversion Unit. Ace's DFM stood out in the gathered company of Officers, which caused not a few enquiring glances. The old ghosts were still there, given substance only by the photographs on the walls, of various crews, few of whom were still in the land of the living. Ace grinned at John as he pointed to his own crew photo.

"Reckon we look any older, Johnny?" he asked.

"Just a bit more dissipated, at least you do."

"Well we'll get it out of our system in the Old Cow." It was Ace's standard remedy for all ills. It was clear that he had changed very little during the past year.

"Sure we will." John's agreement was listless. He was still numbed by the shock of Marion's posting to another station and could not clear his mind of the possibility that it had been a fix.

"Why hello, John." Bert Apsley, the navigation leader was at John's elbow. "Welcome back to the old firm. Good to see you too, Ace. Brings a touch of professionalism back to the Squadron." Ace shook hands accompanying the gesture with a faint smile.

"You're still a fixture then," suggested John.

"Absolutely. Indispensable, you know." It sounded like bragging but Bert was really modest and always the Officer-and-Gentleman. He cocked a questioning eye at Ace.

"Does John know yet?" he asked.

"Do I know what?" John's voice moved up a tone and a half. What more could there be. He had had bad news enough.

"Your WAAF friend." Bert projected concern itself.

"I know, Bert. Ace told me. Sounds just like a fix. Provocative posting."

"No way." Bert was positive. "Your relationship passed into history when you left. Work is the best antidote. There's plenty going on. Nice long stooges down to Bavaria these nights. Piece of cake for you."

"God, poor bloody navigators," replied John soulfully, as if the long trips were just originated to add to his misery.

"Must be off now." Bert was in a hurry to get home to his wife who lived out in the village. "See you tomorrow, John. Got some new techniques to gen you up on."

"Times have changed, hey." Ace was not inclined to say very much on any occasion but his ears were always wide open when there was anything he ought to know.

"They have." Bert was obliged to linger, "But it's a deal easier with our troops on the Continent. Less enemy occupied territory to fly over with radar cover expanded as a direct result." It sounded like a doddle the way Bert expressed it.

"Good show. I could use a good easy tour." John wanted out. And so it turned out to be. Well, more or less, for Ace and his crew rumbled off the runway at night, rising up from poorly lit flare path into total blackness on lengthy 8-hour journeys to Merseburg, Zeitz, Politz, Dresden and Chemnitz, all in the eastern part of the Reich. The tension of taking-off laboriously with a weighty bomb load together with a weighty load of petrol in the wing tanks was still there. So was the fear of an engine cut on take-off and it happened, if not often, then enough times to instil a twitchy feeling in the crews' bellies, for if such failure occurred at the critical point before lift had substantially overcome drag, then, with a bomb load on board it was 'curtains' for the crew in all probability. Even once safely off the ground there was always the risk of collision in the darkness as well as having the enemy to face.

Their first two trips on this second tour of operations to Merseburg and Zeitz were notable. On both occasions when Ace heeled Lancaster M. Mother over to allow Frank, the mid upper gunner to take a gander underneath, Frank was lucky enough to spot vague silhouettes, which was warning enough.

On the first trip the attacking enemy fighter came in finally from the rear, almost dead astern. Jock who by now had the shadow in his sights mouthed instructions to Ace who immediately threw the Lancaster into a corkscrew action throwing the enemy completely who then sheered off to look for easier meat.

On the second of the two operations the enemy came in from the starboard beam. This time, on the rear gunner's command, Ace went into a dive turning starboard sharply at the same time. Again it was a JU88 and it too pushed off without making a further attempt, which was logical enough. Why risk an attack against a wide awake crew when there was the possibility of catching another napping.

Needless to say, the crew were generous in handing out praise to Frank for his effective vigilance. Even Taffy, the taciturn wireless op could not find cause to argue, not even with his Celtic oppo in the rear turret.

They went to Politz, Dresden and Chemnitz on subsequent nights. They saw spurts of tracer in the darkness, there was flak and searchlights over targets but they had seen and experienced it all before and somehow the defences did not seem to have the same powerful bite anymore. In fact, on these distant targets, there was more to fear from bad weather particularly if fog was expected to close in around the home aerodrome. There was nothing to write home about.

Just by way of a change they went on an op of shorter duration, this time to Duisburg, an old enemy, if one could call a defended city thus. Somehow it was no longer fearful. The flak was belted up continually but never getting anywhere near their particular bit of airspace. And that was what was different. On their first tour ack ack shells frequently burst near trailing puffs of smoke, creating associated turbulence and occasionally some damage to the fuselage from shrapnel. Perhaps they were just getting into the dangerous state of being 'flak happy'.

It was only on the following morning when the 'chiefy' announced that two four pound incendiaries had been found in the petrol tanks, clearly dropped from an overflying bomber, that Ace and his crew were taken aback. It was the sort of bald matter-of-fact statement that generated spinal chills and expunged over-confidence. There was an element of luck. The incendiaries must have fallen flat enough to knock off the cast iron heads, rendering them harmless. It could so easily have been otherwise.

Then came the daylight operations. Accustomed generally to night bombing, Bomber Command's heavies joined the USAAF, albeit on different targets, escorted distantly by high-flying Thunderbolts and Mustangs. Each navigator plotted his own courses to the targets, the force of Lancasters proceeding in a sort of gaggle, unlike the USAAF Fortresses which still operated in tight formation. Ace and his crew were amongst those who bombed Mannheim, Cologne and Bremen.

When the weather was good it was possible to roughly fix one's position visually, a benefit rare on night operations, all of which made it a bit of a doddle for John and the other navigators even when they were beyond the now-expanded Gee range. However, Sid was kept busy scanning the deck for pinpoints with the result that he was never able to fall asleep.

There were enemy fighters about but these were very soon engaged by the Thunderbolts and Mustangs, leaving the bomber force to go about its proper business.

Ace relished the relaxed pilotage, free of the fearful tensions of night operations. He would even condescend to put M. Mother onto automatic pilot on the first leg out across the English Channel and on the last leg of the route home.

The Tannoy grated out harshly its early Spring morning message. "All crews on the battle order report for final briefing." Sleepy eyed, twenty three crews reported as ordered, complaining as usual.

"Target 'PADERBORN'" announced the Wing Commander and there was only a semblance of interest. "We aim to wipe out Gestapo HQ in particular, so the need for accurate bombing is paramount." This did raise a few eyebrows and set up vague murmurings. The Wing Co continued: "You will again have fighter cover so you should not have too many problems."

Briefing patterns had changed but little over the years. The various specialist officers spoke in turn including the Met Officer who was supremely confident:

"You will find a thin layer of cloud over your route with tops up to eight to ten thousand feet. Winds are light and generally from the south-east. No weather problems on your return.

Before, during and after briefing a subdued murmuring emanated from the assembled crew members, but there were few wisecracks. Most of the crews sensed that the duration of the War was limited. As a result there was a sense of apathy and a measure of war weariness. What's more, there was no Texel present to stir things up a bit for he was now operating from the Base station, still with Denny Denning who now had his own Squadron to Command with the rank of Wing Commander. For some unknown reason the individualists, the real characters had disappeared. In some measure this situation was due to enlargement of the Squadrons into 3 flights, instead of 2.

In mid-morning, Ace lifted M. Mother off the deck into a brilliant cloudless sky, going straight into a steepish climbing turn which did none of his crew any favours. Ken, the flight engineer had a wary eye on the speed, half anticipating a stall. Jock, from the rear turret complained that he had just swallowed his egg and bacon again, a sort of second unanticipated breakfast, while for once Taffy, the W.Op failed to come up with a rejoinder, probably because he was still re-digesting.

They circled higher clawing for height until 'set course' time. John breached the silence with his first instruction.

"Course 111 True in two mins., Ace."

"OK Johnny boy, 111 T it is. Height 5000. Climbing speed."

It was reasonably straight tracking all the way to the target compared with some of the night routes which dodged about to confuse the enemy as to the ultimate destination of the bomber stream: out at Skegness, across the North Sea to just north of the Hague in Holland and thence to the aiming point North East of the Ruhr.

On this brilliant, sunny morning Sid, the bomb aimer, was in good form. At Skegness he piped up to announce that they were directly over Skegness. Out to sea, the drink appeared to be as smooth as a baby's bottom, the air above wholly free of any turbulence. Ace put George, the automatic pilot, into action by way of celebrating the beauty of the morning. Once again at the Dutch coast Sid happily pinpointed the crossing, but warned the navigator that there was 8/10ths cloud in the distance which appeared to be a consistent blanket stretching out ahead but below, well below their operational height of 20,000 feet. All around, well-spread-out Lancasters in their hundreds seemed to fill the sky in a very loose gaggle, certainly not a formation. Perspex cockpit canopies glinted sharply from the sun's rays as the bombers dipped and rose or yawled a bit from side to side. It was an impressive sight.

Frank, the mid upper gunner, very much more adult now than when he flew with Ace on the first tour and happily now without some of the adolescent acne that marred his face, came onto intercom.

"Mustangs high above and astern," he advised.

"Sure they're Mustangs, Frank?" Ace was cautious, leaving nothing to chance.

"Frank's right," Jock confirmed. "Thunderbolts to starboard too."

"Good show. Rendezvous on time." The pilot relaxed again.

It was the navigator who spoke next:

"15 mins. to ETA, Ace. Any sign of cloud breaking up, Sid?"

"Looks thinner, but still about 8/10ths. Probably have to be a sky marking attack." He did not sound quite so chirpy now. However accurately the sky marker was positioned, it was much less satisfying to bomb on a flare than a visual ground aiming point which was much more positive. A few minutes later he was more confident although not wholly so. "Cloud breaking a little," he advised, "but it may be too late."

"5 minutes to target," called John.

"There's the skymarker." The flight engineer was using his eyes too.

"I've got it." Sid was ready to go. "Course for marker approach 099T."

"OK, Sid. 099T." Ace nudged the rudder bar to slew on to the required heading.

"Hold it, Ace." Sid was back on the air again. "Bomb doors open. There's a big hole in the clouds. I can see Paderborn."

"Bomb doors open," echoed Ace. "Bomb visually."

"Left, left smartly." Sid had his nose to the Mark 1XA bombsight, while Ace slewed M. Mother further to Port

"Bombs going down ahead," the bomb aimer continued. "Left again . . . steady . . . Keep it there."

The Lancaster shot up like a cork as Sid pressed the tit. "Bombs gone," he unnecessarily confirmed. "Keep steady for the photo."

"New course 285T." John could not wait to get home.

"Bomb doors closed. Course 285T. 3000 revs, Ken." Ace was confirming and instructing at one and the same time as he swung round on to the reciprocal heading. 3000 revs it was for at least 5 minutes. Whatever the target, once bombs were away, Ace was at full speed to clear the immediate target area, discretion being the better part of valour. Now they were on the way home. Jock was eloquent from the rear turret:

199

"Bloody good prang. I can see fires burning and there's a hell of a lot of smoke."

"He's looking through bloodshot eyes, drunken sot," suggested Taffy rather unkindly.

"Belt up, you Welsh wonder," was Jock's clincher.

There was little flak so it had to be assumed that the Germans did not expect Paderborn to be a heavy bomber target. Way above the bomber stream was where the real action was with fighter condensation trails criss-crossing the blue celestial ceiling.

"Seen the contrails, John?" Ace asked. "If not come out and have a look. It's quite a sight." If Ace was impressed he thought John ought to be as well, but it was not like that. The navigator was more concerned with the scientific explanation.

"Must be a temperature inversion," he pronounced and retreated to his office.

"We're leaving a trail too," Jock wanted his bit of the action and in any case he was in the best position to see.

They were within 15 minutes of the Dutch coast, cruising at a steady 165 kts indicated and at about 18000 feet when Frank switched on with urgent warning:

"Dive starboard. Go. GO." His voice was almost soprano.

Ace threw M. Mother into a diving right-hand turn in an action that was wholly reflex. One could not wait to see what the trouble was. A dark shadow flashed by between sun and cockpit perspex roof. With immediate danger gone, he redressed the balance of direction and course by turning port and climbing before resuming the laid down course.

"Cripes." Frank could not suppress bubbling excitement. "ME 262 — new German jet fighter and there's a Thunderbolt after it."

"I see them, Frank." Ace was completely cool now, as he watched the Thunderbolt flat out in a steep dive rake the German jet with cannon fire. It was only a momentary sighting for seconds later both aeroplanes disappeared below the cloud. John logged the incident with time and position. It was particularly notable being their first sighting of the new enemy advanced fighter plane. He had to admit, albeit reluctantly, that the Germans were pretty bloody clever, having produced the Doodlebug, the V2 and now the first operational jet. We had to be lucky, he thought, that our ground troops were advancing to make sure Hitler did not have any other nasty tricks up his sleeve.

It was their only thrill of the day. Not much got past the Thunderbolt/Mustang umbrella.

The Dutch coast was obscured by cloud, but John, happy to be in positive GEE range was uncaring. What was more, the downscanning H2S radar showed up the coast line as clear as a topographical map. He just could not go wrong. Four hours and forty five minutes after taking off, Ace monotonously set M. Mother down on 3 points so smoothly that the rear gunner dare not complain.

In the Officers' Mess, Ace and John were now regular drinking partners. Since John no longer had Marion's company, it was natural to socialise with Ace who was essentially a loner. Occasionally Ace struck out to meet Texel in a pub, the latter being based some three miles away and so when they met it was a question of either shank's pony or a bicycle as the means of travel.

John telephoned Marion as often as he could, but sometimes it would take all evening to get a line. Marion reciprocated when she was able.

Marion had taken John to her home in Norfolk on a mutual leave period and he had been well-received by her family. It was a happy relaxed break. Once or twice they had walked down to and along the shore in the early hours after dawn and had seen the trail of V2 rockets setting off for landfall in the London area.

On John's return from leave, Ace observed laconically:

"You really are getting your feet under the table. I hope you know what you're doing." Then he rubbed it in. "Don't forget we've half a second tour to get through yet."

"I know, Ace." John hesitated before continuing carefully. "I do get more confident with each op safely logged and one should always exhibit some optimism."

Ace was not giving an inch. He had his basic theory and it was unchanging.

"Famous last words? I hope not, of course, but anything could go wrong even at this stage — the possibilities are infinite."

"Wouldn't have put you down as a worrier, Ace." John was a little surprised at his pilot's uncompromising "No Future" attitude, although the logic was sound enough.

"No. Not worried, Johnny boy. Wrong word altogether. Don't like jumping bridges until I reach them." It was not altogether a suitable analogy but John got the drift. Ace was right to be cautious.

And so it proved. Sandwiched between some easy daylight stooges to Nordhausen barracks, Heligoland and Bremen they went on a nine-hour trip to Potsdam, then, much more dangerously laid mines at low level in Kiel Harbour. Then, boring away from Kiel, M. Mother was caught in a belt of searchlights and hosed down with light flak which resulted in the loss of one engine and some considerable pepperpotting of the fuselage. To round off this particular incident, as they got close to the English coast, the Royal Navy opened up firing with all barrels. It was hardly a barrel of fun, but good fortune that the Navy's shooting was less accurate than that of the German Command. Not for the first time Ace's crew were aptly chastened. Recurring spells of over-confidence were successively being nose-dived.

Then it was practically all over. The Dutch were in a sad state of semi-starvation and a truce was arranged with the Germans to allow Lancasters to drop canisters of food to the civilian population. Operation MANNA was on.

The Lancasters roared into Holland at about 500 feet to drop canisters on open ground near Rotterdam, each pilot extremely wary in case the Germans broke the uneasy and, in their case, reluctant truce. John made one of his rare appearances up front to peer down through the starboard blister. Lancaster M. Mother was so low that he could clearly see the smiles on a sea of happy faces. The Dutch were waving wildly up at what must have seemed like deliverance from slow starvation. Just here and there was a sullen, grim-looking face which John assumed belonged to Nazi sympathisers who, if the War wrapped up suddenly, were in dead trouble.

They went again the next day to be received, albeit at a distance, with the same ecstatic enthusiasm. For Ace and his crew it was perhaps their most satisfying operation and it was their last. They had, despite constant misgivings, open or subdued, made it to the end of a second tour. Quite suddenly the "No Future" theme had become obsolete. It was time to celebrate in the only way they knew. In the very near future there would have to be a party in the Old Cow. It could not be in the messes because Ace and John were commissioned officers while the rest of the crew remained NCOs.

Ace and John, in best blue, got into the mess at around 18.30 hours. They would dine first to lay a proper intestinal foundation before joining the others in the Old Cow.

"Telephone for Flying Officer Howard, Sir," the steward called.

"I'll be back, Ace. Bound to be Marion. Line me up a first pint will you."

"Sure thing, joker. First of many."

"Is that Flying Officer Howard?" the caller asked.

"Yes. Who is speaking?" John was puzzled, as a result of which he was sharply interrogative. It was a woman's voice, but it was not Marion's.

"I'm Sgt Denise Farrow, Sir." She was speaking slowly and very quietly, so much so that John could scarcely hear her. "Marion and I rotated duties here."

"Yes, I understand, Sergeant. How do y'do. What's the problem?"

There was clear hesitation. Clearly the WAAF did not know how to proceed. For all that, John was not unduly alarmed.

"I'm afraid I have bad news." Denise got it out and there was a momentary silence preceding the vague sound of a stifled sob. And now John's blood ran cold.

"Marion was involved in an accident." The WAAF, slightly more controlled now that she had communicated bad news without breaking down, continued:

"I'm sorry to have to tell you that Marion was killed when a Mosquito crashed into the watchtower."

John could not believe it. He was stupefied, his face ashen.

"It can't be true," he mouthed.

"I'll write to you," Denise said and broke into a fit of sobbing. The line went dead.

John replaced the receiver at his end mechanically. It just could not be. It must be a hoax. No it could not be. No one here except the rest of the crew and Bert Apsley knew of his liaison with Marion. None would have perpetrated such a foul hoax. Texel, over at Base could have set up a false message, for he had always been somewhat jealous, but no — Texel was not that bad. It was true then. Oh, God! The WAAF could just not have been good enough an actress to be party to a dirty trick of this order. Her sobs had been altogether real. Marion was dead.

Ace came over carrying two pints.

"For crying out loud, Johnny, you're as white as a sheet. What's happened?" he asked.

"Marion's dead." He could only just frame the words.

"No." Ace was shocked and it took a deal to achieve that. "How did it happen?"

"Kite crashed into the watchtower and exploded."

The pilot put a long arm round John's shoulder in what he believed was a comforting action. All he said was, "Tough Titty." Ace meant well. He was not much up in the civilities in any circumstances. To John his brief remark said, "I told you so."

Denise Farrow's letter came a couple of days later. It was a carefully phrased, sympathetic letter in which she got around to explaining that Marion had confided her intention to marry John as soon as his tour was completed. She also explained that an over-enthusiastic and foolish young Mosquito pilot had failed to pull out from a diving beat up of the airfield and ploughed straight into the watchtower, his aeroplane exploding in a mass of flaming petrol that incinerated the watchtower occupants. The letter was not couched in such bald terms but the purport was there. Marion had effectively been cremated.

How long John stood staring at the now-desolate WAAFery he could not tell. He saw in his reflections of the past the movement of WAAF personnel in and out of the entrance and heard again their chatter. He saw again the dark-haired head and the slim figure of Marion, his first, his only love in a vision that was reality. He blinked and the vision was gone, but the coagulating pain was still with him years after Marion's tragic and so unnecessary demise.

The bitter irony of it was that he had flown on two tours of operations with Bomber Command, the arm of the service with the outstandingly high chop rate, not expecting to survive, but he had, while Marion had fallen victim. In his own mind there had been no future for him and he knew deep down that Marion had had the same fear. She had prayed for him (he knew that too) with only a slim hope that her prayers would be answered. Instead, she had had her young life rubbed out by a stupid clot right on the brink of cessation of hostilities. What really was the point of it all? For that matter, what was the point of life itself?